D0204754

"Jones owns a fine writer's eye for the kind of details that matter.... It is Jones's skillful straight-from-the-shoulder depiction of [Moon] and his pinched world that resonates and then compels.... The author draws on his disoriented thoughts with dark and excellent detail."

—Daniel Woodrell, *Washington Post*

"Compelling.... Jones is an evocative writer."

—*Winston-Salem Journal*

"The ultimate noir nightmare.... Jones conveys the claustrophobic, dead-end lifestyle of the rural poor with a frightening incisiveness."

—Peter Handel, *San Francisco Sunday Examiner & Chronicle*

"A high-voltage thriller...a gritty, claustrophobic blend of Jim Thompson and James Dickey."

—*Publishers Weekly* (starred review)

"Powerful...compelling and readable.... A violent study of desperation, owing more to Dostoevsky and Faulkner than any suspense writer, the story unfolds like a graphic, slow-motion nightmare from which the protagonist will never awaken."

—Michael Adams, *Library Journal*

"An absolutely riveting read. Jones gives trailer-park minimalism just what it's always needed—a story to tell and one that your mind won't let go of for quite a while."

—Gary Krist, *Smart Money*

"Jones and Daniel Woodrell are the leading contemporary authors of country noir, a subgenre whose roots trace back to James M. Cain's *The Postman Always Rings Twice*."
— Bill Ott, *Booklist* (starred review)

"Jones's writing is vivid, carefully composed, and unadorned, making for a thrilling tale that stays in the mind long after the final page." — Michael A. Green, *Post and Courier*

"A story fraught with suspense that climaxes with an ending that will rivet you to your bed. Forget sleeping that night.... The book stamps Jones as a major talent."
— Scott Rapp, *Syracuse Herald American*

ALSO BY MATTHEW F. JONES

The Cooter Farm

The Elements of Hitting

Blind Pursuit

Deepwater

Boot Tracks

A SINGLE SHOT

Matthew F. Jones

MULHOLLAND BOOKS

LITTLE, BROWN AND COMPANY

NEW YORK BOSTON LONDON

Mulholland Books / Little, Brown and Company
Hachette Book Group
237 Park Avenue, New York, NY 10017
www.hachettebookgroup.com

Originally published by Farrar, Straus and Giroux, 1996
First Mulholland Books paperback edition: September 2011

Mulholland Books is an imprint of Little, Brown and Company, a division of Hachette Book Group, Inc. The Mulholland Books name and logo are trademarks of Hachette Book Group, Inc.

Library of Congress Cataloging-in-Publication Data

Jones, Matthew F.
    A single shot / Matthew F. Jones. — 1st Mulholland Books pbk. ed.
    p. cm.
    "Originally published by Farrar, Straus and Giroux, 1996."
    ISBN 978-0-316-19670-3
    1. Poachers—Fiction.   2. Criminals—Fiction.   I. Title.
    PS3560.O52244S56 2011
    813'.54—dc22   2011027225

10 9 8 7 6 5 4 3 2 1

RRD-C

Printed in the United States of America

To every good life chased from the good life

it was born to.

Six Angles of Wrath

In a time when reliable standards of personal conduct have allegedly eroded and, no longer anchored by religious conviction or cultural cohesion, have diminished to irresolute situational postures and secular mumbles, an older, less elastic code of honor may seem vastly appealing, even heroic. To avert the confusions attendant on choice, such codes are simplified, starkly so, but clearly: Do that to me, you can rely on me to do this to you. Do that to my kin, watch for smoke from your garage. Say that to my wife, and this is the bog where your worried relatives will find you facedown and at peace forever. Should it require the efforts of generations to uphold this code, to respond to the responses, so be it. Such codes ask an awful lot of adherents (my own great grandfather was an adherent and, when a slander on his wife reached his ears, obeyed the code promptly and went door to door with a pistol throughout the neighborhood I still live in, but, shrewdly, no one he encountered would admit to being the source and he did not get the satisfaction of killing some poor wretched gossip, and his wife attempted suicide by drinking Paris Green while he was out thoroughly publicizing the slander) and deliver little, but they yet exist.

John Moon, the resolute, pitiful, and confused man at the heart of *A Single Shot,* one of the finest novels of rural crime and moral horror in the past few decades, has an inherited code of his own, but almost innocently violates it, and experiences a cascade of nightmares in response. He is a hunter, raised on the rules of hunting, the ethics of hunting, and can't let a wounded deer slink into the thicket to die a slow, agonizing death. So he follows as he should, obeying every tenet of the deerslayer code, chases up hills and over rocks, on and on, then down another hill until exhausted, when suddenly a bush wiggles, there's a flash of brown, and he breaks the most important and basic rule of all, pulls that trigger. Moon is the creation of Matthew F. Jones, a hard, wonderful, and very powerful writer you might not know yet, but ought to soon. But be forewarned, dear reader: Jones is a twisted motherfucker when sitting at his keyboard, twisted in the manner so many of us appreciate mightily, and will not spare your tender sensibilities should you be among those poor souls afflicted by such. He rakes you over the coals at a measured pace, unfurls wrath from six angles, and the amen he delivers over John Moon will keep even other twisted motherfuckers awake nights.

Andrei Tarkovsky, the legendary Russian film director, once said, "The allotted function of art is not, as is often assumed, to put across ideas, to propagate thought, to serve as an example. The aim of art is to prepare a person for death, to plough and harrow his soul, rendering it capable of turning to good."

My personal list of nasty country boy and girl writers who so admirably insist on sharing their "ploughing and harrowing" with the wider world, representing, if you will, is select but with room for more: Jim Thompson, Flannery O'Connor, Tom Kromer (*Waiting for Nothing*), Charles Williams, Tillie Olsen (in her fashion; trust me), James Ross, Meridel LeSueur (*The Girl,* a masterpiece), vast acres of Joe Lansdale, Larry Brown, William Gay, and there are others. Matthew F. Jones has a seat at the table and has for a good while, though not everybody noticed. Well, notice now, friends, Jones is major, he's got the piss and vinegar and moral rigor that make books matter, and he's got more books to offer.

Daniel Woodrell

A Single Shot

SUNDAY

BEFORE THE SUN is up, John Moon has showered, drunk two cups of coffee, and changed into his blue jeans, sweatshirt, and Timberland hiking boots. He has eaten two pieces of toast, a bowl of cereal, and put out food for his wandering dog. Before leaving the trailer by the front door, he gets his 12-gauge shotgun and a handful of slugs from the gun cabinet off the kitchen.

The grass is damp with dew and the early-June air is heavy and already warm, promising it will be hot within a few hours. A mourning dove is cooing in a tree somewhere to John's left. Down the road, past the treeline, he hears the gentle clanging of cowbells and the lowing of Cecil Nobie's herd on its way from the pasture to Nobie's barn to be milked. The sun is just starting to peek out over the crest of the mountain directly east of the one John lives two-thirds to the top of.

Gazing down at the converging roads winding like miles of dusty brown carpet through the hollow below him, John sees a set of headlights descending the right fork, piercing the three-quarters dark. He thinks this strange since only he and the Nobies live on the right fork and unless there'd been an accident at Nobies', in which case someone from there would likely have called John, none of them would be driving into town at four-thirty in the morning. John wonders if the vehicle might belong to a conservation officer, then decides he's being paranoid. No green cap is going to get up before dawn to search for would-be poachers. Thinking two teenagers must have fallen asleep parking the night before, John shrugs, then starts walking up the mountain.

He hikes five hundred yards or so up to the road's end, then turns right and heads on a narrow path into a forest of pine trees on the state preserve. There's no wind and it's so quiet in the forest that, even on a soft bed of pine needles, John's footsteps echo in his ears as if he is treading on snow. Every few steps, he stops, listens for several seconds, then, not hearing anything, moves on. He is looking for a ten-point buck he has seen three times in the last week, most recently on the previous afternoon from his back porch, where, through binoculars, he watched it graze for several minutes at the edge of the preserve before it loped into the pines. John has figured the buck has a bed somewhere in the pines. He has balanced in his mind the value of a hundred fifty pounds of dressed venison versus the thousand dollars in fines and possible two months' jail time it would cost him in the unlikely event that he is caught shooting the deer out of season on state land, and has decided the risk is worth it.

As he approaches the far edge of the pines after which the forest turns denser with deciduous trees and brush, in the canopy of pine boughs a crow starts cawing. Several others join in. His senses suddenly heightened, John cocks the shotgun. The sharp click of the engaging mechanism increases the crows' agitation. A squirrel or a chipmunk jumps from one tree to another above him. A pinecone drops near his feet. Several smaller birds—sparrows or swallows—take flight, slicing through the still air, before landing again.

Sensing the presence of a large animal besides himself, John cradles the gun in two hands and starts slowly walking toward the pines' edge, where the half-risen sun gives the trees' upper branches a bejeweled look. A branch suddenly snaps to his left. Then a sound like rushing water. In one motion, John wheels toward the noise, puts the butt of the shotgun to his shoulder, flicks off the safety, and aims at a bouncing tree limb. Just beyond the limb, he sees a tan-and-white flank disappearing into a patch of thistles and, above the thistles, a large rack of antlers. John fires. He hears the buck snort, sees the antlers tilt to the right, below the level of the bushes, then rise up again, and, as he recocks the shotgun, the deer shoot out the other side of the thistles, beyond his range, and disappear.

John pushes the safety in and runs toward the thistles, but before he gets there, he stops next to a large oblong shaped indentation in the pine needles. He kneels down, touches with his fingers the center of the spot, feels the warmth left from the sleeping deer, even sees some of its coat lying there. He feels his heart loudly thumping in his chest, air rushing in and out of his nostrils, beads of sweat rolling down from his armpits. And he can smell the buck, the adrenal surge it's released, like John's own, pungent and harsh.

Holding the gun in one hand, he trots a half circle to the left of the thistles, doubles back on the far side, stops near where the deer came out, squats down, and sees several fresh drops of blood on the ground. So, it was wounded—probably in the right rear flank, given the way it had pitched forward—and is heading deeper into the woods, through thick underbrush and rough terrain, hoping to tire its pursuer out.

John had hoped to down the deer with one bullet, then drag it quickly back to the trailer, afraid that a gunshot, even at this early hour and distance from town, might be overheard by someone—maybe a hiker in the preserve—and rouse suspicion. Now that he has wounded the animal, though, he has no choice but to pursue it. He can't just let it limp off somewhere and die slowly.

He follows the trail of blood down the east side of the mountain on a zigzagging course through a stand of white oak undergrown with witch hazel, sumac, mountain laurel, and nettles that tear at his pants and shirt and painfully rake his face, until, after several hundred yards, the brush thins out and is interlarded with moss-slick rocks and vine-covered boulders. Here the buck has headed north, along a narrow ridge parallel to one fork of the hollow road a half mile below. For a few seconds, John hears in front of him the sound of the deer's hooves clattering noisily against the rocks. It's bleeding thin, sporadic drops, and John fears it might be a while before it gives out.

Winded, he stops for a short blow, looking east where the sun, now completely up, casts a gold trail from the far mountain to the near. A hawk circles over Cecil Nobie's red house and barn, which look doll-sized from this height. The day vows to be perfect, if a little hot, but John doesn't mind hot. He likes to sweat. Taking a deep breath of the warming air, he starts again after the deer.

After nearly an hour more of bushwhacking, he comes to a dry creek bed, crosses it, then follows the deer where it has veered right, up the hill again, toward the west boundary of the preserve. A steep half-hour climb through raspberry bushes and over clear-cut maples and white pine that have been sawed and left by the state brings him finally onto the back side of Hollenbachs' mountain, where Old Man Hollenbach a dozen years before grazed heifers and sheep. Now the old pasture's a maze of crab-apple trees, chokecherries, Scotch pine, and brambles, but at least the terrain levels out.

Breathing heavily, John stops next to a thorn-apple tree where the deer must have rubbed its wound because the trunk is marred by blood, and from there the trail gets redder. From the way the grass and bushes are bent above the blood, John guesses the buck is dragging one leg. He thinks it can't last much longer, and, not for the first time, he worries about how he's going to lug a two-hundred-pound carcass all those miles back to his house. Maybe he can get Simon Breedlove to help by giving him some of the meat. He worries, too, that the farther he has to cart the deer, the more chance he has of stumbling across someone else.

Wiping his brow, he starts across the pasture. It's not even nine o'clock and already the temperature feels like it's gone up twenty degrees. John's clothes are soaked with sweat and he's thirsty enough to wring them out and drink it. A hundred yards ahead, at the pasture's edge, he sees the deep grass swaying back and forth. He guesses it's the deer, but can't see it to shoot, then suddenly the buck stumbles out of the grass onto the abandoned dirt road that winds up the northwest side of the mountain to Old Man Hollenbach's played-out stone quarry. It just stands there, sniffing the air around its knees, looking dazed and ready to cave in. John raises the shotgun to his shoulder but there's too many trees between him and the deer to get a clear shot off, and besides, he figures by now he can pretty much walk up and put the animal out of its misery. Then the buck lets out a loud snort and, dragging its hindquarters, moves off down the road toward the quarry.

John quietly curses, not because he's worried about losing the deer—unless it can scale rock walls, there's only one way in or out of the quarry—but because he's tired of chasing it and is sorry, too, that the buck has had to endure so much suffering. He hears a dog barking off somewhere and starts to worry again about being caught and wishes it were colder so that he could hide the carcass in the quarry out of sight from buzzards and coyotes and come back for it the next day before sunup. Then he decides maybe he ought to butcher the deer right there in the quarry—behind one of the slag heaps—and bring the meat home in two or three trips. A grouse suddenly breaks cover almost beneath his feet and the frantic beating of its wings nearly gives John a heart attack and he thinks, "Get this the hell over with."

When he reaches the road five minutes later, the deer is out of sight, but a trail of blood leads directly from there to the quarry, five hundred yards in the distance. The grass on the road looks slightly impacted to John and some of the smaller rocks freshly dislodged. He kneels down and takes a closer look, but can't tell whether the road has recently been driven on or only disrupted by the hailstorm two days before. "I'm goin' to go kill that deer," John tells himself, standing up and starting down the road in a nervous half-jog. "Take what meat I can easy carry, and clear out pronto."

A flock of blue jays suddenly flies up from the quarry and starts squawking, flat out scaring John until he remembers that right about then the deer, bleeding and snorting, had probably stumbled inside and startled the birds. Still, he can feel his heart pounding in his ears. Slowing to a walk, he raises the gun to his waist. He smells spruce, the trees lining both sides of the road. At the entrance to the quarry, a small canyon with fifty-foot granite walls, he reminds himself that the deer would be crazed enough to charge whatever gets too close, and could, with those antlers, do some damage.

He flicks off the shotgun's safety, then warily enters the canyon overgrown with briars, pine bushes, and crawling vines, stops just inside, looks around, and sees the same half-a-dozen slag heaps, junked truck chassis, gutted genera-tor, plastic-covered lean-to, that have been there for years, and off to the right, the deep water-filled pit where John, as a boy, caught frogs, and behind it, the circular opening in the wall he had never dared enter, on one side of which stands a rusted shovel and pick.

John looks down for the deer's blood and at the same time hears to his left a grunt, then branches cracking. He shoul-ders the gun, wheels toward the sound, spots behind a briar thicket a moving patch of brown-and-white, aims at it, and fires. He figures he's hit the deer in the head or heart because, without a sound, it drops from sight as if its legs have been severed.

John levers out the spent shell. Dangling the shotgun in one hand, he starts walking toward the thicket, when suddenly a loud snort sounds directly behind him. He spins around and sees charging out from behind a slag heap, straight for him, the injured buck.

John doesn't even have time to cock or shoulder the gun before the deer is so close he can feel the phlegm flying from its flared nostrils and read the rage in its pain-maddened eyes.

Instinctively hop-stepping to his left, John grabs the rifle barrel with both hands, then swings it upward as hard as he can. With a loud crack, the butt connects with the deer's jaw a moment before its antlers pierce John's left shoulder. He goes down and the buck, standing above him, lowers its head as if to gore him, then suddenly lets out a pained bleat, starts to tremble as if it's been electrically shocked, and drops in a heap next to John.

He rolls to his right, slowly pushes himself with his hands into a squat, then stands. With the effort, the pain in his gored and bleeding shoulder doesn't increase or radiate. A good sign, thinks John. He extends his arm gradually forward and back, then gingerly loops it in a full circle, heartened that he has full motion in the joint.

At his feet, the deer suddenly twitches, its legs kicking out as if it will rise. Startled, John jumps back. Then the buck lies still. John sees it isn't going anywhere. His shotgun butt has crushed its jaw, forcing its teeth into a grotesque grin; its rear quarters are a mass of blood, thistle-matted fur, and exposed bone; it's exhaling as much fluid as oxygen; its eyes are clouded as though it's already in the afterlife. Looking down at the dying animal, John has the same sad feeling as he did watching his father doing likewise in a hospital bed fourteen years before.

He picks up his shotgun from the grass- and weed-covered gravel, starts to cock it, then, changing his mind, wraps both hands around the barrel, hoists the butt like a post-hole digger above the deer's head, and brings it forcefully down. The deer's skull collapses like a rotten vegetable. The buck groans once, for several seconds twitches again, then lies still. Placing the gun on the ground, John thinks it shouldn't have come to this. The buck should have died in the pines from a single shot.

He reaches up, pulls off his torn sweatshirt, wads it into a ball, then dabs with it at his injured shoulder until enough blood has been removed for him to see a jagged puncture wound, half an inch deep, oozing a slow, steady stream. He unwads the shirt, grips it at both sides of the tear, and rips it in two. He wraps one piece tight around his bicep, just above where he's bleeding, binding it with a square knot, and the other securely around the wound.

Fighting a sudden urge to turn and run from the quarry, he takes a deep breath and tries to calm the fluttery feeling in his stomach. He picks up the shotgun, wipes its butt on the grass, and closes its breech. He looks down once more at the deer, then over at the briars. Holding the gun ready at his side, he slowly walks the twenty-five yards over to the thicket, stops in front of it, and with the shotgun's barrel moves the forward branches aside. He tries to peer through the tangled thicket to the far side, but it's dense as a sponge, and he can't see anything but more branches and briars. Nor can he hear anything, not even the blue jays, which, oddly, have gone mute. "Whatever's there," thinks John, "is bad hurt or dead."

He remembers the flash of brown-and-white he saw, and the shovel and pick standing—not lying—by the hollowed-out spot in the wall behind him. He remembers reading in a book once about how lives are begun, altered, and wiped out in a second, and something else about people only coming to know themselves through tragedy. "Where did that thought come from?" he wonders. "And why? I'm a good hunter," he tells himself. "I followed a wounded, crazed deer into a box canyon, heard an animal grunt behind me, saw it move, then shot it."

He walks rapidly to the right of the patch, ten feet wide at least and almost that tall, and without hesitating rounds the corner. On the far side, on the ground five feet in front of him, he sees the worn bottoms of two sneakered feet, then blue-jean-covered legs, a slim torso adorned by an earth-stained, white T-shirt, and a dirty-blond clump of hair protruding from beneath a floppy brown hat. The body has a circular sweat spot on its lower back and lies facedown behind the brambles, arms thrown out in front of it toward a small denim satchel.

John is hit by a wave of nausea. Instinctively, he flicks on the shotgun's safety, drops the gun at his feet, runs up to the body, kneels next to it, places one hand on the white neck beneath the hair clump, and feels for a pulse. He doesn't find one. "Come on," he says aloud. He reaches his hands beneath the body's warm, damp stomach, then carefully rolls it over. He sees first, in the left center of the chest, the slug's gaping entry wound, then a woman with her eyes wide open. "Please, God," says John. "No."

He raises his balled fists to the sides of his head, closes his eyes, and prays that when he opens them the dead woman will be transposed into a dead deer, dog, or bear. When he looks again, the body is still human, only now John sees a girl. She is maybe sixteen, with crystal-blue eyes, blossom-shaped clumps of freckles on both cheeks, a small space between her upper incisors where a piece of gum or chewable candy is lodged. The clump of blond hair is a ponytail. John looks up at the sky. It looks just as it did five minutes before. He can't figure out how that can be.

He loses sense of time and objectivity. He sits down on a small rock next to the body and, as the sun heats his naked back, declares himself a murderer. For the moment, he forgets that the body is even there. He focuses only upon his act of killing another human being. He would like to spread the blame around, but can find no one else to fault, not even the dead girl for wearing tan and white in the woods, because it's not even hunting season and John, after all, is a trespassing poacher.

He picks a small stick up from the quarry floor and doodles with it in the dirt. The blue jays perched above him begin to sing again. A red fox wanders into the quarry, stops and sniffs the deer carcass, then, possibly sensing John's presence, turns and bounds out again. A hog snake slithers over the dead girl's feet. The crows caw, alerting others to the death.

John thinks about how he has grown up in and around

these woods — on the Nobie side of the mountain — and, like his father and grandfather, has hunted them since he was a boy, and though they fought in wars and he didn't, he is the first among them to kill someone. He thinks that if his father hadn't lost the Moon family farm, with its rolling meadows and three hundred acres of game-rich forest, John would not have to trespass and poach to feed his wife and son. They might even still live with him. He looks at his watch. Almost an hour has passed. His left shoulder throbs. His shirt is damp around the wound, but the bleeding, for the most part, seems to have stopped.

He forces himself to stand up, walk over to the dead girl, look down at her lying in the grass like a rag doll casually tossed aside. Boiling with black flies, wine-colored blood slowly oozes from her open chest. John reaches down, brushes several of the flies away, then pulls back his hand wet with blood starting to congeal. He thinks of the hundreds of animals he has shot, gutted, and cut into strips of meat. All the blood he has seen. The wounded deer that he chased for miles to kill. Blood is blood, he thinks, wiping the girl's on his pants. And dead is dead.

He moves his gaze from her chest to her face. She is beautiful, he thinks, not like a greenhouse flower, but like a wild rose raised in bright sunshine, bitter cold, torrential rain. Sun-chapped lips, parted as if to speak, a bent nose, slightly running, make her seem still alive. A tiny anchor-shaped birthmark mars her right cheek. Kneeling down near her head, John smells orange-blossom perfume, the same three-dollar-a-bottle fragrance he used to buy for his wife. What is your name? he silently asks her. Where are you from? What were you doing in the quarry by yourself? He bends forward and tenderly kisses her lips, then, shocked at his own behavior, quickly rears back and glances around the canyon, up the rock walls, into the white-pine and cedar-tree forest orbiting the upper rim, as if someone might be watching him. Suddenly John feels certain someone is. The thought hits him like a punch: she wasn't alone. He sees nothing to substantiate this, though. He reaches down and with his index fingers gently closes the girl's eyes.

He stands up, walks over to the blue satchel, picks it up, carries it back over to the rock where he had been sitting, sits down again, then opens the satchel. Inside he finds a woman's pink bikini underpants, matching gray socks adorned by galloping horses, a T-shirt with a winding, white-capped river on its front and, on back, "Ride the Wild Snake," a wax-paper bag containing a partially eaten tuna-fish sandwich, a half-filled plastic water bottle, two rolled marijuana cigarettes, an open box of Kools, a nylon tan wallet, and a jackknife.

John takes the items from the satchel, places them in a neat circle on the ground between his feet, and, for several minutes, sits there looking at them, feeling as if he's opened a door to the dead girl's life and not sure he's up to walking through it. Again he's hit with the uneasy feeling that he's not alone, that someone is watching to see what he'll do next. When he hears a small plane fly over the mountain, he wonders, for a panicked moment, if someone might be searching for the girl. He looks up, shielding his eyes from the sun. The plane is so high it's only a silvery dot marring his vision. Beneath it, a hundred or so yards above the quarry, a large pair of turkey vultures casually circle. John silently screams, "Why'd you put her here today, God, of all days?"

He doesn't get an answer.

He picks up the wallet, flips it open, and sees, enclosed in plastic, a photograph of the dead girl sitting with two others about the same age on a large boulder near a waterfall. Smiling, her arms around the others' shoulders, each girl is holding up three fingers of one hand. John pulls the photograph out of the plastic, turns it over, and sees, in a looping scrawl, "All for one, one for all. The Three Senoritas—Man, Tools, and Germ—6/94." Behind the first picture are two others, one of a couple who look to be in their fifties, he burly, with horn-rimmed glasses and a large drinker's nose, she plumpish and smiling in a pantsuit that's too small. The other is of the dead girl again, this time arm in arm with a heavyset man in his late twenties or early thirties, with slick black hair, dark eyes, and tight lips curled upward at the corners in a grudging half smile.

John slips the pictures back into the plastic, then searches the rest of the wallet, and finds fifty-two dollars, two condoms in tinfoil, and a book of stamps. There is no driver's license; no credit, membership, or social security cards; nothing at all with the girl's—or anyone else's—name or address on it. John drops the wallet and for several seconds sits there, the enormity of the situation sweeping like a tidal wave over him, thinking, "Why me?" And, "She couldn't have just dropped out of the sky."

He stands up and walks several fast, tight circles around the rock, stops and kicks it, then hurries back over to the dead girl. He bends over, thrusts a hand into her pants pocket, groping for whatever's there, but finds the pocket gone and his fingers kneading a thigh so warm, soft, and lifelike that he half expects the girl to giggle, moan, or cry out. Panting as if he'd just run a race, he quickly pulls back his hand and shakes it. "Son of a bitch!" he hisses, then quietly to the dead girl, "Sorry. Weren't your fault."

Gritting his teeth, he leans down and rolls the cadaver toward him, causing it to exhale and loudly break wind. John, gasping, feels he ought to apologize to the girl again, but instead goes ahead and searches her other pocket, finding in it several coins, a pencil stub, and a folded piece of paper that he unfolds and discovers is a half-written, unaddressed letter to the girl in the photograph named Tools. Standing over the cadaver, John reads the letter, written in the same awkward scrawl as the note on the back of the photograph.

Dear Tools:

By now I guess you know I'm gone. I couldn't take it no more—not so much Daddy's drinking and losing his temper and Ma pretending nothing was wrong as me bein fraid I'd end up like em which is dead inside. Like a pair of corpses. I wish I could have said goodbye but there weren't no time and that you'd of got to know Waylon's goodside (well, not too well!) He's sweet and treats me better than all them grabass highschool boys (like Donnie LaTrec—the pig!) plus the way he loves me—for the first time I know what all the fuss is about (wow!)—and is smart but got in trouble from bad breaks. Talk about childhoods—you ought to hear bout his! Anyway, I don't hold it gainst him he was in jail—he calls it his college education. And it weren't for naught. He'd kill me if I told you—or even found out I was writing you as he made me throw out my address book—but soon as Waylon gets back tonight we're heading somewhere starts with an H where there's ocean, good weather, lays and coconuts (remember—wasn't me who told you!) I can't say no more, only that it's like we always talked about—I can't believe it's been hardly a week since passing notes in geometry class! I'm not sure how it's going to end up, Tools, and sometimes that scares me but it's like Waylon says, better to go out like a Roman Candle than a wet log. All I know is for the first time ever I feel like I'm really living stead of—I got to stop for awhile, Tools—you won't believe what just come hobbling in here with me, poor, dear thing, looks shot or something...

John refolds the letter, shoves it into his hip pocket, then, having decided what he must do—and quickly, before Waylon returns—glances down uneasily at the dead girl, half fearing she will open her eyes and say, "There's the life you took from me and now you're doing with me worse than you would a shot deer!"

Bending over, John grabs the girl under the arms and starts hauling her toward the near end of the bushes, the cadaver emitting noises like a couple of drunks eating beans around a campfire. John is so embarrassed for her that his cheeks burn and he thinks if the whole world could see itself dead there'd be no vanity left. Near the end of the bushes, one of her sneakers comes off. John stops and puts it back on, and her foot, in a baby-blue socklet, is so warm and alive he suddenly wishes he had known her when she was, a thought too disturbing to dwell on. He hurriedly picks up the corpse again and starts dragging it across the quarry floor, making a trail of blood, urine, and matted grass, toward the small pond and dug-out place on the far side, thinking, "The first thing is to get her hid somewhere, so I can think."

He is halfway across the field when, from directly behind him, comes a loud hiss and a hollow thumping sound. With a startled yelp, he drops the cadaver and wheels around and there, over the dead buck, their huge wings flapping and red wattles trembling, hover the two turkey vultures. John runs at them, waving his arms and sibilating, and the birds, in their lumbering, unhurried way, fly off, one with deer meat dangling from its beak.

John walks back to the girl, bends to pick her up, and is shocked to find her staring straight at him. Her head banging against the ground must have caused her eyes to pop open. "It won't do nobody," John loudly blurts out, "you, your boyfriend, your family wherever they are, me, or my little one countin' on me to feed 'im — one bit a good for me to go to jail which is jis' what'id happen if the law found out 'bout this and even did accept it was an accident!" He reaches down, pushes her eyes shut again, then drags her the rest of the way across the quarry's rock floor, through which grass and weeds sprout, past the water hole, to the opening in the wall, a dynamited cavern maybe four feet high and twice as deep, from which, years before, Old Man Hollenbach mined slate.

Breathing heavily, John lays the girl down on a bluestone

slab in front of the opening, its floor marred by raccoon droppings, bat shit, and two or three cigarette stubs. John bends down, picks up a stub, sniffs it, and smells recently burned tobacco. "What the hell?" he thinks. He drops to his hands and knees in front of the cavern, carefully examines the entrance, and sees several crushed weeds, their broken stems oozing fresh fluid, and a large patch of imploded grass.

He glances at the dead girl, thinking of the Kools in her duffel, then at the cavern, where, past the entrance, it's pitch dark. He looks at the shovel and pick against the near wall, tools left from Old Man Hollenbach's days, and, as he had right before he'd discovered the dead girl, wonders why they are standing, as if recently placed there, rather than lying haphazardly on the ground. He reaches out, grabs the shovel, and sees rust everywhere but at the tip, which is shiny and chipped. He looks at the pick and sees the same thing. He wonders why, other than for the reason he had planned to, anyone would be digging in the cave.

He sticks his head a foot or so into the cavern. Along with the dankness, he smells the faint odor of smoke. He's not sure it's tobacco smoke. It smells more like gunpowder. He thinks of the thousand tons of dirt and stone above him, and suddenly remembers why, as a child, he had never dared enter the cave. "I ought to make me a flare," he thinks. He starts to back out of the opening and his right hand lands on a coil of thick flesh that, from experience, he knows will instantly strike or slither away. It does neither. John, his pulse resonating in his injured shoulder, ears, and belly, gingerly picks the thing up, backs out of the cave, drops it at his feet, and sees a timber rattlesnake, fat as his fist, several feet long, with most of its head blown off.

"What the hell have you all been up to?" John says aloud, glancing down at the dead girl, then disgustedly kicking the snake away from the opening. He runs past her and from beneath a bush near the pond picks up a short stick of iron-wood, then glances around for something to make a flare with, but, other than the girl's clothes or his own, can't find anything, so runs back across the quarry toward the lean-to, realizing as he traverses the gruesome trail left by the dead girl that everything he's done since reaching into her pockets has further undermined his credibility with the law should he get caught or decide to turn himself in, the latter option, under the circumstances and with his prior record, one he's pretty far from considering.

Without hesitating, he pulls back the plastic strip covering the front of the lean-to and plunges inside, hoping to find among the abandoned tools and moth-eaten recliner he knows are there a dry piece of cloth to make his flare with. He is struck first by the smoke-filled air, then by the pungent smell of marijuana smoke mixed with beer and sweat. A few articles of clothing and an open newspaper lie atop a zipped sleeping bag stretched out on one side of the ground. John at first thinks someone is in the bag, until he sees protruding from its top the furry head of a large stuffed lion, the sight of which, when he realizes who must have owned the toy, causes in him a despondent pain, worse even than when he first discovered the dead girl. He pictures her nestled com-fortably in the sleeping bag—like John's own son nestled beneath the covers of his crib — cheek to jowl with the lion, smiling and dreaming about her future, and he feels like going out right then, getting his gun, and shooting himself.

Instead, he sits down on the sleeping bag and, breathing in that putrid air, thinks of his little boy, Nolan, being raised in town without him, and what it would feel like for the kid to learn when he grows up that his father had killed a young girl, then killed himself, and how no one would be there to cast any light on the situation, to put a positive spin on the old man, certainly not his wife, who, from John, wants only child support and an uncontested divorce. This train of thought transports him deeper into self-pity, where he mentally bemoans all he has lost and had taken from him in his thirty years, beginning with his birthright, the family farm, on which he had planned, like his father and grandfather, to raise his family, and followed shortly thereafter by his father, whom John remembers near the end, when the banks were starting to foreclose, grim-faced and determined one day, angry and violent the next, getting thinner, smaller, paler, until, to his sixteen-year-old child, he vanished like a ghost, as if he never was, and John thinks he wouldn't mind dying, but he doesn't want to be a ghost in the mind of a son who never knew him. "The girl is dead," he emphatically tells himself as he stands, "and my bein' so too — or goin' to jail — won't bring her back!"

From the sleeping bag he picks up a T-shirt — a man's size 42 — wraps it twice around one end of the ironwood, and ties it securely. Then, suddenly thinking the girl ought to have some company in that dark hole, he reaches down for the stuffed lion and, in lifting it, pulls back the sleeping bag to reveal inside a cone-shaped flashlight, a carton of 9-millimeter shells, and a Luger pistol. "This ain't here for shooting rattlesnakes," thinks John, picking the pistol up and hefting it in his hand. He ruefully wonders if here is what the girl might have been running for when he shot her, but thinking of the stuffed toy and her half-written letter, he can't fathom it. Then he thinks, "Whoever this Waylon character is, I don't want to be here when he gets back." He drops the gun on the pillow, where it lands with a metallic thud.

John looks at the pillow, bulky and misshapen, thinking he's had enough surprises for one day and he ought to just leave, but like a man falling downstairs who can't stop his own descent, he reaches down and with his knuckles lightly taps it. The pillow is hard. John pushes it. It barely moves. He grabs the closed end of the pillowcase and vigorously pulls it until he's holding in his hands just the case and gazing down at a dented, dirt-stained, large metal container. Feeling like a tumbleweed caught in a tornado whose eye is his own tragic act, John bends down next to the container. Fumbling with trembling hands to open the rusted latch, he hears a voice in his head say every life has a defining moment; here comes your second. He opens the case, looks inside, and sees piles and piles of haphazardly stacked bills in various denominations.

In John's head a flat, practical voice says he ought to drag the girl away from the quarry, maybe to Quentin's swamp, where even hunters don't venture, weigh her down with stones, then drop her in a deep bog. He can't do it, though. He can't even bring himself to dig a hole and put her in it.

The thought of covering her with dirt reinforces in his mind a hundredfold his awful act. Burial has a ring of finality to it he can't yet bear.

This time carrying in one hand the flashlight and in the other the pick poised in front of him like a spear, he duck-walks into the cave, the sleeping bag draped over his shoulders, listening for telltale rattles, knowing that where one snake lives, so may others. Past the entrance, he is able to three-quarters stand, the jagged granite ceiling acting as a painful reminder not to lift his head too high. The silence starts an ominous hum in his ears. Nervously he thinks of the precariousness of his position, imagining himself an egg beneath an elephant's ass.

Crouched near the center of the cave, he moves the light in a slow circle around the oblong interior of dark red and slate-gray rock, two sides of which ooze a moldy dampness. The back wall is dry; in the floor in front of it, John sees a rectangular hole surrounded by freshly dug dirt, gravel, and a long, flat rock. One side of the rock is earth-stained, as if it has recently been removed from the hole, which looks to be slightly bigger than the metal box full of money in the lean-to. A nervous twitch starts in the muscles of John's injured shoulder. He tries to fathom the man who had crawled into a snake-filled cave with a pick, shovel, and Luger to unearth a box of money, and how the money had come to be there in the first place. A rattle sounds to his right.

He flashes the light that way and sees, three feet from him, two eyes like hot coals inches from the ground, and behind them, above a coiled, thick body, a tail rapidly vibrating its cacophonous clatter. He could back out of the cave. The rattler wouldn't bother him. But he thinks of the girl, trapped there with it, and his pent-up emotions from the previous hours coalesce in blind rage.

Keeping the snake lit, he moves the pick in a silent arc through the dark air in front of him, stopping it a foot above, and a few inches behind, the diamond-shaped skull, before swiftly bringing it down lengthwise. He slams one foot on the pick, pinning the reptile to the floor, then lifts and forces down hard the heel of the other on the snake's head and grinds until he hears a dull pop. The rattler lies still. After a minute, John picks it up by its tail. He holds it that way while shining the light around the rest of the interior, searching for more snakes and not finding any. He exits the cave, holds the rattler out like a trophy toward the dead girl, hollers, "That there's the last of 'em," and tosses its body next to the first one.

Then he grabs the cadaver by the shoulders and drags it head-first into the cave. After laying the sleeping bag along the driest wall, he places the body on it, folds its hands beneath one side of its face, and gently tucks its knees in at the waist. For a minute or so, he crouches there, studying the girl's body in the flashlight's beam, seeing on her cherubic face a child's peeved, forlorn expression. Then he runs back across the quarry and retrieves her satchel with its contents, and the stuffed lion. He lays the satchel near her feet and the lion on the sleeping bag next to her. Still not satisfied, he unzips the bag, then spends several minutes wrestling the cadaver and the lion into it, so that, when he's done, just their two heads stick out. Even now, he has trouble leaving the girl. On his knees over her, he prays:

"As you seen, God, her dyin' was an accident. Maybe I

shot too quick and now I gotta live with it. I ain't figured it all out yet. Even 'bout the money, which I could dearly use. Anyway, here she is for you to watch over. Thank you. Amen."

He emerges from the cave into the midday sun covered with the girl's blood and feeling like some misunderstood, tragic figure—a latter-day Frankenstein—who's rapidly evolving into the monster he's widely believed to be. The buzzards are on the deer carcass again and he chases them off, screaming maniacally, then runs straight from there to the lean-to, where he enters, grabs the metal box and the pillowcase, hauls them outside, and transfers the money from the former to the latter, tying the case, when he's finished, with a granny knot.

He looks around at the carnage in the field and thinks if he doesn't clean up the trail of blood and dead bodies even a moron stumbling on the scene could draw a pretty good picture of what's happened and maybe even who did it. He buries the shot rattlesnake beneath a slag heap, then, not wanting to waste good meat, wraps the other up in a pair of men's dungarees that were in the lean-to and brings them and the money over next to the dead deer. Knowing he can't lug back the entire carcass, especially not along with the money and rattler, he decides to make the rest disappear.

He kneels down next to the body, pulls out his hunting knife, and with its serrated edge starts sawing just in front of the buck's hind legs. The torso is hard-boned, gnarled, and muscular from years of fighting and just living and, for nearly thirty minutes, resists John's efforts to sever it. Afterwards he cuts out the deer's tongue and wraps it with the snake in the dungarees.

When he's finished, his muscles are burning; he's sweat-soaked and drenched with gore from a half-dozen bodies; his mouth is parched; and he's weak from hunger and adrenaline overdose. He glances at his watch. Nearly three o'clock. He worries that maybe Waylon will come back early— though if he comes in a vehicle, as he will almost surely have to, it will be a four-wheel drive that John will hear winding up the steep, potholed road a good ten minutes before it arrives, but even that will be cutting it close. He's concerned, too, about somebody else, a hiker maybe, wandering into the quarry, though the likelihood of it seems slim. Mostly, he just wants to be gone.

He hoists the buck's head and upper torso onto his shoulders, walks over to the pond of algae-black water, drops the three-quarters carcass onto the bank, and stuffs it with several pounds of stone. Following the task he is so hot and thirsty that he takes off his pants and shoes, walks into the tepid water, and laps at it. After taking two steps, he drops in over his head. He stays beneath the surface, scrubbing himself, seeing only a few suspended weeds inches in front of his face, until his lungs threaten to burst. He emerges, screaming out the air still in his chest, sucks in some more, then goes down again. He goes down and comes up half a dozen times, before swimming over to the water's edge to retrieve the rock-laden torso. He hauls the body into the pond with him, then sinks with it to the bottom. When he's satisfied it will stay there, he swims to the top, climbs from the water, dries himself, and dresses.

Using the T-shirt he found in the lean-to and a fallen spruce branch, he spends several minutes cleaning up, then smoothing over the grass around and beneath the dead deer, then the path made by the human cadaver from the briars to the cave. When he looks at the field afterwards, he has to remind himself that the girl or the deer ever existed.

With the sleeping-bag cover he ties the shotgun around his waist; then he drapes over his shoulders the buck's hindquarters and the snake-and-tongue-filled dungarees, whose combined weight is maybe sixty pounds. He carries the money by his side, on the long walk home alternating the heavy pillowcase between his left and right hand every few minutes.

He hangs the deer's hindquarters and the rattlesnake from the rafters in the woodshed, then, carrying the money sack and a length of bailing twine, slithers on his stomach into the crawl space beneath the shed and lashes the pillowcase to the top of one of the heavy foundation beams.

Too exhausted to move afterwards, he lies there, imagining the girl doing likewise in her dank tomb, and wondering if at the quarry he left unattended some minor detail that, like a loose thread in a suit, could lead to a mass unraveling. The wondering, he knows, will end only with his surrender, capture, or death, which leads to his feeling that events are being orchestrated by some higher force and that, like a caged rat, he is the subject of some bizarre experiment.

Halfway down the mountain, Cecil Nobie begins loudly calling in his cows for evening milking—"Cow-bossie! Cow-bossie!"—just as John's father used to do years ago from the same rear open doorway in the barn. Though it's fourteen years since he bought the Moon farm at auction from the bank, Nobie's hollow shout can still give John chills, especially when the foliage blocks, as it does for half the year, his view below the treeline, so that the spectral voice floating up through the heavily leaved terrain might indeed be that of Robert Moon's ghost. This afternoon, though, John is only amazed that anybody—Cecil Nobie included—is going about his or her everyday affairs as if yesterday's world were unaltered.

Only after he crawls out from beneath the shed and starts walking down the sloping lawn to the trailer does he realize how much his muscles ache and his shoulder burns. He inwardly vows to show up for work the following day, regardless of the pain. It's important, he thinks, for him to act and appear normal to the world.

The sun, three-quarters concealed behind the mountain at his back, casts a dark shadow, like a diving whale, on the opposite mountain. A swirl of dust from an ascending vehicle is visible above the hollow road, and John wonders if Waylon might be on his way up to the quarry to retrieve his girl and money and how he will react to losing both.

In the trailer bathroom, he gets undressed, then into the shower, where for several minutes he steels himself against a coarse blast of freezing water. Subsequently, he cleans his shoulder wound with peroxide and wraps it in an aerated bandage.

After drawing the blinds against the dying light, he lies down naked on his bed and tries unsuccessfully to convince himself that it is the morning of the same day and he has just awakened. He thinks about his wife and son, insulated for three months now in their village apartment, making for themselves a new life in which John is to have no part, and he remembers his wife's departing words to the effect that she doesn't want the boy to grow up, like his father, thinking there is no life beyond a small patch of mountain that is the last vestige of his ancestors' homestead.

In the end, thinks John, in a stuporous half sleep, everything boils down to money and death. The whole world. As if he's counting sheep, he silently repeats, "Money and death, money and death." The phone rings. He doesn't answer it. He closes his eyes and sleeps fitfully, dreaming not about the girl or money, but of the wounded buck that like a dying pied piper led him through the woods into a box canyon from which nothing that enters leaves unchanged. Around 3 a.m., he wakes up sweating and disoriented. He puts on his clothes and goes out to the woodshed.

He skins and butchers the buck's hindquarters, then the rattlesnake. He carries the meat and the deer's tongue into the cellar beneath the trailer and tosses them into the standup freezer. Afterwards, he sits for several minutes on the front deck with an open beer that he doesn't drink, and, by the star-filled sky, is reminded of the insignificance of all earthly acts, including his own.

He empties the beer over the deck railing, then goes back to bed. He sleeps until his alarm wakes him two hours later.

MONDAY

H E WORKS most of the morning next to Levi Dean, both of them with shovels, smoothing out the gravel as it slowly slides from the back of Cole Howard's dump truck onto the undertaker's driveway. Except for Dean's mumbled curses, neither man says much while working, both seemingly hypnotized by their own monotonous motions and the metallic ping made by the rearranging pebbles. The hot, hard work is made more so for John by the dull pain radiating from his injured shoulder to his fingers that with nearly every scoop causes him to wince and grunt, and by an apprehensive feeling that someone is watching and judging him. By ten o'clock it is hotter than the day before. Dean and John strip off their shirts, the former's mammoth, jiggly upper torso sun-pink and obscene against John's short, compact body, which is, but for his gauze-covered shoulder, deeply tanned.

"Who bit ya?" asks Dean, nodding at the shoulder.

"Ax head broke off."

"So what?"

"Jumped up and jabbed me."

"Jumped up from where?"

"What are you, a goddamn cop? The ax head come off, hit a stone, jumped up, and jabbed me! What else you want to know?"

"I'm just asking."

"Now you ain't got to."

John doesn't trust his own thoughts. He is uncomfortable in his own head, as if on his first full day in a new life he hasn't got used to an altered way of thinking. He suspects that people looking at him will discern that he is a man with a deep dark secret. He keeps seeing in his mind the flash of brown-and-white that was the dead girl and the impacted grass on the road he had noticed before he shot her, followed by the pick and shovel standing against the quarry wall. Is there an evil speck on his soul, he wonders, that had foreseen the murder and driven him to it? Could this be the life, that of a thief and murderer, he was meant to live? He thinks of the money that could change his life, that might even bring back his wife and child. But how could he possibly spend it without raising suspicion? Levi Dean slaps the side of the truck loudly to indicate the load is out.

"This goddamn undertaker's got an airstrip for a driveway," he says to John. "Must be he flies in the corpses."

John grunts.

"Who the fuck needs a driveway this long?"

John shrugs.

"You get laid this weekend?"

John doesn't say.

"I did," says Dean. "I never seen nobody do what she done. She got down on her hands and knees and backed my prick into her then had me pick up her ass and legs and wheel her around the room like that till she got off. So I did. Then she blew me."

"Ask him how much it cost him," Howard yells out the truck window.

"Yeah," says Dean. "Go over to Cole's house and ask his wife how much."

"Two men together couldn't hold up my wife's ass," says Howard.

"She wanted me to slap her ass, too," says Dean, "and yell giddyup. But I told her she'd have to get Cole to do that."

"Did she french-fuck your tits, Dean?"

"I think this is gonna be my last day," says John.

"What?" says Howard.

"I ain't sure yet. I'll let ya know."

"Let me know?"

"I'm pretty sure it will be."

"Yeah, right," says Howard. "Three months. That's about how long I heard you were good for."

Dean laughs. "Give him a raise, Cole," he says. "Bring him up to minimum. Maybe he'll change his mind."

"I'll give him shit," says Howard, lowering the truck's rear end onto the bed. "He can work for a living or sit on the side that goddamn mountain he holes up on and keep feeding his wife and kid with jacked deer meat. It's no skin off my ass."

He spends his lunch hour in the office of Daggard Pitt, the attorney he had made an appointment with last week, on Simon Breedlove's recommendation, to discuss his divorce. Pitt turns out to be a tiny, maimed man who drags one shriveled leg like a tail when he walks and always seems to be apologizing. He occupies two rooms above J. J. Newberry's. His receptionist/secretary, who looks like she might be Pitt's sister, for the entire half hour of John's visit talks loudly on the outer-office telephone to a veterinary hospital about scheduling her cat to have a tumor removed.

John shoves the papers he'd been served across the desk at Pitt, who, fidgeting like a small child on one side of his chair and periodically rubbing his shrunken leg with a dwarfed hand frozen in the shape of a claw, surveys them, making disapproving grunts and groans. John sits there looking past the lawyer, out the window, at the traffic light above Main Street, imagining himself a porous wall through which his guilt oozes like sweat, and thinks, "Maybe I ought to just lay the whole thing on this lawyer," then, remembering his prior convictions—three for poaching, two for driving under the influence—tells himself no lawyer in the world could convince a judge or jury not to send him to jail for a good long time. Daggard Pitt says something about the papers having been served thirty days ago and the law allowing only twenty days to answer them.

"They got under somethin'," says John.

"The problem, thankfully, is not fatal."

"I ain't interested in a divorce. We don't see eye to eye on that."

"I'm awfully sorry," says Daggard Pitt, slumping in his chair.

"I'm ready to end this thing."

"How so?"

"She mentioned couns'lin' once—I'd go now, if it'll bring her home. Tell her lawyer that."

"At any rate," says Daggard Pitt. "We ought to serve them an answer."

"I never hit her nor nothing."

"I'm glad to hear that. I certainly am."

"It ain't about that."

"Nor does she allege so."

"She's got this idea about the boy."

"Your son?"

"Nolan. After he—she started to see things different."

"Different?"

"Suddenly my way of doing things—not that I'm lazy. I always provide—she can't say I don't provide."

"She says you have trouble keeping a job."

"I've kep' plenty of 'em, just not for long."

Daggard Pitt smiles encouragingly.

"I was raised to farm—suddenly she wanted me to get a full-time factory job, work nine-to-five indoors like some..." John lets his voice trail off. He thinks of Gerhard Lane, the former college football player who represents his wife, then tries to imagine the Lilliputian Daggard Pitt, with his hang-dog look and shriveled limbs and the way he wheezes and makes funny little noises to himself, in the same courtroom with Lane, and his heart sinks. He actually starts to feel sorry for Daggard Pitt. "Look," he says, "what's the use? She wants a divorce she's gonna get one sooner or later, I know that much. If it comes to that, the boy ought to be with her. I'll pay what I can. There's no money, only the acre and a half that my trailer's on that I inher'ted fair and square from my mother."

"I was acquainted with your parents," says the lawyer.

John stares blankly at him.

"I wish I had realized it before—I didn't put the names together."

"Acquainted how?"

"I represented the bank when it foreclosed. I felt awful about it—we all did. The bank did what it could to keep your father afloat—but the economy at that time, and his having overextended himself, then, of course, him taking sick..." Daggard Pitt stops in midsentence, reaches down, and firmly grasps the emaciated midpoint of his bum leg as if to assure himself it's still there. When he looks up again, John can see the pain from the leg in the lawyer's face. "I thought I ought to tell you, in case—though, from my point of view, John, I would like nothing better than to represent you to the absolute best of my lawyerly abilities."

"How'd you get yourself all mangled up?"

"What?"

"Was you born like it?"

Daggard Pitt frowns sardonically. " 'Twas the hand I was dealt. Indeed."

"Least you didn't have to get used to it later."

"Pardon?"

"To havin' to walk crooked."

Daggard Pitt smiles pleasantly. "I thought it was the rest of the world did."

"My father was a good farmer," John says, "and a shit businessman. He died so long ago I can't hardly remember him."

"You'd have been in your midteens, as I recall."

"You still whoring for the bank?"

"Not for almost fourteen years."

"You're cheaper than the rest of 'em I called. That mean you ain't as good?"

"Compensation takes many forms, John."

"Better not take more'n the half grand I was told."

"I only meant I have no wife, John. No family. Only my clients and their often sticky and heartfelt situations. Simon Breedlove and I, for example, have known each other for years."

"He says you got almost a heart."

"He's in a position to know."

John stands up, reaches into his pocket, pulls out the five $100 bills he had taken this morning from the pillowcase, and drops them on Daggard Pitt's desk. "There's for your retainer," he says. "All's I want's for you to delay matters long's ya can, while I try to work things out."

"Work things out?"

"Get her thinkin' turned around 'fore the water's all over the dam."

"I'll draft an answer to her complaint—a general denial—for your signature. We'll get it to Gerhard Lane, then go from there."

"Don't do nothin' fancy," says John, walking toward the door.

He has the uneasy feeling that he is the focus of the sun's glare. He stops at the drugstore and buys a bottle of aspirin and a pair of mirrored sunglasses that he puts on. The thought of pouring blacktop in the afternoon heat next to Levi Dean causes the pain in his head to radiate backward from his eyes. He eats three aspirins.

At the municipal parking lot, he sits in his idling pickup truck, its engine growling through an aerated muffler, tormented by images of money and death. He pictures his own guilt as an animal hollowing out his insides and wonders if it's true what he's heard that keeping a big enough secret can kill you. He pictures his wife, in cotton smock and jeans, leaning against their open trailer doorway, her long, walnut-colored hair blown back by a gentle summer wind; and the boy, all eyes and facial expressions and herky-jerky movements. He imagines Moira cradling him in her arms the way she does that tiny, fragile body and him telling her all about yesterday's awful events and the horror then magically vanishing.

Leaving the parking lot, instead of turning right onto Main Street and heading for the undertaker's, he turns left, toward Puffy's Diner, the first floor of a two-story red-brick building wedged between two others of like design, to see if Moira is working the lunch shift.

Cruising slowly past the diner, he is unable to see through the foggy plate-glass windows in front, so turns right onto Broad Street and peers in at the dirt parking lot behind Puffy's. Among a dozen or so vehicles, he spots Moira's salt-eaten Ford Escort sitting near the building's far corner, next to Jerry Puffer's Olds 88, with its busted driver-side shocks.

Now he's not sure what to do. It's lunch hour and busy in the diner. Moira will get all flustered and upset if he approaches her. Then John will get upset, and that will make matters worse. John, though, feels driven to speak to her. Or at least to see her. His mind, overloaded with data, is temporarily closed to other options.

Twice more, he cruises by the diner, trying to decide how to proceed. He shoves a Hank Williams, Jr., tape into the cassette deck and turns up the volume. He thinks of Moira's freckled, spherical face; her strong, angular body, soft only where she is most a woman; her dark brown eyes that remind John, depending on her mood, of gently caressing or sharply probing fingers; the rounded smooth curve of her buttocks where they merge, then sharply intersect with her plump vaginal lips.

He'll walk into the diner like an ordinary customer, he tells himself, order coffee and a sandwich, and when he catches Moira's ear, cordially whisper to her that after the lunch crowd thins out, he'd like very much to speak to her. In the meantime, he'll just sit there, drinking his coffee, hoping that just the sight of her will clear up the ambiguities in his head. She couldn't, thinks John, driving by Puffy's for the fourth time, get angry at that.

Puffy's front door opens and two men emerge—one tall and blond; the other, who is vaguely familiar to John, dark-haired and stocky with a duck-billed cap pulled low over his eyes. They start to cross the street, then, at the same time that John, making the turn onto Broad Street, spots a police car approaching from downtown, change their minds and quickly walk off in the opposite direction.

Still trying to place the second man, John hears a short siren burst. He looks back and sees the police car, its bubble light flashing, follow him onto Broad Street. John turns into

Puffy's parking lot. The police car does the same thing. John feels his heart leap into his throat. He considers slapping the truck into reverse and heading as fast as he can out of town. Then the cruiser comes to a stop in the exit, blocking his retreat.

John sits in the middle of the lot, one foot on the clutch, glancing frantically around the cab, wondering if he should open the door and run for it. He hears laughter to his right and sees two kids, standing in the alley between Puffy's and the barbershop next door, holding up their middle fingers at the police car. Another short blast of the siren, then a microphoned voice calls out, "I know you, you little hellraisers."

The kids run off down the alley. Above the music in the cab, John hears someone yell, "Fuck you, chief!"

Then the microphoned voice says, "Park her, Moon, shut her the hell down and sit there with your hands on the wheel!"

John slowly pulls the pickup into a space between a flatbed truck and a minivan. He ejects the tape and shuts off the engine. If this is how it's meant to be, he thinks, okay. He even feels a little relieved.

The cruiser's driver door opens. Undersheriff Ralph Dolan steps out, yanks his belt and holster up over his melon-shaped gut, and, in his exaggerated hip roll, starts walking the fifty feet to John's truck. John thinks, "Of all the cops in the world, goddamn Ralph Dolan." He tells himself not to mouth off, though knows that around Ralph Dolan he sometimes can't help it. Dolan pokes his big head through the window.

"What's in the cooler, John?"

"Popsicles," says John.

"Wouldn't be beer, would it?"

"Might be one or two in there, Undersheriff. I can't remember."

"How many of 'em you already drunk?"

"None so far. Wouldn't take much to start, though."

"You puffing me, John?"

"No, sir, Undersheriff." John emphasizes the "Under," though he knows better. "I ain't puffing you." Grimacing, he waves his hand at Dolan's breath, which smells like a taco burger. "I'm inhaling you."

Dolan backs out of the truck and glares at him. "Take off those fucking sunglasses, Moon."

John takes off the glasses, blinking in the sudden glare.

"You look shit-faced, Moon."

"I been workin' too hard. Ain't had enough sleep."

"Maybe you been working on jackin' deer and that's why you ain't slept. That right, jacker? You the one was heard blasting away in the preserve early yesterday morning?"

"Weren't me, Undersheriff, on account of you scared me so bad last time I sold all my guns. I don't even eat meat no more."

"How 'bout I take a look in that cooler, John?"

"I don't guess today. Less'n of course you got a warrant."

Dolan leans back on his heels and surveys John's truck. By now John figures it's just one of Dolan's pull-over-and-harass stops, though he's not sure if there's any substance to the comment about the preserve or if Dolan was just fishing. As he watches himself being written up, John curses himself for not holding his tongue. "Got you a bad muffler, John," says

Dolan, ripping off the ticket and handing it to him. "Heard ya clear to the other end of town."

John bites his tongue. He folds the ticket, then puts it in his wallet. "Can I get out now?" he asks, reaching for the door. "Go about my business?"

"Maybe I ought to see if you can walk a straight line."

"I'll piss one if you want me to."

Dolan closes his ticket book, then slips it into his back pocket. "Just don't cause no trouble at Puffy's, John."

"I'm gonna eat lunch."

"Way I hear it," says Dolan, adjusting his wide-brimmed hat, "she don't want to be bothered." John steps out of the truck. "Not by you, anyway."

John smiles, though it's the last thing he feels like doing. "You oughta run for sheriff again next time around, Ralph," he says. "I'll bet the same two people voted for ya before would again."

"Fix that goddamn muffler, Moon," says Dolan, waddling back to the cruiser.

His three hundred twenty pounds engulfed in a cloud of blue-white smoke, Jerry Puffer bobs the burning cigarette between his lips at John, who answers with a curt nod. In response to a few other greetings, he barely grunts.

He sits in Moira's station, at the end of the counter opposite Puffer, and next to a thin, toothless man eating soup.

He grabs a menu, pretends to read it, then puts it back on the counter. He drinks some water, then picks up a napkin and coughs into it. He puts his fingers onto his temples where his head still hurts, and pushes. The smoke is stifling around the counter. He wonders how Moira, who wouldn't allow smoking in the trailer, stands it.

Carrying a tray of sandwiches and french fries on one shoulder, she abruptly bursts through the swinging kitchen doors. Spotting John, she raises her eyes, gives a tiny side-to-side shake of her head, then charges right past him, twenty feet or so down the aisle, where she starts distributing food to patrons in three or four different booths.

Seeing her, John feels his spirits raised and lowered at the same time. He remembers her once saying that she loved in him what the world couldn't see—a gentle soul and a kind heart that injured easily and took forever to heal. She was good with words and could easily have gone to college, yet had married John, who didn't even graduate from high school. John thinks now that he had always believed she would one day tire of him and leave and that this became a self-fulfilling prophecy. Watching her going about her job, he imagines that her movements now contain a self-assuredness that says, louder than words, "I am going forward into the world and not looking back."

She comes around the counter again, passes the tray she's carrying to a set of hands behind the swinging doors, then walks over to where John sits, pulls from the front pocket of her wrap-around green smock a pencil and paper pad, and as if John is just another customer, asks him what he would like.

"A cheeseburger," says John. "Medium rare. Fries. Coffee."

"What kind of cheese."

"You know what kind."

"And a side of slaw, right?"

"I don't want slaw."

"No slaw?"

"Tossed salad."

"Tossed salad? You hate tossed salad."

"I'm going to give it another shot. Doctor says it's good for me. Make it a large tossed salad."

She smiles, barely, and writes down tossed salad. John sees Puffer owlishly peering through the smoke at them. "I just come from my lawyer's."

She blows at a strand of hair that's fallen from the bun atop her head into her eyes. "Who'd you get?"

"Daggard Pitt." John studies her face for signs of inward laughter, but doesn't see any. "I told him to tell your guy I'm ready to go to one them couns'lors."

"Well. I think you ought to."

"I mean together."

"Oh, John."

"Was you who wanted to."

"That was before."

"Before what?"

"We separated."

"We didn't separate. You moved out."

"Whatever."

"I got some things home for you and the boy. I'll drop them by later."

"What things?"

"Food things. And money."

"Can't you give it to me now?"

"What?"

"I've got a class until eight o'clock."

"What sort of class?"

"I told you, John."

"Tell me again. I forgot."

"A college class. Night school. I'm studying to be a teacher."

"I'll come by after, then."

"I'd rather you wouldn't tonight, John. I might not be there."

"Why? You got a date?"

"I don't want to talk about this now, John."

"And you don't want to talk about it later. When do you want to talk about it?" Lifting one hand to gesture with, John accidentally nudges the toothless man just as he's lifting a spoon to his mouth. The spoon flies from his hand, clattering onto the counter. Soup splashes into the man's lap.

"Sorry," says John.

"The hell you say."

Moira picks up John's spoon and hands it to the man. "Chris' mighty," he mouths. "Go fetch me another bowl of soup there, missy. On the house."

"I don't know," says Moira.

"You don't need more soup," says John. He sees Puffer grimacing at him through the smoke, his ox-like head angled precariously forward. "You didn't lose but a spoonful." He looks at Moira. "I'll come by and see Nolan then. He'll be there, right?"

"It's not such a good time, John. I wish you'd called ahead."

"I need to see him. And you."

"We been there all week and you haven't needed to see us."

John puts a hand up to his mouth, and whispers, "I got somethin' important to tell you. 'Bout our future."

"John, I..." He watches her face, her whole posture sag. His heart sinks. He wants to bury his head in her lap and cry.

"How 'bout my pants?" says the man.

John glares at him. "What about your goddamn pants?"

"They look pissed in."

John reaches into his pocket, pulls out his wallet, withdraws a ten-dollar bill, and slaps it on the counter in front of the man. "There," he says. "Go get 'em cleaned!" He looks up to see Moira disappearing through the swinging doors and Jerry Puffer laboriously rising from his stool. John gives him a half wave. "Don't trouble yourself, Puffy," he says. "We're good over here." He pats the toothless man on the back. "Ain't we good?"

"We got her straightened out, Puffy," yips the man. He picks up the ten dollars and shoves it into his pants pocket, then goes back to eating his soup. Puffer silently lowers himself back onto his stool, picks up his cigarette, sucks it with his fat lips down to the filter.

John stands up and walks toward the exit. Everyone in the place, it seems to him, is waiting for him to do something. He pulls his dark glasses from his shirt pocket and puts them on. His head throbs. He senses rather than sees Moira reenter the dining room through the swinging doors behind him. Pushing open the glass door to the street, he barks over his shoulder, "Cancel my order, Puffy!"

Harsh laughter behind him. The afternoon heat in his face.

The two men he had earlier seen leaving Puffy's are back

where they had started. They glance left, right, then cross the street in front of John and climb into a black Chevy Blazer. John definitely remembers the dark one from somewhere—his small, piercing eyes, the blocky look of his skull.

He hears the Blazer start up, then watches it pull into the street and drive off toward the east edge of town. John feels haunted, pursued. He turns onto Broad Street and heads for Puffy's parking lot. A minute or so later, as he's climbing into his truck, it hits him—Waylon. The man in the dead girl's photograph.

The tree was felled by spring lightning. Three months before, John had dragged it with Cecil Nobie's John Deere in four pieces into his back yard, then sawed the pieces into logs. A quarter of the wood will go to Nobie. The rest John will burn or sell. He owns a gas log splitter and chain saw, but this afternoon he uses an ax. The work is as hard or harder than laying blacktop and he doesn't get a paycheck. Neither, though, does he have to listen to Levi Dean or Cole Howard, and from his mountain perch he has a grand view of the valley.

About an hour into the work, he begins to marvel at the multitudinous ways in which chopped wood splits. Two nearly identical-looking logs when struck with equal force in their direct center by an ax head will splinter in entirely different manners. He finds this as intriguing as the varied echoes produced by his chopping. Thump. Bang. Whop. Like the rumblings from a giant's belly. For a while, he even manages to block out the pain in his shoulder. He works shirtless, stopping only to wipe his brow or to drink a beer from the cooler on the grass near him. He is as impressed with his own physical stamina and prowess as he would be watching a horse or a tractor at work.

He thinks about the land, how it shouldn't be bought or sold for money, but possessed, as in pioneer days, by those best able to work it. His father, thinks John — and he, too — should have lived back then, before dairy co-ops, sixty-thousand-dollar tractors, milk inspectors, grain monopolies, double-digit interest rates, major land developers. He feels his anger slowly boiling, as it hasn't for years. More chronic than acute, it is directed at everything, but at nothing specific. Even after all these years, he isn't astute enough to know for sure if losing the farm was the fault of his father's reckless spending, the bank's greed, the economy's collapse, or cursed luck landing like an incubus on the Moon family.

The loss of the land. His birthright. Every misfortune or failure, every hurt and tragedy, John sees as being born of that deprivation: his father's death — never mind the doctor's talk about cancer and metastasizing tumors — and, four years later, his mother's, whose heart just quit in the middle of dinner one night; his own hermetic existence, living like Cecil Nobie's serf on an acre and a half of mountain, forced to pilfer and poach from the land that should be his; his abandonment by his wife and son. In this roundabout way, his errant, self-pitying anger meanders and slowly comes back to its fuse, that black, impenetrable spot in his mind that he wishes were a dream.

The same questions over and over. Could he, an experienced hunter, have prevented her death? Could he have

S M T W T F S

foreseen it? In some unconscious way, even wished for it? In his mind he has already separated the money from the tragedy that begat it. Much has been taken from him in his life and very little returned. He sees the money not as a road to a more exorbitant life but as the way back to his wife and son. Maybe he could even buy a large parcel of land—start his own farm, off this mountain—for the three of them. Then he thinks again of Waylon. Had he already returned to the quarry, or might he have been on his way there when John saw him? And what has John left behind that might lead Waylon to him?

He chops until he has produced half a cord of firewood, and, at his back, the descending sun is a huge, fiery ball. His naked torso is a knotted, slick muscle. Now he is aware again of the pain in his shoulder. He takes off the blood-damp bandage, dabs at the open wound with his T-shirt, then, deciding to let the cut air, sits down on the grass near the cooler. He eats three more aspirins, washing them down with beer.

He thinks of the deer carcass sitting with his 12-gauge slug in it at the bottom of Hollenbachs' pond. And the dead girl in the cave. If Waylon finds her, wonders John, how long will it take him to figure out some local hunter had killed her and stolen his money?

Only the stars and Nobies' houselights, filtering up through the trees, illuminate the mountain. The temperature has dropped fifteen degrees. John's slick sweat has dried, penetrated his skin, and turned rank. Where it has sat for three hours on the back-yard grass, his rear is stiff and sore. The empties from two six-packs form a roofless, four-sided building between his feet. Somewhere back on the hill, a coyote yips. Nocturnal birds and animals fly and scurry through the woods to his right. From the spring-fed pond below the trailer comes a cacophony of peeps and croaks.

John takes off his shoes, then shakily stands up, pulls off his jeans and underwear, and walks naked into the trailer. He gets a rattlesnake strip steak from the refrigerator, fillets it, cooks it for five minutes beneath the broiler, then rolls it in olive oil and cornmeal, and leaves it to slowly panfry on the stove while he showers, dresses his wound, and puts on clean clothes.

Before leaving the bedroom, he takes from the closet, then carefully lays on the bed, one of the few articles of clothing Moira had overlooked when packing to leave: a long, blue-and-white-striped, country-style dress that John best remembers her wearing, six months after they were married, to a heart fund benefit square dance at the old armory. He puts his face to the dress and smells her. Then he sees her, stately and beautiful. Her hair up and in dancing clogs, she is several inches taller than John this evening. John feels the envious eyes of the other men — eyes envying him. Moira wins a cake in the raffle, three layers of sour-cream chocolate. Later, lounging naked where the dress now rests, they feed the cake to each other, then spend half the night in a lingering, nerve-tingling, impacted embrace from which Moira occasionally reaches down, gently squeezes the leaking tip of John's inflamed penis, and whispers, "Rein it in, cowboy. Rein it in. This ain't no race. It's a swoon!"

John never knew love could last that long. When, finally,

he comes, he is a river, emptying into her not just his seed but all the words describing what he feels for her but is not adept enough to say. Looking at the dress now, he sees the moment as clear as if he were watching it on film: Moira's wide-open eyes, like full moons in the dark; lean hands clutching his buttocks; vaginal muscles firmly milking him. Her throaty voice passionately urging, "Okay, John! Now!" A pulsating throb, like a crashing wave. Warm breath. That musky, just-fucked smell...John charges across the room and rummages through her bureau until he finds an overlooked pair of her briefs. Smothering his face in them, he inhales.

Then he drops his pants, lies down on the bed, and, ardently calling out her name, masturbates into the underwear.

He feels embarrassed afterwards. Then cuckolded. Looking at himself in the bureau mirror, he imagines his face is slowly evolving into a coarser, meaner him. Then he thinks, no. It looks like a clay lump that could turn out to be anything. He thinks of the crippled Daggard Pitt, who had helped steal John's birthright, suddenly showing up in his life at this time, of all times. "I'm drunk," he says aloud, as if that explains something. He thinks his face looks too predictable. He decides he will grow a beard. He puts Moira's underwear on the headboard, goes out to the kitchen, and finds it engulfed in smoke.

He throws open the door to the front deck, then runs over to the stove, where his strip steak and the pan it's in are in flames. John douses them both with water, then opens all the trailer windows and, loudly cursing, charges around waving at the smoke with a towel. In a few minutes, coughing heavily, he stumbles out to the deck to breathe. Collapsed in a plastic chair, he watches stodgy black smoke twist lazily into the night sky. He thinks about what he went through to get that rattlesnake back to the trailer, then butchered and filleted, and decides it wasn't meant for him to eat. He goes back into the trailer, gets the burned strip steak and his .45 pistol, comes back out to the porch, tosses the steak onto the lawn, and empties his gun into it.

Then he goes downcellar, pulls from the big freezer what's left of the rattlesnake, half a dozen venison steaks, and a bag of ice, and takes them all out to his truck, where he tosses everything into the portable cooler. Standing in the driveway afterwards, still three-quarters drunk, he decides that offering mere meat to his family is not enough. A much bigger gesture is needed. He runs up to the woodshed, crawls beneath it, pulls out the pillowcase, withdraws several packets of money, then reattaches the pillowcase to the foundation beam.

Sitting at the kitchen table, he counts the money. Five thousand six hundred dollars. A lot. Much more, certainly, than he's ever seen at one time. Yet only a tiny percentage of the whole. He wonders, though, if it's too much. If word got out that he was giving away sums that big, what then? Still, the gesture must be big. A big—great big—not tiny, cash wad is the point. Like John's cataclysmic orgasms, the gift is meant to speak volumes; to say more than he is able to say in words about his love and concern for his family. He eats two bologna-and-cheese sandwiches, washes them down with a quart of raw milk. He thinks himself nearly sober. He looks around at the kitchen walls streaked with soot. The whole trailer smells like burning charcoal. He decides to give Moira all the money but a thousand dollars. Before he leaves, he rolls up the latter amount and stuffs it into the sugar jar above the sink.

He drives the eight miles to town in a blindered, half-drunk state, foreseeing from his mission only positive results—a grateful Moira, an impressed Moira, a contrite Moira, begging for him to take her back. He parks in front of a liquor store at one end of the street, then, carrying in a paper bag the deer and snake meat and the cash, he walks the two hundred yards to where she lives on the top floor of a three-story, white, flaking clapboard building, half obscured by spruce trees. Her car is out front.

Looking up at the third-floor windows, dark except for a single flickering light, John is suddenly not so sure he's doing the right thing. It's later than he thought. Nearly ten o'clock. What if Moira is in bed? Worse yet, what if there's someone up there with her? The street behind him is so quiet he can hear the buzz of the streetlights. An occasional car passes. John walks back up the street to the liquor store, goes inside, buys a pint of schnapps, then walks back to Moira's, and, drinking the schnapps, leans against her car, staring at the flickering light, imagining it to be about anything. A firefly lights several times in front of his face. John tries unsuccessfully to catch it in his hand. He wonders what it would feel like to fly, to bypass walking altogether.

A vehicle comes fast down the street, slows up, then turns into the dirt driveway next to the house. It's a small compact car. Rap music pours from its open windows. While the engine's still running, the driver's door opens. A long-haired kid holding a square, flat box steps out. He glances at John, then quickly walks to the outside stairs on the side of the house and starts up them, two at a time. A dog starts barking somewhere in the building. A voice tells it to shut up. John watches the kid climb past the second floor and head for the third. He drops the empty schnapps bottle onto the grass. A horrible image of Moira naked beneath another man flashes into his head. "She don't even like pizza," he thinks. "I've never seen her eat even a single goddamn slice."

He starts on a half trot toward the stairs.

He reaches the bottom of the first platform just as the kid, guffawing to himself, steps onto it from above. "Unfucking real, man," he says, shaking his head. "Some dudes got all the luck!" More to steady himself than anything else, John puts his hand not holding the paper bag on the kid's chest. The kid stops laughing. "What's the deal, man?"

The world spins around John. He asks the kid, "Who ordered it?"

"Huh?"

"Who ordered the fucking pizza?"

The kid nods up the stairs. "She did, man. The chick."

John pushes past the kid. Holding on to both rails for support, he lurches up the wooden stairs to the third-floor platform. He leans against the entrance-way door, hearing inside, above soft music, piggish grunts, moans, one- and two-syllable verbal barks. Through the door he sees past the kitchen into the living room, where the light flickers. He thinks, "How can the world end in a single day?" He is past reason, several drinks beyond thought. He puts his hand on the door handle and turns. The door is locked. He smashes the paper bag into the lowest section of glass, reaches through the hole, unlocks the door, yanks it open, and runs through the kitchen into the living room, where a naked woman holding a pizza slice sits cross-legged on the floor before a television set. John starts to speak, then hears behind him a click and a man's voice. "Drop the goddamn bag."

John doesn't recognize the voice or the woman. He's not sure he recognizes the house. People are fucking on the television. He says, "Is this 1201 Belmont?"

The woman giggles.

The voice says, "I'm not shitting you, man."

John drops the bag.

"Now, who the fuck are you and what do you want?"

"I think I got the wrong house," says John.

"Most fucking likely."

"No," says the woman. She tosses the half-eaten pizza slice into the box next to her. She looks sweat-soaked or greased. Her nipples are red flares. She's bald between her legs. "No, he don't."

"How do you know?" says the voice.

"That's John."

"John?"

"The husband."

John hears a baby cry in back. "What's going on here?"

Frowning sheepishly, the woman pulls a blanket from the couch, wraps it around herself from the neck down. "I'm Moira's friend, Carla. From Puffy's?"

John's thoughts can't find anywhere to land. He looks

more closely at the woman and thinks maybe he's seen her around. He recognizes the blanket covering her as the one Moira's mother made them for a wedding present. That's their television set playing. Their couch. "What are you doing in Moira's house?"

"Babysitting."

"Babysitting?"

"For Nolan." The woman stands up. "Moira's out."

"Out where?"

"I didn't ask."

"Christ," says John. "You're watching porno movies."

"We got a constitutional right," says the voice.

"You got a fucking gun on me?"

"I put it away."

John doesn't turn around. "And fucking in front of my kid!"

"He was asleep," says the woman.

"Till you woke him, John."

"Fuck you," says John. He glances at the television screen, on which three men in wolves' masks are screwing Little Red Riding-Hood. "Both of you!"

"I'll get him," says the woman, starting for the back bedroom.

"No, you don't," says John. "You don't go in there with my kid!" He looks around at the room filled with empty beer cans, a half-full vodka bottle, ashtrays with butts of something smoked in them. "You better have your clothes on when I come back," he barks over his shoulder at the man. "I don't want to see your sorry ass naked in my wife's house! Christ, what's the matter with Moira?" He reaches down, switches off the television set. In the ensuing hush, the kid's wail becomes more pronounced. John starts toward it.

"Better let me," says the woman.

"What?"

"He ain't used to seeing you."

"Ain't what?"

"You're apt to scare him."

"I'd punch you in the mouth," says John, pushing past her, toward the sound. " 'Cept I been taught better!"

"Okay," says John. "Okay. Easy now." His arms and legs pedaling madly, the kid lies on his back, squawking like a bird begging for a worm. John's words have no effect on him. He's like a lump of wood standing there. "Daddy's here."

Above the crib hangs a mobile of small animals. Pushing one with his finger, John makes them spin. The kid wails louder. John grabs the animals to stop them. The mobile pulls free from its mooring and lands in the crib. The kid screams like he's dying. John tosses the mobile onto the vanity. A Vaseline jar is knocked to the floor. The kid hollers, "Mommy!"

John didn't know he could talk. Part of him is elated. He leans into the crib and gushes, "I'm Daddy. Can you say Daddy?"

The kid looks mortified.

He hates me, thinks John. Already he's decided. Probably thinks I abandoned him. Or he knows I'm evil inside. Can see right into my soul. Christ, he tells himself, he ain't a year old. How can he know anything? Why won't he stop crying, though. What would Moira do? Pick him up, maybe? He reaches down, puts his arms beneath Nolan's back. He lifts him. The boy goes completely still. A moment later, he lets out such a scream John nearly drops him. "What's the matter?" he asks, in a panicked voice that petrifies both of them. "Did I hurt you? Did someone else? For Christ sake. Show me where!"

The wailing builds to a crescendo. John turns the boy over in his hands several times, looking for bruises or cuts, some sign of an injury. Then he thinks maybe it's one of those scars you can't see, some mental pain having to do with the fucking he must have overheard in the next room. He thinks about Moira leaving their son with these people. And he'd always believed she was a perfect mother. I'll go for custody, he thinks. Raise the boy myself. "Stop now," he begs. "Cut it out, Nolan. You're scaring Daddy!" He puts the boy against one shoulder, starts patting his back. Then the woman, Carla, is there, her hands reaching out. "Easy now, John. Just give 'im over gentle."

She's wearing blue jeans and a pullover black jersey. Her wild, frizzy hair is still sweaty at the temples. John says, "What's the matter with him? What did you people do to him!"

"He's fine. Just a little scared's all. And hungry. Poor little man." John hands her the boy. She deftly cradles him in one arm. With her free hand, she places a bottle in his mouth. He stops crying, then starts making wet suckling noises. The woman softly rubs his back, rocks him to and fro, coos gibberish in his ear. John glares at her. He wants to say something but isn't sure what. Reaching out a hand, he gingerly touches one of his son's socked feet. The whole foot is smaller than John's finger. He touches the other foot. He counts five tiny toes through the cloth. There's tears in his eyes. Incredible, he thinks. Absolutely unbelievable what Moira and I done. "He looks like you," says the woman.

John grimaces at her.

"Yeah. You know, round the eyes."

"I'm gonna tell Moira what I found here," says John.

The woman shrugs.

John places a hand on the boy's head, feels the heat there, the silk-soft hair. He thinks about taking him back, but is afraid his son will cry again.

"Got Moira's long legs, though," says the woman, "and gentle temperament."

John walks past her into the living room.

His mouth drops open. Before the television set, holding the bag he brought for Moira, stands the lanky man with bulging eyes, veiny, tattooed arms, and collar-length, thin blond hair who earlier today John saw crossing the street with Waylon.

"You remember me, John?"

John doesn't say. He looks for the gun and sees it protruding above the left side of the man's belt.

"Way you looked at me, I thought maybe."

"I seen you comin' out a' Puffy's today."

"I didn't see you."

"Maybe you was too busy watching somethin' else." John jerks his head toward the bedroom. Suddenly he is struck by the smallness of the world. He imagines himself the bull's-eye at the center of a shrinking target.

"We got something in common there, don't we, John?"

"I can't guess what."

"Oh, come on, John. We fish in the same pond!" The man laughs. He's clothes-coordinated with Carla, except for his steel-toed boots. "Old Puffy, that chain-smoking lard-ass, got himself some hired help, I'd say."

"Some reason you can't fuck in your own place?"

"You know how it is, John. My dick's a basset hound." He shrugs. "I'm just the poor sumbitch holding its chain."

"I can't figure out why you're still here."

"Nobody lives here's asked me to leave."

"Most guys make assholes of themselves don't wait to be."

"Hell, John, that was nothing. You shoulda come few minutes earlier—got the show the pizza man did." He smiles, then holds up the bag. John wonders if he's looked inside. "You want me to put this in the fridge? It feels like maybe it needs it."

John strides forward and snatches the bag. Fighting an impulse to check its contents, he shoves it beneath one arm and glares up at the man, who leans casually back against the doorframe. "You mad at me for some reason, John?"

"I don't like guns being pulled on me."

"A fucking madman breaks into the place, what would you do?"

"I don't like 'em around my kid."

"A lifelong hunter like you, John? I can't believe that!" John thinks fleetingly of grabbing for the pistol, which is making him more and more nervous, then tells himself that alcohol and recent events are making him paranoid. "Truth is, John, I'm like you. A person who makes good use of what he kills shouldn't have to worry what time a' year it is or whose fucking land he's on. Christ, can you imagine if our ancestors who discovered this fine country could only hunt when the government told 'em to? Jesus, wouldn't none of us be here!"

"Moira know you're here?" says John.

"Why don't you ask her?"

"I might."

"Do that, John. When you give Moira her bag of goodies, ask her if she knows Obie—that's short for Obadiah—Cornish—that's like the hen!" He sticks out a hand, which John doesn't take. "No shit, John, we might actually be acquainted, seeing as how a number a' years back old Obie Cornish spent many a day busting his ass for peanuts around and about that old mountain you're on. Though I've moved on to a more lucrative line of work, I'll never forget those days, or that terrain. Jesus Christ, steeper than a hard-on, it was!" He pulls back his hand, places it onto the butt of his pistol. "Yup. Back in town after a lot of years, only to find out not much has changed, 'cept I understand you and yours had a string of bad luck. Money must be pretty tight these days, huh, John?"

"I don't recognize you from a clump of cow shit," says John.

The man laughs.

John walks past him into the kitchen, then over to the front door, his feet crunching against the broken glass. In the bedroom, the woman, in a low, throaty voice, starts singing a lullaby.

John opens the door and steps into the night, quieter even

than when he'd stepped out half an hour before. "What about the bag, John?" asks the man. "Ain't you gonna leave the bag?"

John doesn't answer.

Descending the stairs, he has an odd feeling the man was never there. At the same time, he worries about being shot in the back. He glances in the bag and sees the meat and, beneath it, three rolls of cash, just as there had been.

The same dog starts barking again. This time, though, no one tells it to stop. A light breeze rustles the spruce trees; higher up, thin clouds blow across the moon. A pickup truck peels out from in front of the liquor store. John uses his key to open Moira's car, then carefully wedges the bag beneath the accelerator, where Moira will be sure to find it.

Tuesday

O N T H E B A C K of the dead girl's neck, at the base of
her skull, is a star-shaped birthmark. Had he seen it
when he first discovered her, prior to turning her over?
Couldn't be! She had a ponytail and was wearing a hat. The
rest of the time, she lay on her back. So how does he know
it's there?

Her breasts are milky-colored and large, the consistency
of a soft pudding, more those of a mature woman than of a
teenager; their centers are blood-red bull's-eyes with cuspate
nipples that, when sucked on, pop up like bulbs. He had not!
When had he?

She has the hard, muscular calves of an athlete. A bike
rider maybe. Or a field-hockey player. Her left knee, marred
by a four-inch butterfly scar like that on his own right
elbow, has been surgically repaired. The tissue is raised
and slightly swollen, as if the operation was recent. Impossible for him to know! He certainly hadn't removed her jeans!
Why, then, does he recall the smooth, lacquered feel of
her thighs? Her neatly manicured pubic bush, emanating
the smell of apple-essence shampoo? The wet, musky taste
of her?

★   ★   ★

In his sleep, John thrashes out with an arm, pushes open the truck door, and, with several empty beer cans and a schnapps bottle, tumbles onto the dew-covered grass surrounding the trailer, now convinced that his crime is more atrocious, even, than murder. His head hurts. His vision is blurry, though clear enough to see that the truck sits in the center of his unmowed lawn, a few feet from the trailer's front door. He has no memory of parking it there. He can't recall driving it home.

A damp, dew-marred morning breathes an earthen, fresh smell, slightly tempered by the odor of just-spread cow shit. Sitting like a pillow on the valley, fog obliterates the world past a hundred yards. Nobies' electric barn cleaner drones beneath the bone-white canopy. Their yellow, toothless hound howls. John wonders if following his discovery of the dead girl he went into a trance-like state during which he committed horrendous, unforgivable acts he can't consciously recall. The thought is nearly unbearable. He picks up the schnapps bottle and knocks himself over the head with it. The bottle's refusal to break infuriates him. He flings it at the pond. The splash starts the frogs croaking. Two ducks lift off.

Drinking coffee later at the kitchen table, he consciously summons her face and finds it lacking in particularities, those individual nuances that make a person unique. This strikes him as being as sad almost as her death itself. He feels intimate with her, a closeness beyond his ability to understand. A familiarity that has nothing to do with sex. The coffee tastes bitter to him. He throws it out and opens his first beer of the day. He picks up a deck of cards, aimlessly shuffles them, starts playing solitaire. At the very least, he thinks, he owes her loyalty, which requires that in his memory she be forever preserved as the person she truly was and not as he dreams her. The implications of this are muddled and horrible.

The phone rings six times and stops.

The deck screen door creaks open. Something enters. The door bangs shut. Mutt, the three-colored stray that lives at John's when it feels like it, shoves its wet nose in his lap. "Where you been, Mutt?"

Mutt wags its tail.

John stands up, walks to the refrigerator, pulls out leftover spaghetti, dumps it with milk in Mutt's bowl. Mutt greedily gulps the food. Idly scratching the dog's burr-impacted neck, John gazes down the valley at the slowly rising fog while mentally trying to reconstruct the previous evening, which in response to his thoughts roils like a quagmire of ambiguities. He remembers Obadiah Cornish openly referring to John's poaching and, later—had he been dreaming?—the dead girl's transmogrifying body and his orgasmic spasm entering it like a gunshot.

The phone rings again. This time he answers it. It's Cecil Nobie wanting John to come down and give him a hand pulling a heifer out of the muck.

"Anne and the kids is to her sister's for the day's why I troubled ya." Nobie spits, then shakes his head, too large for his bandy-legged little body that's wearing fishing waders. The cow's in up to the tops of its legs in a quag at the rear side of the barn where runoff from the meadow and mountain pools.

"What happened the fence?"

"Power went dead."

"And she walked right through her?"

"Like muck was molasses."

"Goddamn dumb."

"As a tongueless Polack. Figured we didn't get a rope round her pretty quick, she'd be clear to China."

Standing at the edge of the quag, John grips Nobie's left hand while he wanders as far as he can into the slime before tossing the looped rope he's holding at the cow. He tries unsuccessfully several times to lasso the animal, which lows, exhales phlegm, and sinks deeper. With each failure, Nobie's ruddy, sun-chapped face gets redder. In John's injured shoulder, the burn intensifies.

"Widen the goddamn loop, Cecil."

"She's wider'n a whore's legs a'ready. She's so covered with muck, though, I can't toss her straight!"

When finally he gets the rope around the cow, it slips down onto her neck, so pulling on it would strangle her. "Now I can't reach the friggin' thing to get it off, John."

"Let me run get a pitchfork. We'll get a prong into that loop, then run it back over her ass."

"Just don't leave me here in the goddamn quag, John. I might not be here when ye get back."

After yanking Nobie from the muck, John gets a pitchfork from the barn. Ten minutes later, the loop surrounds the cow, though only her head and the upper third of her torso are still above the muck. Nobie and John are slime-covered. The pitchfork is lost to the quag. When the two men pull on the rope, the cow doesn't budge.

"I better run get the John Deere."

"I wouldn't spend much time talkin' 'bout it," says John.

Nobie runs for the barn, his waders making wet, sloshing sounds.

Kneeling by the quag's edge, John, watching fog patches move like ghosts over the damp meadow, talks softly to the cow. Working to break through the haze, the sun tinges the grass gold. The organic smell of that world is an opiate to John's frayed nerves. He daydreams being fifteen years old and working, not with Cecil Nobie, but with his father.

As Nobie backs the John Deere up to the quag, half his herd gathers round. John ties the loose end of the rope to the tractor's drawbar. He pulls the rope until the loop closes tightly around the cow. "Ease her forward till she's taut, Cecil. I'll sit down on her. Maybe keep her from jumping."

Nobie drives the tractor ahead until the rope is like a tightwire over the slime. Feeling the loop's pressure, the cow moos protestingly. Still gripping the rope, John sits down on it. "Steady she goes, Cecil."

Nobie gives the tractor a little gas.

"Don't jerk her, now."

Nobie eases out the clutch. The rear wheels briefly spin, then take hold. The cow groans. It lifts up some, comes forward a foot or so, lifts up higher, then, bellowing, falls on one side in the muck and is pulled free. "Whoooa!" yells John.

Nobie stops the tractor. He lets it roll back a little. With the clutch in, he guns the engine victoriously.

John jumps from the rope, pulls the loop from the muck-encrusted heifer, then stands back as the animal scrabbles to its feet. Blowing its nose, shitting and pissing at the same time, it angrily charges toward the pasture, while John, watching it go, thinks if only he'd had a similar chance to save the dead girl.

Stinking to high heaven, they stand in the back yard of the house John grew up in, while the last of the fog lifts.

"Got ye any work, John?"

"Just chopped up that old lightning-struck oak."

"Any a' the paying kind?"

"That'll pay me something come fall when I can sell her."

"Thought you was doing some blacktopping."

"Nah."

Nobie strips off his waders, then, in his skivvies, leans back against the porch railing and starts scratching different parts of his wiry, hair-covered self. "My oldest boy, Eban, he's done with school come spring. Already got hisself into college. Place in Rochester."

"Good for him."

"Got hisself some smarts from his mother, I guess. Wants to do something with computers—make 'em think or something."

John nods.

"Never used one myself."

"Me neither."

"He thinks they're the best thing since sliced bread. Says I ought to have one for the farm. Keep all my records on it."

"Maybe ya ought to."

"I got me an old shoe box works plenty good enough." Nobie hunches forward, pulls his dick out of his underwear, and starts pissing into the yard. "Once he goes to Rochester, John, I don't expect we'll be seeing much of him 'cept Christmas and summertime, when, if we're lucky, he might help bring the hay in. I'm proud as can be a' that boy, John, but he ain't never took to farming and I can't say his sister do neither. Guess I don't blame 'em. World out there looks pretty exciting these days and, for sure, there's no money in farming." He puts his dick away, then turns toward John. Out on the hollow road an approaching vehicle whines. "We never had us a need for a full-time man before, John, but when Eban goes, it ain't right his mother should have to take up the slack."

John throws the last of the coffee he'd been drinking onto the lawn. He hears the vehicle downshift as it heads into the J-curve parallel to Nobies', then a basso growl as it starts the long ascent up to Ira Hollenbach's old place.

"If you could see your way round it, John, I'm offering you a job."

John doesn't answer.

"A good job. Long-term."

John nods his head, just to show he's heard. Nobie's a fine farmer and, unlike John's father, a good businessman too. To buy the Moon place, he'd sold, for plenty more than it was worth, the hilly, rock-infested one hundred fifty acres on Briar Hollow he'd grown up on to a real-estate developer who'd put up town houses. He kept John's parents' place looking as good or better than when they'd been alive. But work for him? As a hired hand? No way, thinks John. He'd as soon lay blacktop.

"Ain't that a persistent sumbitch," says Nobie, nodding at the road several hundred yards above his place.

"Huh?"

"That one nosin' round Hollenbachs'." He points a quarter of the way up the hill, beyond the thick foliage, where, glimmering like a beetle in the unobscured sun, a black Chevy Blazer climbs. John's stomach rolls over. He feels like that heifer, neck deep in the quag. "Second time I seen it go by in twenty-four hours."

John looks down at the coffee-soaked patch of sunburned grass at his feet, thinking how, from the single pull of a shotgun's trigger, the world's turned upside down.

"Maybe after five years somebody's finally looking to buy the place. Got to be from out the area, though. Wouldn't ya say, John?"

John shrugs.

"Hell yes! Nobody local, 'specially ones that remember Old Ira and Molly, gon' move into that place knowing its history. Be like walkin' on their grave! You believe in ghosts, John?"

"As much as I don't."

"Sure. Me too." Nobie starts stripping off his skivvies. "Course it's a nice piece a' land and I s'pose somebody might buy it, tear the house down, and put up a new one, but I don't think that somebody'd be me." Naked, holding his underpants in one hand, he nods toward the garden hose. "How 'bout we hose some this muck off, John?"

"I'll jis' go up to the trailer," says John. "Dive in the pond."

"You sure?"

"Pos'tive."

Nobie tosses his skivvies on the porch. "I hear Ira's sister lives down in Philadelphia inher'ted the place and ain't set foot on it since the murders." Nobie walks over to the spigot, turns on the water, then bends down and picks up the hose. When the water starts coming out the end, he brings the hose up to his mouth and drinks. Then he aims the spray at his feet. "You let yourself think about it, it can give you the creeps knowing whoever done it could still be living hereabouts."

"Why would they be?"

"Gotta be living somewhere, ain't they?"

"Yeah," says John. He turns, starts walking toward the front of the house, and is stopped by Nobie's voice.

"Maybe you'll think 'bout it, huh, John? 'Bout the job?"

"Yeah."

"Sure. Think it over. There ain't no hurry."

Glamorous women in nightgowns, underwear, bathing suits. Marble-skinned, haunted-eyed women. Women dressed in striped ties and suits. Starved-looking women. Women with sour pouts, bored frowns, mad, toothless smiles. Women with weight-trained muscles and gnarly-looking breasts coiled like jack-in-the-boxes beneath their skin-tight outfits. Women who beckon alluringly. Laugh haughtily. Jut out their chins, asses, elbows. Shave their heads. Wear tattoos. Show their nipples beneath their shirts. Dance, sing, stride like race-horses around tartan tracks. Who look right through him as if he is the air they breathe.

Dozens of Moira's old *Redbooks* and *Glamours* lie among empty beer cans on the front deck beneath where John sits leafing through them, searching for a look similar to the dead girl's, a face to recall hers, with its novelties and nuances. Straining the limits of his memory, he seeks to contradict his unconscious, nightmarish revelations from the previous night. But he can't make her complete. She is inchoate in his mind—a pretty face, an adolescent's evolving body, pale blue eyes, dirty-blond ponytail.

The sun sits straight over the mountain. Puffy white clouds, shaped like beanbags, rest above both horizons. The heat from the last several days is unabated. There is almost no breeze to temper it. John thinks he might not recognize her were she to walk this very minute into the trailer, so intent had he been after killing her not just to conceal her death from the world but to expunge her life, to act as if she'd never been. That, he realizes, was a worse crime than shooting her. People who loved her—her parents, her two girlfriends, Tools and Germ—even now must be wondering where she is. And Waylon? Maybe he'd loved her also.

He stands up, walks inside and over to the kitchen wall phone, not sure whom he intends to call, until he picks up the receiver and dials the county sheriff's department.

"I'm calling 'bout that girl," he says, then, thinking he ought to disguise his voice, jerks the phone from his ear and reaches above the sink for a dish towel.

"Hello?" says a woman's voice.

"Just a minute," says John. He puts the towel over the phone's mouthpiece. " 'Bout that girl..."

"What girl?"

"The one lost."

"Please speak up, sir. I can't hear you."

"The girl."

"I heard that part. What girl?"

"The one reported missing—the runaway—I'm calling 'bout her."

"About who?"

"The missing girl."

"Which one?"

"Ain't somebody reported a girl'd run off recent?"

"We've got an envelope full of flyers, sir. In country and out."

"Flyers?"

"About missing kids. Runaways. Are you talking about a particular girl."

"One 'bout sixteen? Blond ponytail? Blue eyes?"

"Does she have a name?"

"That's what I'd like to find out."

"What?"

"I don't know her name."

"What's yours?"

"Why?"

"I'd like to call you something."

"You ain't got to call me nothin'."

"How do you know she's run away?"

"Was in her pants."

"What?"

"Was a note in her pants pocket. Said she'd run off."

"Note from who?"

"Her."

"To who?"

"Somebody else."

"Do you know who she ran from?"

73

"If I did, I w'udn't be calling the goddamn sheriff."

"How'd you happen onto the note?"

"What?"

"What were you doing in her pocket?"

"Somethin' bad happened her. An accident."

"What sort of accident."

The phone starts shaking in John's hand.

"Sir?"

"Yes?"

"Does she need an ambulance?"

"What?"

"Does the girl need medical assistance?"

"No."

"Would you hold on for a minute, please, sir?"

"What for?"

"I'm going to let you speak to an officer."

"I'm just tryin' to find out her name. That's all."

"Hello?" says a male voice.

John hangs up the phone.

Paralyzed by his predicament, he sits in one of the plastic deck chairs, with the beer cooler resting at his feet, and watches through binoculars for the black Chevy Blazer to descend from Hollenbachs'.

The kitchen clock ticks loudly behind him. Mutt endlessly stalks a woodchuck at the upper edge of Nobies' pasture. The sun slowly heads for the horizon. John gets drunker. His thoughts fragment. Waylon, the dead girl, the money, Obadiah Cornish, Moira's leaving him — each, alone, is horrible to consider. Their combined weight is staggering.

He thinks about Ira and Molly Hollenbach's murder, how the police had questioned about everyone in the area, including John, who'd ever heard Ira brag that hidden in his house was a safe containing over twenty years' worth of undeclared profits from the quarry and farm that Ira would retire on. Like most of the county's populace, John theorized that being a blowhard is what got Ira killed. He figured that whoever had cut up Molly to get Ira to open that safe was so enraged at discovering its piddling contents he'd slit both their throats. Now, though, he wonders if Ira really had been loaded and the money John has found was his. But why would the robber have hauled it all the way up to the quarry and buried it? And why would he have left it there for five years?

Through the glare of the late-afternoon sun, he follows the slow descent of the black Chevy Blazer. A quarter mile above Nobies', it passes by the treeline on that side of the hill and disappears. Why was it up there so long? wonders John. Did he—or they—find the deer carcass? Maybe even the girl's body? If so, now what? John remembers how, in front of Puffy's, Waylon and Obadiah Cornish had suddenly changed their minds about crossing the street in front of a police car. Could one—or both of them—be wanted by the law? The phone's ring makes him jump. He knocks a half-filled beer bottle onto the deck.

"My lawyer's going for an order of protection tomorrow, John. From now on, you're to stay away from the house." Moira's calling from a pay phone. John hears voices in the background. "You can't just go around breaking windows and leaving rancid meat in people's—John?"

"Yes?"

She lowers her voice some. "Are you in trouble?"

"What?"

"Did you...?" Her voice becomes a whisper. "John, for God's sake, where did all that money come from?"

"It's for you and Nolan."

"There's over four thousand dollars there!"

"A few months' advance."

"Advance?"

"There'll be more."

"More?"

"We can buy a new home if we want, Moira."

"What's going on, John? Are you all right?"

"You at school?"

"Yes. Look, John—I can't spend this."

John watches out the window as Mutt makes a blind rush for the woodchuck, which whistles harshly, then dives into its hole. Mutt puts its nose to the hole and starts sniffing.

"Some son of a bitch looks like Ichabod Crane was fucking the babysitter when I showed up."

"Carla told me..."

"I had every right to call the social services."

"You can't believe I knew about it!"

"I could go for a change in custody."

"You don't want custody, John. You don't even want to babysit!"

"Who's Obadiah Cornish?"

"Some friend of Carla's. I didn't ask him over."

"What else?"

S M T W T F S

"I don't know what else. I only met him a few days ago. He used to live around here, he said."

"He ask about me?"

"Just chitchat—about hunting, that sort of thing. He said he remembered you were quite a hunter—made some joke about your poaching."

"What do you know about the guy he hangs around with?"

"Who?"

"Heavyset guy, dark—they came out of Puffy's together."

"I don't know anything about him." A recorded voice comes on the line and tells Moira to deposit another twenty-five cents. "John—I'm giving the money back."

"I won't take it."

"I'll put it away someplace, then. I don't know what you've done, John, but..."

"What's it like there?"

"Where?"

"School?"

"I don't know. It's school, John. That's all. A lot of work..."

John hears what sounds like a rifle shot outside. He watches Mutt's body lift a foot in the air, fall to the ground, and lie still. "Jesus..."

"John?"

"I got to go. They shot Mutt!"

John cries when he sees him. Half his head's been blown off. He's got a mouthful of grass and foam and lies on his side like he's been thrown there. The bullet's buried itself in the dirt or flown off into the woods. The shot looks to have come from down the hill, on the town side of Nobies'.

Cecil answers John's call on the barn phone. John hears mooing, buckets clanging, the whir of milking machines. "He leave?"

"What, John?"

"The son of a bitch shot Mutt!"

"Who shot Mutt?"

"Who was there?"

"The one in the black Chevy Blazer. Had a picture of some girl. Wanted to know if we'd seen her."

"What'd he look like?"

"Long drink a' water. Said he was a private investigator hired by the girl's family. Her boyfriend's from these parts. S'posedly they was seen two days ago headin' into the east entrance the preserve. That's why he's been nosin' round."

"He show ya a badge?"

"Somethin' in plastic. Said the parents are offerin' twenty thousand dollars to whoever helps find the girl. I said he ought to talk to you, seeing as how half your life's lived in the woods round. He didn't come see ya?"

"No."

"If the girl's found—dead or alive—with all her b'longings, the twenty thousand, he said, 'll be paid no questions asked."

"What's that mean?"

"Go figure."

"He involve the law?"

"Weren't my bus'ness ta ask."

"Bastard killed my dog, Cecil! Didn't ya hear the shot?"

"I can't hear nothin' 'bove this racket. Why would he shoot Mutt?"

"I'd like to know. You watch him leave?"

"Had better things to do. I saw him walk out the barn, get in his car, and head for the hollow road's all. You gon' call the sheriff?"

"I ain't. Don't you neither."

"I got nothin' ta say to him."

The first time he showed up at the trailer he had a faceful of porcupine quills. Moira and John had been married less than a year. They spent two hours with pliers, pulling the quills out. Mutt, who was only half grown, never even whimpered. "You're one tough mutt, Mutt," Moira kept telling him.

He was a fighter. He fought for fun—raccoons, foxes, even a bobcat once. Following his bouts, he'd drop in at the trailer, showing off his wounds, looking to be patched up, fed, patted, bedded down for a few nights on the living-room floor. Then he'd get restless. He was a good dog. Never caused any problems. Just lived his life. Someone had house-trained him once or he'd learned himself. Moira was real impressed with his cleanliness. She called him "a mannered rogue."

John picks the dog up in his arms, carries him over next to the garden, lays him on the grass. He digs a hole in the soft loam there, places Mutt in the hole, then slowly covers him with dirt. Afterwards, he sticks a large flat stone vertically into the soil. Standing above the grave, he folds his hands, closes his eyes, and thinks about Mutt's wagging tail causing his whole body to whip side to side like a rod yanked by a hooked fish. He thinks of the three of them—Mutt, Moira, and John—lying together in front of a fire on cold winter nights. He says a short prayer. He asks God to let Mutt fight in heaven.

He sits in the kitchen, listening to crazed bugs battering the screens. It's dark down the hill. Frogs croak. They sound like giant frogs. Monstrous frogs. The Night of the Frogs.

He turns on the television set, tunes it to the one station he gets. Something's wrong with the horizontal hold. He switches the set off. He's aware of the bugs again. Then the frogs. He plays a game of quarters against himself. He wonders how, in this world, he could ever have thought his luck would be good enough to allow him to walk away unscathed with a case full of cash. The phone rings. He answers after the third one. On the other end, someone hangs up.

Five minutes later, it happens again. Beyond the lighted window, darkness cresting in a watery black wave. Minutes that feel like hours. Hours that feel like days.

He brings the radio over to the kitchen table, sits down, tunes the radio to country music. He listens to three songs. Four. His feet and armpits start to sweat. He kicks off his sneakers, pulls off his T-shirt. A commercial for Delco batteries plays. The phone rings once more. He picks it up. A man's voice says, "The dog got in the way."

"Who is this?"

"You know, right?"

"What?"

"How things get in the way."

"What things?"

The phone clicks dead.

A set of headlights slowly serpentine their way up the hollow. They turn onto Nobies' road, then continue on up the hill. Sitting on the deck, drinking the last beer in a six-pack, John is too tired and drunk to stand. He reaches down, picks up the .45 from beneath his chair, and flicks off the safety.

The vehicle lurches before skidding to an uncertain stop adjacent to the trailer. It backfires once, then stops running. A loud fart from inside. Raucous laughter. A female voice baying, "Gawd!"

Doors open to a loud creak. Another fart. "Je-zus!"

Simon Breedlove and two naked women exit Simon's beat-up old Cadillac. "Pool open, John?"

John waveringly sticks his arm holding the pistol straight up into the air and squeezes the trigger. In the still night air, the report is deafening. "He's worse than you, Simun!"

More laughter.

"I'll get the lights," says Simon.

John fires again.

Their loose flesh glabrous and silvery in the moonlight, the women charge hell-bent for the water.

"You must remember big Colette," Simon insists from the pond's grassy banks, where they watch the women, yipping and laughing, frolic in the water like overfed seals. "Is married to Ralph Gans."

"She ain't familiar."

"Colette Gans! Ralph's missus?"

Watching them water-wrestle beneath Simon's jerry-rigged lights, John has the feeling that this day and night are an eternal hell to which he is doomed. "Don't know him, either."

"Sure you do! He's got that scrap-metal yard outside Blenham. Three, four years ago we hauled a couple demo wrecks over there—was right after the Fair. Bunch of us tied one on after with Gans. I know you remember. Ralph Gans? Had that half ear?"

"I don't remember."

"You don't remember that set a' inner tubes she's carrying? Christ, you got to! She comes sashaying into Gans's living room 'round midnight wearing this little-bitty nightshirt could see right through and says, 'Raaaa-lph, these boys gotta go home now! Colette needs tendin' to!' Christ, we 'bout died. Who even knew the man was married? Don't you remember? Said it just like that—Raaaaalph!—funny thing is come to find out that's how she really talks—takes her 'bout an hour to get a sentence out."

"Nuh-uh," says John.

"You're bullshitting me, right?"

"I don't remember."

"The hell you say!"

John shrugs.

"I ran into her earlier this evening at Benders with this other one who's her cousin and a daughter to Beano Dixon, the mechanic down to the Chevron station? I didn't even know Beano had a daughter, but turns out he's got three he's been sendin' regular support to all these years up in Red Hook and this one here's the oldest. She's got a mountain lion tattooed to her ass. Got its teeth bared and its claws open. She gets out and shakes herself dry, you'll see." Simon caps the gin bottle he's been drinking from and tosses it into John's lap. "Figured I'd roust ya. Shape I'm in, don't know as I'd been able to handle the pair of 'em." Smiling broadly, he places his elbows into the bank and leans back. "What happened your arm, Johnno?"

"Buck gored me."

"No shit?"

"Dry-gulched me after I wounded it, then chased it for miles. Keep it yourself."

Simon grunts. "When haven't I?"

"I mean, don't even breathe it."

"You thinking it's like a vampire buck or what?"

John flicks his eyes at him.

"It's the middle of the night, Johnno."

"Yeah."

"You're sitting here shit-faced with a loaded pistol."

"And you're sitting next to me." John plucks a piece of hay from the field and starts chewing on it.

"I guess Moira ain't changed her mind?"

"She's educating herself. Worries about missing classes."

"That ain't so bad. Wished I'd had a little more."

"Why didn't ya?"

"Vietnam come along fucked with my aspiration. I was gonna be a nuclear fizzy—you know like Einstein was?"

"I think she's got a boyfriend."

"That ain't the end of nobody's world neither. The end of the world's when your heart stops beating."

"Yeah," says John. He thinks of the dead girl, the end of

her world a 12-gauge slug. He remembers Simon, thirteen years older than John, once saying that the world is divided into those who've killed someone and those who haven't and that the second group doesn't know how lucky it is or about the danger it's in. That was the closest he'd ever come to discussing the war with John. "You ever heard of a guy named Obadiah Cornish?"

Simon raises his eyes at John. "I don't brag on it. Why?"

"He pulled a gun on me last night over to Moira's."

"You don't mean to say, Moira...?"

John waves dismissively. "Cornish was over there balling the babysitter. He seemed to know a lot about me. I don't know diddly 'bout him."

"Last I heard, he was upstate, though that was a lot of years ago."

"How come I can't place him and he can place me?"

"He ain't much to place is why you can't him. Probably why he can you is 'cause he was foster kid one summer to Old Ira Hollenbach. This was back 'fore the killings—when Ira had the stone quarry. Cornish I guess got sent to Ira's after he wore out 'bout every other family in the county. Reason I know is I used to work for Ira. I was there when this psycho Obadiah stabs one Ira's cows to death."

"A cow?"

"One of Ira's top milkers. Kicks a pail of milk over onto Cornish and he runs and gets a pitchfork and jabs it straight through the cow's heart."

"Jesus."

"Yeah. Ira sent him the hell back the county after that."

John spits out the grass.

"He was one the hundreds the police talked to after Old Ira and Molly got sliced up. Has himself little Daggard Pitt for a lawyer, same as me." Simon pulls off his boots, then lies back on the bank and wriggles out of his jeans. Beefier and taller than John, he's got a long scar on his leg that he brought back from Vietnam and never talks about. As much as John's father, he'd taught John how to hunt. "Rule numero uno, Johnno," he used to say. "Don't shoot at rustlin' branches, footsteps, farts, or hallucinations." A few years back, after a downstate hunter had shot and killed his companion for a deer, Simon claimed the guy must've done it on purpose. Nobody, he'd said, could make a mistake that bad. And John had agreed with him. "Where's that three-colored mutt a' yourn?"

John whips his head around. He stares wordlessly down at Simon.

"He's usually slobbering all over me, I show up."

"I don't remember you ever giving a rat's ass."

"Still don't." Pantless, Simon stands up. He starts unbuttoning his shirt. "Just wonderin' where it's at, that's all." When he came back from the war, he'd gone to work for John's father, milking cows. He had a temper back then— once he'd gotten mad, punched a breed bull in the snout, and nearly killed it, and later spent time in jail for having similar run-ins with people. For weeks at a time he would disappear, then show up looking for his job back, and John's father would give it to him because finding good help was nearly impossible and Simon Breedlove, John's father used to say, could work the tits off a mule. He hadn't stayed long, maybe a year or two, but by then he'd become like an older brother to John, sometimes like a father, even though John didn't have any idea, and still doesn't, what Simon did on his long absences.

"Was shot," says John.

"Dead?"

"Yeah." John gazes down at the pond, where the smaller woman, her naked backside to the bank, has climbed on the shoulders of Colette, standing waist-high in the water. "Don't know by who."

"When?"

"Earlier this evening."

"What for?"

John's seeing tracers in front of his eyes. "How would I know?"

"I mean, might somebody had a reason?"

"I'd guess not."

"Well, shit."

"I buried him up by the garden."

"Musta been a reason."

Now John's ears are ringing. He doesn't answer.

"Nothing you can think of?"

"I loved that dog, Simon."

"Yeah, well, I know, John, but the thing to remember is—he was just a dog—not a human being—ya know?"

"We're getting awful lonely down here, boys!" The small woman, gyrating her backside, stands on Colette's shoulders. Simon shakes his head admiringly.

"Ain't that Colette a strong one, John?"

John doesn't say.

"With that equipment she must've fucked little-bitty Ralph

Gans right down to a carrot stub. 'Member how godawful small he was? Like a mouse. Had that half ear?"

"Can't place him," says John.

"Me, I never forget a face," says Simon. "You want to go swimming?"

John slowly gets to his feet. His head spins.

"Way you stink, she ain't gon' get near you less'n you do." Simon nods at the pond just as the small woman dives head-first into the water, yelling, "Banzai!"

"Did you see the mountain lion, John?"

John unbuckles his pants.

"Later she'll make it roar for ya."

"Me?"

"She's too young and skinny for me. I'm gon' tangle with big Colette see if we can't liven up the valley with tit-farts." Simon turns and sprints for the water.

On a blanket in the high grass above the pond, the girl moistens an index finger and presses it to her upraised nip-ples, one, then the other, as if she's playing pinball. Her taut, water-slick body reminds John of a coiled spring ready to pop. She tells him her younger sisters nicknamed her Mincy because when she used to get mad at them she would threaten to make them into mincemeat. She makes him feel her arm muscles, gnarly knots about the size of handballs, and says in her senior year of high school she wrestled with the boys' varsity and didn't lose a match. In the moonlight, her swol-len areolae look to John like plump red tomatoes. He tells her he's married and wouldn't be here if he wasn't drunk. She laughs and says that's most men's story, then helps him to remove his underpants. Naked, on their backs, they count shooting stars to the groveling, baying, flesh-quacking sounds of Simon and Colette on the opposite shore.

Rolling a leg onto John, Mincy tells him he's got a nice muscular little body, then reaches down and, while in his ear wetly whispering that the fucking across the water is making her as horny as she's ever been, plays like a kitten with his genitals. John says he's never cheated on his wife and Mincy places her pinky finger at the base of his balls, stretches her thumb as far up his penis as she can, which is nowhere near the tip, and coquettishly asks if maybe he's exaggerating a few inches. Then she's sitting up on John's knees, sliding his penis slowly back and forth between her squeezed-together breasts and saying that in her wallet is a condom she ought to slip on him, and John says okay, but instead of making a move to get it, she groans, "Oh, Christ," rolls off him onto her stomach, hoists her bottom with its snarling green-and-purple mountain lion an inch or two off the blanket, and with a self-conscious little smile says, "Like this, 'kay, little John? Hard as ya can, and deep."

Then John is inside of her and she's bucking backward into him and screaming for him to do it harder, and John, violently striking out with his groin, as lost in that world as he had been earlier in his wood-chopping, fixates on the back of her flying hair, which in front of his amazed eyes suddenly turns from an auburn pageboy to a dirty-blond clump.

He lets out a terrified scream.

Mincy, thinking he's about ready to come, barks over her shoulder for him to pull out, so John pitches back and she deftly rolls onto her back beneath him, then takes his penis deep into her throat, where John explodes, and in his mind sees a 12-gauge slug tearing into the chest of the dead girl.

He lies there, loudly gasping, too petrified to look, inhaling mud-stink, mountain lilacs, blood, and sexual juices, and hearing what sounds like a light wind rustling a bluestone-based field of nettles and brush. A voice moans, "You 'bout halved me!"

He opens his eyes and sees her, a dead weight on his groin, blankly staring, and imagines a gaping red wound between her breasts.

He tries to scream, but something blocks his throat. He gets up and in the gray, starlit field blindly stumbles toward the pond, retching out the impediment that is everything he's eaten and drunk since the morning before. He flops belly-down in the mud, lapping at the water, knowing that in this world once familiar to him he is now an alien.

WEDNESDAY

"Where's my foot! Who took my lucky god-damned foot!"

John wakes up in a pelting rain. The girl is on her hands and knees next to him, shrieking like a starving bird. In the semidarkness, with her pale, mud-streaked skin and hair plastered to her head, she looks like a living cadaver. He reaches out and touches her shoulder. She snarls, "The rain'll ruin it! Turn it to shit!"

He looks down and sees both her bare feet, mud-stained, but where they ought to be. He wonders if she's gone insane. Or if he has. "Leave it," he screams. "We'll come back for it later!"

A thunderclap blots out her answer.

"Come on! Run for the trailer!"

"Not without my foot!"

She throws his hand off, starts rifling the grass again. John glances up at the trailer. Several lights are on. A shadow fills the basement window, a head and two hands next to the cabinets where his tools are stored, another light in the master bedroom. John tries to stand, but in the slick grass his feet slip out from beneath him. He lands on the girl. She curses and starts punching him. He stifles her with one hand, then, with his knees, pins her to the grass. Her body feels electrified beneath him. John shouts, "What's the matter with you!"

She furiously whips her head from side to side, tries to bite him. With his free hand, John twice slaps her face. Her eyes look ready to pop out of her head. Her breath dampens his palm. John fears she is suffocating. He pulls his hand from her mouth. "You cocksucker! Where's my foot?"

"How would I know!"

She spits at him. "If you don't give it to me, you'll burn in hell!"

John is hit with a wave of nausea. His eyes, he thinks, are conspiring against him. He looks at the trailer, where the basement light has just gone out, then back at the girl. A lightning flash illuminates her face. She looks possessed. "My money's all in there!"

"I ain't got it!"

"Help me find it, then. Please!" She sobs. Snot trails from her nostrils. She sniffs it back in. John now realizes she is severely addlebrained, if not retarded. "The rain'll piss it away!"

She quits struggling. John backs off her arms. She rolls her head to one side, pinches a nostril, and blows, then does the same with the other. The surrounding trees sway in a brisk wind. In the trailer, two more lights blink off. Only the kitchen is lit now. John thinks, "On the road to hell I am alone and friendless." He rolls away from the girl. "Where'd you have it last?"

"Was tied to one my belt loops."

She gets to her knees. Her slick, nodular breasts bob like

drenched minks' heads. Water pours from the end of her nose. She starts patting the ground. Three feet away, John does the same. The rain lands like pellets against his back. Night crawlers and slugs intertwine with the wet grass. At regular intervals, lightning fractures the sky. He finds the foot beneath her cutoffs. An orange, furry thing with a zipper in it, attached to a rawhide string. He hands it to the girl. She unzips it, looks inside, and breathes a deep sigh. "It's still dry," she says to John.

John nods. He has an urge to apologize, though isn't sure for what. If he had something left to throw up, he would. "Beano Dixon's got himself three daughters," he says. "Unfucking-believable."

"I had this foot since I was five," she tells him. "Gettin' it wet inside's worse luck than losing it."

His shoes and boots are at odd angles in the bottom of the bedroom closet. The bureau drawers are not quite shut. One corner of the mattress spread is hanging from the spring as if, it seems to John, someone had lifted it to look under the bed.

In the bathroom, the towels in the linen closet seem to have been hastily rearranged. Beneath the sink, a can of Ajax lies on its side. Someone has taken his 12-gauge from the living-room rack and returned it to a different slot. Each oddity has a reasonable explanation. Simon and Colette were up early. After showering and using John's bedroom to change into their clothes, Simon had gone down-cellar to get some venison sausage from the big freezer, while Colette had started breakfast.

After changing his clothes, he enters a subdued kitchen.

The others have eaten. He's not hungry. The four of them sit there quietly drinking coffee. John wonders if he has interrupted a conversation about himself or if, like him, they are just hungover, now sober, seeing one another clearly, and not liking it much. Maybe they're just let down. He suspects they know his darkest secret and are conspiring against him. He trusts no one, not even Simon. The phone rings. Before he can answer it, Simon does, listens for a few seconds, then slowly hangs up.

"Nobody, Johnno." He wrinkles his brow. "Wrong number."

"Don't ya hate that shit," says Big Colette. She gulps her coffee, half a cup at one time, whereas Mincy lowers her face to hers and laps like a dog at it.

"'Specially," she says, "when you're just settin' there, waiting for it to ring so's you can talk somebody—anybody—'fore you go out your fuckin' mind, then 'brrrriiing!'—the asshole slams down on ya!"

John thinks if she's not retarded she's on hard drugs.

"Had me this breather one time," says Colette, in her constipated drawl, "so I breathed right back to 'im, started huffin' like I was 'bouht gon' blow my nuht. Mistah puhdpuller gets so scared he hangs upon me."

"Cops'll trace that shit, ya ask 'em."

"I w'udn't ask 'em."

"Was in *The Star* 'bout a prevert had 'em walk right in with the phone in one hand and his little red pencil in t'other. Was talkin' to Joan Collins."

"Gawd! Talk 'bout red-faced!"

"Red-penciled, ya mean."

94

"I wish you girls'd shut up," says Simon. "I got a headache."

"That ain't the tone you used last night, Si-mun!"

"Last night I was so drunk I could hardly see."

"Well, I don't much like what I'm lookin' at here this mornin' neither."

John walks over to the gun rack and gets down the 12-gauge.

"Still huntin' with them slugs, Johnno?"

John nods.

"They don't leave much question, do they?"

"Nuh-uh."

"Men and their great big guhns," says Colette.

Mincy laps at her coffee. "Or eensy beensy 'uns."

Simon frowns sardonically. "I just got off a two-month bridge construction job up near Syracuse. This here's my vacation. Ain't that a pisser."

John removes the shotgun's bolt, stares down the barrel, sees tiny filaments lining the bore. He gets out his cleaning rod, cloth patches, and solvent. He starts cleaning the gun. The girl puts her head down on the table. She looks asleep. Simon throws out a cold cup of coffee and pours a fresh one. Rain loudly pummels the windows and trailer roof. Light slowly comes to the mountain.

"Ain't this fun," says Colette.

"Shut up," says Simon.

"You ask me nihce."

"Please don't open your big fat mouth again until we're back to town and you're dropped off someplace I ain't got to listen to it." Simon finishes his coffee and stands up. He claps John on the back. "One day it just hits ya, Johnno," he says.

"I'm too old for this shit. Too fucking old." He walks out the door. The two females get up and follow him. The girl walks into the doorframe on her way out, but doesn't seem to feel it. She gazes over her shoulder at John, smiles dumbly, and wiggles the tips of her fingers at him.

A minute later, through rain-streaked glass, John watches the Cadillac slowly wind its way down the mountain.

The potent, wet smell of the woods affirms in his mind life's cyclic nature. What is beaten down does or doesn't sprout back up. Lingering dampness accentuates the forest's darker colors—the greens, auburns, onyxes, browns. Brightness hides beneath a thin ground cover of mist. Bowing tree limbs, leaden with water, issue an eerie cacophony of protesting creaks and groans. The pulpy soil gives beneath him, each ground-sucking step confirming his live weight. The rain has abated to a slow drizzle. In the muggy air, beneath his waterproof poncho, he sweats profusely the alcohol he has consumed in recent days.

Just beyond the border of the preserve, from a wet swale of tangled goldenrod and dogbane, comes a pained mewl, like a baby's cry. John looks into the swale and sees, pinned beneath a tree limb, a spring fawn with faded spots still on its coat. The limb is maybe six inches in circumference and has fallen from a white pine standing at one edge of the swale onto the left hindquarters of the deer.

At John's approach the fawn thrashes so that he fears if its back or legs aren't already broken they soon will be. Its round glistening eyes stare at death and, through the power and mystery of evolution, are terrified of the view. He wonders where its mother is. Another clueless enigma. To the fawn he talks soothingly as he is unable to do with his own son, though he is oblivious to the dichotomy. It's likely crippled, thinks John, and if he frees it, with or without its mother, it will die slowly or fall prey to wild dogs or a bobcat. He ought to kill it and be on his way. Four days ago, he would have. Now, though, he fixates on its frantic stare and sees, beyond its trepidation, a nameless plea.

He lays down his shotgun, tosses aside his pack, and, to keep the fawn from thrashing, heavily places one hand on its steaming, rain- and perspiration-soaked chest, then runs the other back along its spine until he reaches the tree limb. He tries to lift the limb, but it's too heavy for his one hand.

Still holding the deer, he sits down with his back against the swale's edge and extends his legs until, with his knees slightly bent, his feet are against the limb. His head is so close to the deer's that the latter's warm breath, with its sharp, musky smell, dampens his cheek. Now the animal quits struggling as if understanding that John is there to help. John straightens his legs, then, pushing with his back, tries to move the limb. It edges forward a few inches, then stops. The deer groans. John pushes harder. The log rolls off the deer. For a few seconds the fawn lies there, failing to comprehend its good fortune. Then, trembling, it gets to its feet, glances once at John, and, without a noticeable limp, bounds up out of the swale and off through the woods. Listening to it go, John allows himself to think, "Might maybe make it, after all."

Before he reaches the quarry road, on the near side of the abandoned pasture, he turns left and bushwhacks through a tangle of vines and brush that border the woods. On one of the sharp needles of a thorn-apple tree, blown there by the recent gale, a skewered purple finch twists. A three-legged fox plunges into the brush. There's still no sign of the sun. The sky is the color of slate.

He enters a forest of virgin pine. Inside, it's dark and steamy. John can't see his feet for the mist. The canopy leaks water. Needles, cones, dislodged branches drop all around him. He stumbles into an elderberry thicket. Before finding his way out, he fills his hat with the sweet fruit. On the far side, he sits on a tree stump and eats what he's picked. Perched overhead, a pair of grackles angrily squawk at him. He watches a pileated woodpecker drill for bugs in a rotten stump. Idly he wonders if, in these mountains, he might forever elude his pursuers. He knows he could survive. And what of his current life would he miss? His wife, who is trying to divorce him? His son, who cries at the sight of him? Yes. He would miss them both, but that would be all he would miss, and they might be better off without him.

Past the forest, he turns right again. Now several hundred yards beyond the quarry, he walks parallel to it. He crosses over a small stream, made bigger by the rain, then quickly skirts the outer edge of Quentin's swamp, where the mosquitoes and black flies are thick, passes through an older stand of birch, oak, and elm, the last half-devoured by caterpillars, and emerges on the back side of the hill leading to the cliffs above the quarry. He walks along the spine of the wooded hill, undergrown with field grass, hawkweed, and patches of soft moss, until he reaches the quarry's upper lip, where he lies down on his stomach between two mountain-laurel bushes, places the 12-gauge on the ground next to him, and through binoculars gazes a hundred feet down into the rock bowl.

Not exactly sure what he is looking for or how to react if he sees something unusual, he peers behind the bushes and into the crevices in the quarry walls. Everything looks the same as it did three days before, except the stone is water-stained, the plastic top of the lean-to sags beneath the recent rain, and John doesn't remember if he left the pick and shovel lying, as they are now, in the entrance to the cave or standing next to it.

He lets the binoculars dangle from his neck and, delaying the inevitable for close to an hour, stares with his naked eyes into the quarry. He curses himself for being so stupid as to have left the body aboveground, even temporarily, with a slug from his gun in it and covered with his fingerprints. Then he remembers that when he should have buried the girl the thought felt like killing her all over again. Doing so now will be even harder, but he must. This time he'll keep her photograph and personal items so that when she is lost to the rest of the world she won't be to him. The money is a separate issue. It had been no more hers than John's, Waylon's, Obadiah Cornish's, or whoever else might know of its existence. Despairingly John thinks again of Simon Breedlove showing up in the middle of the night, asking after Mutt, and of his feeling that morning that the trailer had been searched.

He walks the two hundred yards around the rim to the west edge of the bowl, where he stops and through the binoculars gazes down the mountain toward Hollenbachs'. The farm is hidden around a sharp bend a mile below, though

John can see a short stretch of the rock-infested dirt road winding from there up to the quarry. He puts the binoculars away, then picks his way down the front side of the slope to where the cliff ends in less than a ten-foot drop near the quarry's entrance. The road is puddled and muddy. Any tire tracks have been obliterated.

His ingress commences a cacophony of caws and squawks. To his left, a Scotch pine shimmers and bounces beneath the weight of hundreds of crows that have gathered there to escape from the storm. Sweeping his eyes and the shotgun left-to-right, John feels an edgy, life-lived-in-a-second adrenaline tug that must be what soldiers feel when going into battle. Barely glancing at the patch of nettles behind which he shot the girl, he walks straight for the cave, stopping before he gets there next to the pond, which is roily and brown from the recent rain. There is no sign of the deer carcass. No footprints mar the bank, though mostly it's rock, and where it isn't, the rain would have washed them away.

John wishes he were a smoker so that he could sit and slowly smoke a cigarette before going farther. He pulls out his water bottle, drinks, then puts the bottle away. The drizzle is now a mist more than a rain. Heavy, post-storm air covers the bowl like a warm, drenched blanket. John's sweat smells of beer. He considers removing his poncho, but doesn't want to carry it. The cave's entrance is mostly fog-filled. Approaching it, John wonders if the cadaver will be at all decomposed.

He picks up the shovel and pick, leans them and his shotgun against the quarry wall, then pulls off his pack, takes out his flashlight, and lays the pack on the ground.

He squats down, switches on the light, and cautiously enters the cave. Water is trickling somewhere. John shines his light at the sound. In the back of the cavern, a thin, sporadic drip comes through the ceiling. He directs the beam farther right, then blinks his eyes several times to make sure he is seeing correctly. Hadn't he left the girl's face undraped? Now the sleeping bag is covering it. In his agitation, he tries to stand up and bangs his head against the ceiling. He curses and rubs the hurt. Then he waddles over to the sleeping bag, grabs the top, and yanks it back. The lion grins up at him. The girl is gone.

He sits on the hill above the trailer, watching it through his binoculars. Dampness stiffens his joints like the beginning of a flu. Melancholy—for the girl's lost body, for his solitary life, for what he foresees as a quick or imprisoned end to it— takes hold like the germ itself. His thoughts dance arrhythmically, whirl like drunks trying to do a four-step. His senses play tricks on him. Shrouded by fog, the silver-white trailer floats like a ghost in and out of his vision. Flying birds look like rocks hurled into the mist. Whole trees disappear. Nobie's hollow shout, at exactly 4 p.m., echoes up from the valley like the reverberating clank of hell's gate.

He watches the herd, like a row of condemned souls, sullenly parade in single file from the upper pasture toward the barn. Later, he hears the electric milkers whir and watches steam rise up from where he knows the barn to be, then vanish in the mist.

He eats an apple and the two remaining peanut-butter-and-jelly sandwiches in his pack. With his Bowie knife, he files his fingernails to the quick. In the damp grass between his legs, he draws a circle, then repeatedly throws the knife into its center. Later, touching his three-day growth of beard, he remembers his father had worn one for maybe six months. It made him look old. Then he turned mean, got sick, and died. John hacks with the knife blade at the growth. He cuts his cheek. He dabs with his shirttail at the spot until the bleeding stops. He puts the knife away. He folds his hands, closes his eyes, wonders if there's a God and, if so, what His plans for John's future are. The gray day gets grayer, darker. Dusk comes to the mountain. The drizzle stops, but the fog stays put. No one approaches the trailer. No one leaves. John remembers his little son crying, "Mommy." He wishes it were so easy.

Down the hill to his left, from a thick patch of fog, sound the stomp and suck of footsteps in the wet ground. He grabs the 12-gauge, cocks it, flicks off the safety, and dives behind a spruce bush. Ten feet above the dirt path, he nervously waits for whatever it is to emerge from the mist.

Clomp-suck. Clomp-suck.

Slowly comes a horse's head, with its pointy ears and sloping snout, then its long neck and muscular torso, atop which elegantly sits the dead girl.

John drops his gun and screams.

The horse shies. Then rears. The girl tries to rein him in.

"Whoa! Easy, boy! Easy, now!" The horse comes back down onto its four feet, hop-steps sideways, then stands there in the path, skittishly tossing its head. "Steady, Diablo. Stea-dee." Now she talks soothingly to the animal, while rubbing its neck. "John Moon," she says.

John's heart echoes loud in his ears. He leans down and

picks up his gun. The girl shakes her head. "What do you mean, calling out like that?"

"Thought you was somebody else."

"Who'd make you scream that way?"

"A ghost."

"Jesus, John Moon."

"Sorry 'bout it." He steps forward, kisses the wet nose of the horse, Nobie's big dappled-gray Arabian. "Was sleepin'."

"In the rain?"

"Nappin's all."

"You and Mr. 12-gauge?"

"Thought I might see a rabbit or somethin'."

"On the preserve or on my daddy's land?"

"Neither. I was back in further. Headin' for home I 'bout gave out."

"Look at you, John Moon."

"I know it."

"You look like you've seen a ghost!"

"I told ya."

"And you're soaked!"

"Was some storm."

"I wouldn't tell on you even if you were stalking a deer, John Moon. Daddy says you put to good use everything you take, which is more than can be said for most of the world." She smiles. She's half John's age, but already so much he isn't— intelligent, good-looking, self-assured. In a few years, like her brother, she will go off to college and then only occasionally come home to ride Diablo up past John's trailer toward the woods, when she will smile and call out, "John Moon!"

"You gonna take the job Daddy offered you?"

"Ain't decided."

"You ought to." She turns red, looking then like the fifteen-year-old she is. "Not everybody gets a chance to do what they love and get paid for it, too."

"Shoveling shit and milking cows?"

"Uh-huh, John Moon."

"How you figure?"

"'Cause I'm daughter to one just like you."

John grunts.

"Daddy'd be lost without farming. He had to work in a factory, he'd die." The horse shakes its head and blows. John steadies it with his hand. "I'm taking an economics course in summer school, John, and you know what we're studying on?"

"What?"

"Profit sharing."

"Good you're gettin' educated."

"You know what that is?"

"Nope."

"It's when employees own a piece of the companies they work at. The bosses figure they'll get more for their money from workers who share in the profits and workers work harder because they got a stake in things. What do you think about that, John?"

"Nifty."

She laughs. "Nifty?"

"Ain't that your word?"

"Sure. I just never heard you use it before." The horse dances backward. John takes hold of its rein. Abbie says,

"Cool your jets, Diablo." She looks at John. "Was me, I'd suggest something like that to Daddy."

"Like what?"

"What I just said."

"Somethin' 'bout jets?"

"Don't act stupid, John Moon!"

John spits.

"I'd tell him I'd take the job if part of my pay could go toward buying a piece of his farm."

John laughs.

"There's nothing funny about it, John. Our professor says workers with leverage ought to use it to empower themselves."

"What's your daddy think about what they're teaching you in school?"

"I didn't discuss this particular matter with him and don't you dare tell him I did with you!" She purses her lips. "I wouldn't ask for too much at first, maybe just that Daddy let you buy some heifers from him and raise them up in the barn, then—you know, after that—a piece of the land, and Daddy would listen too, John, because he's real worried that after Eban and I go off to college he and my mom won't be able to keep up with the work."

"Buy back a piece of my own farm, you mean?"

She pushes hair out of her eyes. "John Moon. If you keep looking back, you'll never get ahead!"

"Maybe you ought to worry 'bout losin' your inheritance."

"I won't need one because I'm going to be a millionaire before I'm thirty. I got a thousand ideas how to do it, like making you my daddy's partner."

"Huh?"

"I have faith in you, John Moon." She giggles. "You'll only make my inheritance bigger."

"Glad I ain't married to you."

"Me too. We're not at all compatible."

"No, we ain't."

"We can still be friends, though, can't we?"

"Uh-huh." John lets go of the horse. "Be careful back in them woods. It's nearly dark and is slippery underfoot."

"Don't worry about me, John Moon. I'm an experienced horsewoman." She starts to ride off, then reins Diablo in. "What'd that man you told Daddy shot Mutt have to say?"

"Huh?"

"When he was up to your trailer today?"

John raises his eyes at her.

"An hour or so after the Cadillac left. His car went up by, then come back down a while later. You weren't there?"

"Nuh-uh."

"You think he's telling the truth about what he's doing around?"

"Don't know."

"I told Daddy we ought to call the sheriff, but he didn't want to."

"That's probably for the best."

"I only hope none of us regret it later."

"Me too."

"Think about empowerment, John Moon. Daddy's feeling a lot of pressure. And, same as me, he likes you." She turns in the saddle, nudges the horse's belly with her feet, and slowly rides off in the direction of the pines.

*　　*　　*

Against his tired body, the heavy wet branches feel like grasping arms, then bullwhips, so, going down the hill, he cuts right through the woods and, from there, walks the dirt road running like a funnel through thick forest that impedes his view of the valley.

Less than fifty yards from the trailer, he sees, in the not quite dark, moving on the grass below the pond, several large, ominous shapes. As if by instinct, he veers left and, stealthily as he can, slogs through the rain-battered meadow to the near corner of the trailer, where he crouches down to watch and listen to, with their distinctive gobbles, half a dozen wild turkeys picking at the drenched timothy. Among them are two large males. He thumbs off the shotgun's safety and, to keep from tainting the meat, aims for the head of the larger. In his mind he hears the shot loudly shatter the still air and sees the headless bird fall sideways onto the grass, but before vision becomes reality, his hands begin to tremble, his teeth to chatter, and his heart wildly palpitates.

He opens the gun's breech and, panting heavily, lays it on the grass next to him. He remembers his father telling him that the Indians native to this region believed turkeys to be cowardly and stupid and for fear of becoming so themselves refused to kill or eat them. Seeming to have little instinct for danger and with their fantailing and loud prattle constantly calling attention to themselves, the birds are, John agrees, dumb. He sits there watching the flock until it is dark and he can't see it anymore, but can only hear its inane patter. Still, he sits. He wonders if he'll ever again be the hunter he was. If ever again he'll be who he was. He hears Abbie Nobie slowly walking Diablo back down the hollow road, her earnestly conversing about star constellations, and the horse's brusque snort. After its footsteps have faded away, he picks up the shotgun, stands, and walks through the kitchen entrance into the trailer.

Lying on the floor are pots, pans, silverware, dishes, letters, canned goods, condiments. Every drawer and cabinet looks rifled. The cushions are thrown from the couch. The back of his father's old recliner is sliced open and its stuffing torn out. Beyond the grease fire's lingering stench, a faint, unpleasant odor mars the air. Moira's breakfront is trashed; lying beneath it, atop bank statements, personal letters, photo albums, and John's Instamatic camera, are his Polaroids of Moira posing nude, and others of him holding Nolan as a newborn, of Moira nursing the boy, of John giving him a bath. A stabbing pain breaches John's chest. He kneels down, slides the snapshots back into the envelopes from which they had come, then carefully places the envelopes back into the breakfront.

He stands up and walks down the hallway, the stench getting stronger, into the bathroom, where the medicine cabinet is ransacked, the ballcock to the toilet ripped out and its porcelain top smashed on the floor. Every sheet and towel is thrown from the linen closet. Bottles and cans of cleaning solvents roll on the floor. The trapdoor covering the pipes is open.

He steps back into the hallway, turns left, glances into Nolan's old nursery, where the closet doors are thrown back and the empty toy chest is turned upside down.

Halfway down the corridor toward the master bedroom,

he sees, through the open doorway, clothes, magazines, and bureau drawers littering the floor. He smells what he smells more distinctly. In a frightened half-jog he enters the room. Lying face up on the bed, her body wrapped below the neck in clear plastic, is the dead girl. Attached to her chest a yellow sheet of paper declares: "John Moon murdered me!" In the middle of the rug, John drops to his knees, puts his hands to his face, and blathers in a mysteriously poignant way.

Beyond cerebration is a place clearer than thought. Equivocations don't exist in this realm. There is no moral compass. Inside, only him and the dead girl. Outside, the world circling like vultures.

Oblivious to the stench, he sits down on the mattress near her head and studies her pale, bloated face. Her mouth is slightly open and a small particle of food is still lodged between her teeth. Her eyes are closed, her nostrils exaggeratedly flared. The ponytail lies like a thick nest beneath her head. Mashed to her forehead is a dead mosquito. He imagines her voice, medium-pitched and resonant, sounding beyond her years. She laughed often, a free-flowing verse, occasionally at things that others didn't find amusing. She sometimes cried without provocation. The world struck her as ridiculous or tragic. She wasn't sure why. She had a weakness for bad men. Mean men. Men who beat her up, then brought her roses.

He reaches down with his forefingers and gently pushes at her eyelids. They're swollen shut. He pushes harder. The lids open with a quiet pop to eyes the color of deer hide. She kept getting into situations. Her parents were pathetic. Her friends were the world. She liked sex because they did and she was supposed to, but what really got her hot was pushing things to the limit. She had trouble seeing a point beyond that. She didn't like to hurt people, though, or to see them hurt. She was compassionate toward those who were helpless. If she could, she would avoid stepping on an ant. She didn't like to think about growing old. She had a sneaking suspicion she wouldn't. Old people were like robots. She once dreamed her parents ran on batteries. She wrote a short story about this and while reading it to her English class felt so liberated she thought of becoming a writer but decided she couldn't spend that much time sitting down.

John lies down next to the girl. He stares up at the ceiling and softly talks to her. He tells her he is sorry he shot her and that most of the time he believes it was an accident but occasionally, when he thinks about how angry the world sometimes makes him and how little he seems able to change things, he's afraid it wasn't. He tells her that when he was her age his only plan had been to marry the girl he loved, move her back to his family's farm, be the best farmer he could be, and raise his children to do the same, and that his father's having lost everything when John was sixteen crippled John the same as if he'd been in a car accident and lost the use of his legs. He tells her about the many failures in his life and that the only things in it worth holding on to are his wife and son, but that they had left him.

The body is bloated with gas. It occasionally burps or breaks wind. Sometimes it shifts on the mattress. When its right arm jerks out and hits John's elbow, he stops speaking and gets up from the bed.

Standing over her, he apologizes for talking only about his problems when he at least was alive. He tells her that, no matter what else happens, he will try to find out her name and where she was from and that, if he succeeds, he will somehow notify her family about her death and let them know either where her body can be picked up or that she has received a proper burial.

He lifts up the cadaver, stiff with rigor mortis, and slides the plastic out from around it. He takes off the dead girl's shoes and socks, then wrestles her out of her jeans and blood-soaked T-shirt. She isn't wearing a bra. He pulls off her panties because they are soiled and wet. He drops everything into the plastic. Then he takes out his hunting knife. After rolling the cadaver onto its back and eyeballing the bullet's course through the torso, he goes after the slug with his knife. He locates it just beneath the skin's surface, embedded in soft flesh. He quickly cuts it out, then drops it onto the clothes.

He walks down the hall to the bathroom, picks up from the floor a towel and washcloth, dampens the latter with soap and water, then returns to the bedroom and spends several minutes scrubbing blood, sweat, and dirt from the cadaver. He sees no star-shaped birthmark; no scar on her knee; no blood-red bull's-eyes. Far from being large and womanly, her breasts, surrounding the bullet hole, are small and girl-ish. She has almost no pubic bush. For these things alone, he is thankful.

He pulls on a pair of Moira's rubber cleaning gloves, then from the floor takes one of her combs, a tube of red lipstick, black eyeliner, and blush. After combing several hair strands away from the dead girl's forehead, he unties her ponytail, combs out the snarls, and catches the hair again in a rubber band. He applies the eyeliner and a thin gloss of lipstick. Still, he thinks, she is too pale. He dabs blush on her cheeks and, less so, her temples.

After tearing the tags from one of Moira's panties and a T-shirt, he puts the underwear on the dead girl. He considers outfitting her in a blouse and skirt, but is afraid they might somehow be traced to Moira, so settles for a label-less pair of her jeans. He dresses the corpse one side at a time, using a hand to hold the rigid body upright and another to slowly thread a leg into the pants. It takes him close to half an hour. All the while, the cadaver makes noises and jumps. The smell starts to make him nauseous. He rolls up the jeans, slightly long on the dead girl, then snaps them. He puts her old socks and sneakers back on, then props the body in a mostly sitting position against the headboard. He pushes with his fingers at the corners of her mouth, removing some of its slackness.

Afterwards, he stands back to appraise her. He thinks she looks almost alive and that if she were, she'd be beautiful. He tells her so. Then he runs and gets the Polaroid. Eight shots remain in the camera. He uses them all in a dull light, taking her portrait from midchest up at three different angles. He lays the photographs on the bureau. Now he's not sure what to do with the body. What would make things worse or better? And for which of them? A part of him feels as dead as the girl. He's tired enough to fall over. He wonders if in the morning the sun will shine everywhere but on the trailer, and in that sliver of darkness the world will see what awful secrets he is hiding.

He crouches down, puts his arms beneath the girl's knees and chest, and lifts her off the bed. Her unbending weight is staggering. That close to his nose, the smell nearly gags him. He labors with her over to the bedroom door, then down the corridor to the top of the basement stairs, where, after leaning her against the wall to switch on the light, he carts her down-cellar and over to the stand-up freezer, the door to which is open, its melting contents scattered on the floor. The compartment is just five feet high. To get the cadaver inside, he vigorously bends and twists it for several minutes, until finally there is the sharp snap of breaking bone and the body folds half-inward from the waist. John pushes it to the back wall, then stacks around and in front of it pieces of the butchered deer and snake so that, when he's done, what is visible of the cadaver is nearly indistinguishable from the rest of the meat.

Upstairs, he wraps the girl's old clothes, the bloody sheets and towels, the note, and the rubber gloves in the plastic strip, then takes the plastic out to the incinerator and burns it. He hurls the slug deep into the woods. He enters the woodshed. His tools are on the floor among garden mulch and fertilizer from several sliced-open sacks and rock salt from a tipped-over fifty-pound barrel. He shovels the mulch and fertilizer into trash bins and the rock salt back into the barrel, then rearranges the tools exactly as they had been.

He goes back outside and crawls beneath the shed, where the sack is still attached to the fourth beam. He unties it, carries it into the trailer, dumps the money on the floor, and tries to count it, but after reaching eighty thousand dollars loses his place. He is too tired to start over. He thinks that even if he were to give the money back to the thieves, they would kill him, especially if it came from Ira Hollenbach's. And if he handed it over to the law, he would implicate himself in at least one death. He puts the money back in the sack, carries it outside, and ties it beneath the truck bed, between the axle and one wheel.

He spends over two hours cleaning up the trailer, repairing what he can, and putting most of his and Moira's belongings back where they had been. With the dead girl there, he thinks he won't sleep, but he does. He turns on the television set, lies on the couch, and for less than five minutes watches the horizontally distorted images of a man shooting a pistol at a giant fly.

THURSDAY

The unrestful dead, those who have not by their loved ones been laid to earthly rest, inhabit the trees, bushes, birds, and animals of the mountainside. Their eyes are the sun and moon; when one shuts, the other opens. Their words are the stars. Their sadness the clouds. Their fingers the wind. They watch, talk, and touch, but are not felt by the living . . .

H E W A K E S, in a cold sweat, to the sound of shattering glass. Sensing another's presence, he lies there in the still-dark morning anticipating a gunshot, a black shadow, or the touch of cold steel against his neck, but hears only the tick of the living-room clock and, through the screened windows, a light wind moving the trees.

Had he been hallucinating? Or dreaming? If he hadn't, and in a second was killed, would he come face-to-face with the dead girl? Would she forgive him? Would her soul in the afterlife be as beautiful as her body in death? He pictures a place following life—a wood-paneled bar maybe, playing soft country music—where souls, good and bad, dance a few slow ones and reminisce before receiving their permanent assignments to heaven or hell. A place where life's hatchet is buried and all drink to eternity. He remembers his father, reduced to skin and bones, after wordless weeks, rousing himself to scream at the visiting Pastor McLean, "Weren't never your call, Reverend! Was mine! Now it's His!"

An engine roars to life outside.

In one motion, he rolls off the couch and fumbles beneath it for the .45. Powerful lights intrude through the trailer's back windows. The engine exhorts a labored whine. The lights get brighter. John grasps the gun, cocks it, and jumps up. The engine's pitch ascends to a high-revved torque. "Son of a bitch'll ram the trailer!" thinks John.

He dashes away from the sound toward the front deck door. He's three-quarters there when the bottom of his bare foot feels as if it's been shot. He goes down. Behind him, the lights blink off. The engine upshifts, reaches a crescendo, then slowly recedes.

Through the broken glass of the deck door, John watches the outline of the vehicle, darker even than the surrounding dark, vanish down the hollow road.

Panting heavily, he gets to his knees. He fumbles for the wall switch and turns on the light. Glass from the door's middle panel lies in fragments on the linoleum floor. A piece of it has lodged in his foot, which is bleeding.

He stands up, then, trailing blood, tiptoes through the glass and down the hall to the bathroom, where he gets a towel, tweezers, gauze, waterproof tape, and a bottle of peroxide. He brings everything back to the couch, sits down, and, mumbling a string of pained curses, with the tweezers pokes around in the wound for the glass. His foot trembles. So do his hands. He laughs giddily from pain and at his shaking extremities, then loudly commands himself to shut up and act like a man. Soon he finds the glass, a half-a-peanut-sized chunk, and pulls it out. He pours peroxide on the towel and, wincing, cleans the wound, which is not very deep, then tapes gauze around it.

Afterwards, he is drenched in sweat. His heart beats loud in his ears. He pinches the glass chunk in the tweezers, holds it up to the light, and stares at it. He imagines himself as the glass, the dead girl his wound, and Waylon, Obadiah Cornish—and maybe Simon Breedlove—the tweezers. Aloud, he asks the girl how she had ever fallen for a guy like Waylon, who obviously grieved more for his lost money than for her. He gets mad thinking about it and tells her so. "Look how he disrespected your body and even when you was alive made you throw out your history like it didn't matter!"

He places the glass chunk on the coffee table, then leans back against the couch, and, gazing at the blank television set, remembers it playing when he fell asleep. He leans forward and sees that the set is still turned on and plugged in. "Ain't that great? Along with the rest of it, the fuckin' tube is shot!" Then, lowering his voice, he tells the girl, "This Waylon guy's a loser. You should never a' run off with him in the first place, then you w'udn't a' been in the quarry and 'id still be alive and I w'udn't be respons'ble for ya!"

He straightens up, leans forward, puts on his socks and boots, then gets up, goes into the kitchen, and makes a pot of coffee. He turns on the deck light. The sky is starting to lighten some. The fog is still thick. In places, it's as high as the trees. From the upper pasture comes the invisible mooing and bell-jangling of Nobie's herd. Any minute will sound his hollow shout. John thinks of Abbie Nobie and her empowerment theory. "I'd guess she's about the same age as you," he tells the dead girl. "She worries after me. Reckon she thinks I've become like a hermit without Moira. When Nolan was here, she used to come up and beg Moira to hold him and sometimes Moira would call her 'count of Nolan was colicky and Abbie was so good at gettin' him to stop crying. Moira said she's got a love in her heart and the kid could feel it."

From the kitchen closet he takes the broom and dustpan, then carries them over to the deck doorway, lays the dustpan on the counter, and starts sweeping up the glass. "Long's we got the money," he tells the girl, "I guess they won't kill me." He sweeps out from beneath the table, along with several small chunks of glass, a fist-sized stone that is wrapped in yellow paper and circled by a rubber band. John kneels down, picks up the stone, and removes the paper. Ink writing appears on one side. John smooths it out on the floor and reads:

Two eyes fer an eye. Two teeth fer a tooth. We gut your wife, murdrer. We gut your kid. Git the package the Hen. Or Bang! Bang!
P.S. Why don't ya call the law? Hah. Hah.

Suddenly he is aware of his own mental denseness, of his intellectual shortcomings. His stupidity looms like a brick wall between uncentered anger and thought. He tries to remember ever getting an A in school for anything but gym, and can't. The unfairness of the world hangs before his unconscious gaze like a grotesque masterpiece.

Beneath him at the kitchen table, his legs hop up and down. His hands shake. His vision is marred by floating cells. Adrenaline courses like a drug through him. He can't sit still, yet his energy is unfocused. He jumps up, runs over to the gun rack, removes every weapon and shell box, then sits down on the living-room floor, tests the mechanism of each gun, looks down its barrel to see that it's clean, then loads it. He cocks the Winchester thirty-aught-six and returns it to the rack. Then he puts the .45 in his belt, the 12-gauge in a cabinet next to the refrigerator, the .22 pistol behind the bathroom toilet, the .30-30 Greener beneath his bed, and the 16-gauge behind the basement freezer.

He runs back upstairs and dials Moira's number. The sky out the kitchen window is gray. What wind there was has died down. It will take most of the day for the fog to move. The phone rings four times. Five. The air through the screens is warm and filled with birdcalls. Seven rings. Eight. John rubs his eyes, removes his hand, and waits for his vision to clear. The phone is picked up. A man says, "Hello?"

"Let me talk my son," says John.

"What?"

"Put him on."

"I'm afraid you've got the wrong number."

"He better be there, you bastard."

"The only child here, friend, has a vocabulary of less than half-a-dozen words."

"Wait!"

"What?"

"You didn't tell me where to leave the money."

The phone clicks dead.

He sits naked in the unstoppered bathtub beneath the shower's hard stream of cold water, unconsciously reflecting on how the world's lee and sway is as paralyzing to him as it had been to his father. He remembers his father pacing back and forth in the kitchen at night, loudly cursing while blindly punching and kicking appliances as if the machines were his creditors and cancer, "The bastards! The dirty, fucking bastards!"

When he steps from the tub, he is beet-red. He rebandages his foot and shoulder, then puts on a clean pair of jeans and T-shirt. The dull light of the heavily fog-shrouded morning comes through the bedroom window. "Nothing off this mountain is real," he thinks. "If I sit here and do nothing, nothing will be lost." Then he looks at Moira's and Nolan's pictures on the headboard and knows it's not so. In the living room, he calls their apartment again. This time there is no answer. He redials, lets the phone ring twenty times, then hangs up. He has no idea what to do. He wishes the whole world were as easy as tracking something down and shooting it. He goes down-cellar.

He opens the freezer, takes out a couple of venison steaks, and stares at one side of the girl's made-up face with its wide-open eye. The smell has dissipated. "I'm trying to figure things out," he says, "but I got no fuckin' idea." He puts the steaks back, closes the freezer, and locks it. He runs around collecting the guns that he had hidden, then starts rehiding them in different places. He is on his way out to the woodshed with the 16-gauge when the phone rings. He goes back and answers it.

"How's John Moon getting on?"

"You ain't said your name."

"Sorry, John. Daggard Pitt. Thought you recognized my voice."

"What d'you want?"

"I have those papers ready for you to sign."

"Did we talk 'bout this?"

"You're not agreeing to anything. We're just protecting your rights. Remember?"

John's not sure if he hears an engine's whine down the road. He can't see through the fog beyond a hundred yards.

"Is it convenient for you to stop in this afternoon, John?"

"It ain't."

"Are you sure?"

"I can't make it."

"Maybe you've got another matter you want to discuss?"

"What?"

"Other than the divorce, I mean."

"What matter?"

"I hope I'm not stepping over the line, John. It's just that I know lately you've been under a lot of pressure and, well—I hear things." The lawyer pants breathily. "I'd hate to see your whole life get ruined because of a mistake or two." Suddenly John's pulse goes ballistic. He feels it rapping like a snare drum against his temple. "And it wouldn't be just your life, John."

"What?"

"There's the boy to think of. Nolan..."

"He ain't in this!"

"Of course he's in it, John. He's your son."

"You leave my family out of it!"

"I'm sorry I've angered you, John, but I'd be less than honest if I didn't tell you that, for me, your family has always been very much in it. Very much so." Pitt coughs anemically. Down the road, the whine gets louder. The phone is trembling in John's hand. "Most problems aren't as big as they first seem, John. The thing is to deal with them before people get backed into corners."

"What people?"

The lawyer exhales doggily. "Well, the law for one..."

"The law!"

"I'd hate to think..."

"Who are you whoring for now, Pitt?"

"John?"

"Tell the bastards stay way from my wife and kid or they'll never get what they want!"

John slams down the phone. Down the road, above the engine's increased drone, the fog radiates yellow. A vehicle slowly takes shape in the thinning mist, then, two hundred feet below the trailer, a black-and-white county sheriff's car emerges above the treeline.

Dolan's wearing mirrored sunglasses, though there's no sun. He spits on the grass driveway, where John has met him, then strides forward and slaps a folded paper into his hand. "You been legal served."

John glances down at the paper without reading it.

"The judge don't want ya around her no more. Your kid, neither. First time I hear of it, I'll slap the cuffs on ya."

John starts tapping the paper rapidly against his forehead. He can't think quick enough to keep up with the images in his head. His thoughts swim in a consciousness dark as mud. Dolan points at the .45 in his belt.

"You got a license for that, Moon?"

John steps toward him. "She's loaded too, Ralph."

"Is that some kind of threat?"

"You just come from there?"

"Where?"

"Pitt's?"

"Who?"

"My fucking lawyer, crook!"

"Why would I?"

"Who give ya this, then?"

"I'm an officer of the court, Moon."

"That who sent ya here?"

"Who the hell else?"

"I tried to talk my kid and some guy answered the phone." Taking a step forward, John puts his mouth six inches from Dolan's. "I don't s'pose you or Pitt know 'bout that or 'bout the fuckin' rock through my window!"

Backing against the car, Dolan puts a hand on his holster. John slaps the hand away. "What the hell are you talking about, Moon?"

"I don't feel good."

"What?"

"I see shit everywhere."

"You're jumpy as a bug, Moon." Again he puts his hand on his holster. Again John slaps it away. "Just calm down."

"I'm tryin' to figure out why you're here. You want me to hand the package o'er you! Is that it?"

Dolan gets his hand on his holster a third time and starts fumbling with the strap. John knocks his sunglasses off. Dolan gives up on the strap to grab the glasses. He shoves them into his pocket.

"Where's my wife and kid, Ralph?"

Dolan tries to slide out around John. His lips are working, but nothing's coming out.

"I'm holdin' you 'countable."

"Wha?"

"They ain't better be a hair touched on their heads!" John uses his chest to pin Dolan to the side of the car.

"I'm just serving a court order, Moon."

John backs up, turns around, and walks into the trailer.

The village is still heavily shrouded in haze when he arrives at the municipal parking lot. He wanders like a ghost in that soup down Main Street to Puffy's, enters through the front door, nods at Puffer, who seems not to have moved in the preceding three days, sits down opposite the fat proprietor at the counter, and of Carla demands, "Coffee."

"'Bout the other night," she says, trying to hand him a menu, which John lets drop on the counter. "Moira weren't aware..."

"Where's she at?"

"She don't work this morning."

John raises his eyes at her.

"Said somethin' 'bout going out of town."

"Where to?"

Carla shrugs.

"How 'bout Nolan?"

"With them, I'd guess."

"Them?"

"I don't know nothin' 'bout it."

"I'm askin'."

"Not the right person, you ain't."

"I guess you know your boyfriend's a psycho."

She pours coffee into a cup, puts it down in front of him, then heads into the dining room. Smoke hovers below the ceiling like fog oozing through the vents. Voices drone like static. John gulps down half his coffee. The whole world feels to him like a whisper, with him stone-deaf. Someone drops a plate in the kitchen. Puffy rolls his thick head at the sound. Carla walks back up the aisle from the dining room. Spinning round, John catches her by the arm. "You as dumb as you act?"

"Mitts off, John."

"Where's he at?"

"Why?"

"We got business."

"Then I guess he knows where to find ya."

John gives her arm a squeeze.

"Hey!"

"What's goin' on, John?" Puffy's smoke-raggedy voice floats quietly across the counter. John glances at him, but doesn't answer. The pharmacist, Leonard Pine, walks in and sits down two stools from John. John grimaces menacingly at him. Pine gets up and moves to a booth. Carla tries to pull her arm free. John pinches it harder. Puffy says, "How can I help?"

"It's up to her," says John.

Puffer casually blows smoke Carla's way.

"I don't even know what he wants."

"I'd as soon break your arm," whispers John.

"If he's got a question, Carla," Puffer says, crunching out his cigarette and slowly pulling another from the pack in his shirt pocket, "why not give him an answer?"

"I ain't got the one he's wantin'."

"Try, though," says Puffer.

"'Bliged to ya, fat man," says Carla. "You're a real prince."

Puffer ignites the fresh cigarette, drags on it, then, folding his hands on the counter, lets it dangle from one corner of his mouth while exhaling twin lines of smoke through his nose. "Leonard Pine sets over there in a booth 'stead of at the counter where he has for ten years waitin' for his coffee to drink and a menu to read."

"Coffee black, eggs over easy, rye toast with grape jelly!" Carla barks into the kitchen. "'Kay, Puffy?"

"Had a pretty young thing in here the other day wants to waitress," Puffy rasps barely above a whisper. "Had tits the size of cantaloupes. I told her leave her number."

"Bet she's just holding her breath, too," hisses Carla. She frowns loathsomely at John. "Last I knew, he was staying over to the Oaks."

"What room?"

"My memory ain't what it was. Somethin' in the two-twenties."

John lets go her arm and stands up. Puffy says, "Best you don't come back in for a while, John."

"Big man," snorts Carla.

John strides past her toward the exit.

At the south end of town, he turns left and heads through Shantytown, a single dirt street of unpainted clapboard shacks and grassless, junk-marred yards, where yapping dogs and half-naked kids run in the street. From behind a gutted jalopy something flies out and lands loudly in the back of the truck. The kids start laughing and hooting. A few of them yell at John to stop. He keeps driving, not slowing down until after he comes to the top of the gradual, mile-long hill where sits the Oaks.

He's above the fog. The unimpeded sun illuminates the two-story, paint-chipped motel, L-shaped and most recently yellow. Half a dozen cars sit in the lot. None of them is the black Chevy Blazer, though at the far end of the longest row of rooms sits a rusted-out blue-white Cadillac that at a glance John thinks might be Simon Breedlove's.

He pulls the truck around behind the building where it can't be seen from the front, shuts off the engine, shoves the .45 down his pants, covers it with his shirt, and steps out. Immediately he hears something moving about in the truck's bed. He looks inside. Scurrying around in there is a large black Shantytown rat. John reaches in, grabs the squirming rodent by its tail, whips it in a fast circle over his head, and hurls it at the bushes bordering the motel. The rat lands on the pavement just short of the bushes, shakes itself, then runs off squealing. John walks to the building's rear entrance and enters the office, where on a crippled recliner behind the desk sits Skinny Leak, watching television. Leak waves at the set. "You b'lieve them titties is real?"

John doesn't say.

"Well, they ain't. It's a man got plastic tits and a pussy made from the skin off'n his own leg!"

"Obadiah Cornish staying here?"

"Doctor cut off his dick and sewed them things on."

John reaches down and turns around the register so that he can read it. Skinny nods at him.

"A Moon, ain't ya?"

"The on'y one."

"What ta hell happened your brothers?"

"Never had none."

"Who ta hell am I thinkin' you is, then?"

"Somebody I ain't."

"Fer Christ sake! Your old man worked to the mill sure as I sit here."

"He was a farmer," says John, running his finger down the names on the register, but seeing no Cornish.

"Let me get this straight now—you're a Moon"—Skinny pushes his bird-like body out of the chair and hobbles over to the desk—"but there ain't but one of ya and your old man was a farmer and never worked to the mill?"

John nods.

"Mickey Moon, right?"

"John."

"Shit."

"I know he's in room two-twenty-somethin'," says John.

"Know what that makes you?"

John wordlessly glances at the old man, running his pink tongue over black, toothless gums.

"Makes you the man in the moon!" He slaps his knee and hisses. "Got to be, don't it? You the on'y fucking one?" He reaches out and turns the book back around. "Who you looking for there, man in the moon?"

John tells him.

"No hens in this house. What's he look like?"

"Tall, gangly son of a bitch."

"Got him an alias."

"Okay."

"That's why he ain't in the book."

"Where is he?"

"Guess he's expectin' ya, is he?"

"I aim to find out."

"Want me to call ahead?"

"I'll just go on down and knock." John pulls out his wallet, withdraws from it a ten-dollar bill, and lays the bill on the desk, with his hand still on it. "Who b'longs that Cadillac yonder?"

"Which one?"

"Ain't but one." John nods his head at the wall beyond which, obscured from his view, lies the long side of the L. "Down the end. All beat to hell."

Leak cranes his head back and peeks out through a little porthole-shaped window behind the desk. He hisses again. "Musta beamed up, man in the moon."

"Gone?"

Leak throws his bony little fingers into the air.

"Was here how long?"

"On'y you says it e'er was."

John lifts his hand from the bill. Leak reaches for it. John slams his other hand down on Leak's. "Let me guess. Cornish's down there all the way the end."

Leak tugs free his hand gripping the bill, folds the bill, and slips it into his shirt pocket. "Twenty-two-niner, man in the moon. Coulda saved yerself a sawbuck."

At the building's front, John walks down the long cement corridor facing the rooms, each one fronted by a dead or dying spruce bush planted in gravel, to a set of metal stairs adjacent to where the Cadillac had been parked. He climbs to the second floor, again turns left, quietly tiptoes up to room 229, and puts his ear to the scratched wood door. Inside, a television loudly plays the same talk show Leak was watching. What sounds like a fan or air conditioner blows. Intermingling with the din is a gurgling noise, like running water or percolating coffee. John starts to knock, then, changing his mind, reaches down and with one hand pulls the .45 from his belt. He raises his foot to kick in the door, when, two rooms down, another door suddenly opens. He jumps back, holding the pistol out in front of him.

"Jesus God! Don't shoot!" Dangling a Tiparillo from her mouth, a breast-sagging, middle-aged blond woman freezes in midstride.

John puts a finger to his lips.

"Huh?"

"Who's in here?" he whispers.

"I don't know." The woman gasps. The cigar drops from her mouth. "And I don't fucking want to know." One of her eyes looks like a clump of frog's eggs. The other is half taken up by its dilated pupil. Her sweatsuit's too tight. "I'm from Oklahoma. This shit's all new to me. I ain't had no breakfast, no coffee—I just got in last night."

With his pistol John waves her back into her room.

"I gotta go breakfast," she whines.

John walks toward her, vaguely aware that his life is spiraling downward from bad to worse, and against the descent, his own sense of powerlessness. A part of his mind, already faded, blinks off. He thinks if the whole world boils down to a person's last view of it, his won't be of the Oaks, but someone's might. He's three steps from the woman before she moves, then she does so hesitantly, backing into the room as if she's forgotten something inside but not sure what. John follows her in, then quietly shuts the door.

The woman moans.

The air smells of cheap perfume over cheap detergent and cigar smoke. A faucet drips in the bathroom. In the center of the stained yellow rug lies a large, open suitcase. John reaches into it and picks up a pair of stockings and underpants. The woman's mouth falls open. She keeps backing up until her knees hit the bed. She lets out a little groan and sits down. "What happened your eye?" asks John.

"My eye?"

"Are you blind in it?"

"A man..."

"What man?"

"Some guy in a bar where I was dancing..." She takes a deep breath like she's having trouble breathing. John shoves the pistol into his belt. "I was a dancer..."

"A dancer?"

"You're scaring me."

"I ain't tryin' to."

"You are, though."

"I know it. Me too."

The woman looks at him confusedly.

"Was you with your clothes off?"

"What?"

"Dancing?"

"Nobody'd pay me otherwise..."

John moves farther into the room. His balance seems affected. He has a feeling he's listing to the right. The framed vase of flowers on the wall appears to get shorter and fatter as he looks at it. "It's like when I shot the girl," he says, barely aware of his own words. "We was all there."

"What?"

"Her. The deer. Me." He wads the underpants into a tight ball. "Who knows why? Just happened that way."

The woman pants a little maniacally. John pictures in his mind a set of dull claws scratching at a smooth wall. He's back in the quarry maybe, trying to scale its sheer sides. He thinks the woman's probably a mother. Her drooping breasts and wide hips. Her disconsolate gaze. Her breathlessness. "A beer bottle." She huffs. "Some guy..."

"What?" says John. He moves closer to her.

She half sobs, "My eye."

"You cain't see out it?"

She shakes her head.

"Can you see these?" John holds the wadded underpants out to the side of the woman's bad eye. She doesn't even try to look. She starts to cry hysterically. John leans down and claps a hand over her mouth, warm and moist as a hot sponge. In his mind he sees only the pointlessly scraping claws. "Shhh," he whispers, bringing the underpants down and putting them where his spit-damp hand had been. "Shhh. This ain't gon' hurt you much. And that's a promise."

Her blond wig falls off. John carefully replaces it, as if later he might point to this small act as proof of something. He lays her in the bathtub and pulls shut the curtain. Before leaving her room, he hangs out the "Do Not Disturb" sign.

The sun is heating up. On John's shoulders it rests like flesh warmer than his. Below him, last night's moisture steams from the cracked parking lot, where a half-bald dog simultaneously laps and pisses into an oil-filmed puddle and four cars sit, all but one on the short side of the L. From the roof's overhang, several filthy-looking pigeons coo. Laughter sounds down near the office and John watches two maids emerge from there and disappear around back.

He takes out the .45, again walks to room 229, and crouches next to the door's keyhole. He hears what he did before, except now a soap opera plays and the gurgling sound has stopped. He is overcome by the same unbalanced sensation as earlier in the woman's room. He thinks of Simon Breedlove, the closest person to a father he still has, and of his wife and son, whom he experiences now as bodiless dreams from which he has awakened desiring to reenter while sadly realizing he can't. He decides he will buy the boy a gift. A thing they can enjoy together. A replica of a farm maybe, with lifelike animals that neigh, moo, or oink.

Then, suddenly remembering about the money, he thinks, "Why not buy him a real horse, cow, and pig?" A phone begins to ring in the room, abruptly returning John to the present. Ten times it rings, then stops.

John stands up. He knocks on the door. No one answers. John backs up a step and lifts his foot to his waist. He kicks in the door and rushes in after it.

Belted to a wooden desk chair, Obadiah Cornish is naked from the waist up, his head inclining precariously to one side and his mouth agape as if in stunned disbelief, reacting to what's playing on the television in front of him. Cut clear to the spine, his throat oozes a thin line of his blood, and the rug beneath him is soaked where much of it has already pumped out. His face and chest are marred by circular red lesions that look like cigarette burns. The tip of his nose, his upper lip, and his left ear have been sliced off.

John shuts the door, sits down on the bed, closes his eyes, and pictures the boy, in wide-eyed wonderment, petting, naming, and feeding these real-life creatures that John will buy for him. He imagines him asking questions about the animals, questions for which John actually will be able to provide answers. He imagines his son regarding him in awe for his vast knowledge of the world.

He opens his eyes, leans forward, and switches off the television set. He becomes acutely aware of the leaky-faucet-like noise of Obadiah Cornish's blood sporadically hitting the floor. He walks over and studies the mutilated corpse, not so much shocked or unnerved by what he sees as curious.

He walks over to the bureau, but there is nothing on it. He rifles the drawers and finds only clothes. In the bathroom, he finds atop the sink a wallet belonging to Cornish and inside it a paper containing a list of telephone numbers, among them Moira's, his own, and another that is familiar to him, though he can't immediately think why. The phone rings again. Following the fourth ring, John walks back into the bedroom and picks it up.

"I'm very disappointed in your behavior," a voice says.

"Wha...?" mumbles John.

"Your making threats has put me in a very delicate situation. I thought we'd agreed that I would handle things..."

Then John recognizes the voice and recalls to whom the third number belongs. The phone's mouthpiece smells like diseased breath. He hangs it up and, not touching anything else, leaves the room.

Upon seeing him again, the woman starts to squirm, gnaw at her gag, and frantically roll her head from side to side. Her obvious fear of him makes John wonder if his looks are as frightening as her reaction to them and he peers in the bathroom mirror and thinks, "No, they ain't." On the contrary, he sees, as clear as pimples on his face, a kind nature, tempered some by the bad hand he's been dealt. "Cut it out," he tells the woman, slightly perturbed, as he leans down to straighten her wig, which, skewed again, reveals beneath it a red patch of moss-thin hair on an onion-colored scalp. "I tol' ya I ain't gon' hurt ya none."

He helps her out of the tub, removes the stockings binding her wrists and ankles, leads her over to the bed, and sits her down on the edge of it. The room's light is dull. One of the two overhead bulbs is burned out; crawling in the dirt-smeared lamp, half-dead houseflies cast gray shadows on the woman's thighs. She smells of terror, emitted like a tomcat's perfumed scent, and urine where she's peed herself. On all accounts, John feels awful—for her, himself, and the situation in general. "I'm in a terr'ble bind," he tells her.

She reaches up and claws at the underpants in her mouth.

"No! No! No!" says John. He grabs her hand and slaps it firmly back in her lap. He realizes in doing so he's frightened her even more, but he thinks hearing a hysterical voice right now would push him over an abyss whose edge he is barely clinging to. "Let me tell ya why I am, first."

She opens wide at him her good eye with its already dilated pupil, but John can't tell if it's wide with fear, curiosity, or disbelief. "It's been one thing after 'nother," he says. Not sure where to go from there, he sighs and drops his forearms on his legs. He sees his hands are shaking and so are his knees. "It all started less'n a week ago, but it feels more like a year." He looks at the woman and imagines her being quite pretty once, before she got hit with the beer bottle maybe, and then he envisions her life as a water droplet rolling north to south toward the edge of a map. "You e'er had a spell like that? When one thing keeps foll'wing 'nother and everythin' you do to change it just digs a hole deeper till you're so far in, you can't see the top?"

She slowly nods, but John already knows in looking at her that she's had more than one such spell and likely considers herself to be in one now. "If I told ya half of it, you wouldn't even believe me," he says.

She shrugs.

"No. You w'udn't." John runs a hand back through his hair. "But I ain't never killed nobody purposeful," he says. "Though nobody in the world 'id b'lieve that. Sometimes it's even hard for me to b'lieve." Suddenly it strikes him that maybe he's going insane, if he hasn't already; then he remembers once hearing that a person who really is insane never thinks he is. But he's not convinced. "You can see why I cain't just let you go, cain't you?" he asks the woman.

She vigorously shakes her head no.

John points his chin at the wall. "'Sides me, you see anybody this morning goin' in or out that room I was?"

Again the woman shakes her head.

"See what I mean?"

This time he can read in her eye and furrowed brow, along with her fear, confusion.

John says, "What's your name?"

The woman tries to tell him, but it comes out all garbled. John reaches up and pulls the underwear to one side. She gasps, "Florence!"

John puts the underwear back in her mouth. "Florence," he says. Then he repeats the name several times, breaking it into two crisp syllables, and thinking you don't often hear someone below the age of seventy named Florence. "Was it your mother's name?"

She shakes her head.

John's sweating profusely. He rubs the back of his hand over his forehead, then shakes the hand. Drops of perspiration fly against the near wall. Suddenly he has the feeling he may be performing acts—even mundane ones, like wiping his brow—for the last time. His thoughts don't expound upon the feeling. Then he's not sure that he felt it at all. "A relative, though?"

The woman doesn't respond, just shivers like somebody's opened a freezer in front of her. "It's a beautiful name. Someone took some time picking it out. Not like mine—John. John Moon—that's a real simple, common kinda name." John feels horrible, actually physically sick. He pictures Obadiah Cornish's head with an ear, lip, and its nose sliced off and his little baby and Moira in the hands of the madman who did it. He nods solemnly at the woman. "Fella sits in the next room with his throat cut who's got somethin' to do with stealin' my wife and kid and even if I was you or the cops, Florence—I'd think I'd done it."

The woman's good eye madly squirts left to right like a guppy.

"I don't know what to do," says John. Abruptly his legs start hopping up and down as if they're run by little motors and he feels, between its vicious pounding, his heart whispering extra little beats like the flapping of a sparrow's wings. He wonders if maybe he's having a heart attack, only nothing really hurts. He feels more like a jet revving up to take off. "But I got to do somethin'."

He looks down at the woman's fingers and they're white where they're digging into her pink sweatpants above the pee stains on her thighs. It strikes him that she's more petrified than he is and that he's the reason why; realizing this angers John, as he's twice told her he doesn't intend to hurt her. A knock sounds on the door and a female voice with a Spanish accent says, "Clean room, okay?"

Florence precipitately bolts up from the bed and bounds for the door. From his sitting position, John dives headlong and tackles her. For several seconds they grapple on the rug, she squealing through her gag and kicking and punching at him, until finally John gets on top of her and pancakes her to the floor. He barks at the hallway, "No room service!"

"Later, you want?" asks the voice.

Suddenly, in the midst of her exhortative squirming, the underpants pop out of Florence's mouth. She starts to scream, but John points a threatening finger at her, and she stops, her mouth a frozen pink gash. "Later, no!" John calls out, sitting up and, with his knees, pinning Florence's arms to the rug. "We'll make our own beds!"

"Sí," says the woman.

"Wait!" hollers John.

"Eh?"

"I'm in room 229. I don't want no room service there neither!"

For several seconds there's no answer.

John yells, "No towels. Nothin'!"

The voice says, "You stay there?"

"Right. Two doors down! Don't even knock! Comprende?"

"Two-twenty-nine. Sí."

He hears her walk off down the corridor, stop at the room before Obadiah Cornish's, knock, and in a few seconds the door open, then close again. He says to the woman, "I guess I got to put you back in the tub."

"No," she whispers.

"I cain't see 'nother way."

"I won't tell nobody what I seen."

"You won't have a choice once they find ya."

"I could say there was a stocking over your head and I didn't see your face."

John thinks about it. "They'll know a'ready I was here."

"What's it matter, then?"

"I need time."

"To do what?"

"Get back my wife and kid."

"From who?"

"I ain't sure."

"Mis...John—listen...please?"

"What?"

"You're hurtin' my arms."

John rolls off her, flops his arms out to the sides, and gazes up at the ceiling. The woman sits up next to him. "Can I reach in my sweats?"

John rolls his head toward her. "What for?"

"I got a joint in there. You wanta smoke a joint with me?"

John doesn't say, but doesn't stop her when she reaches into a side pocket of her sweatsuit and pulls out a fat cigarette and a Cricket lighter. She puts the cigarette in her mouth, ignites it, inhales deeply, then withdraws it and places it between John's lips. They smoke the whole joint without talking. Afterwards, John is just as confused as he was, but a little calmer, and the woman acts so, too. "You got bus fare to Enid, Oklahoma?" she asks.

John blankly stares at her.

"I come back East to visit my sister in Boston but couldn't find her. Somebody there said maybe she's dead." She reaches into her sweats for a Tiparillo, places it between her lips, and lights it. "What I seen a' the East, I could easily forget."

Her makeup is smeared and now John sees that it had been partly used to conceal a whirligig-shaped scar on the cheek below her bad eye. "How much would ya need?"

"Couple hundred—three, make it—for food 'n all." She sucks on the cigar, then rolls the smoke out over her tongue. "But you gotta let me take a shower first and change."

John frowns at her.

"I ain't gon' go out in public smelling like piss."

"You wouldn't say nothing?"

"Who'd want to hear 'bout it out in Enid?"

John scratches an ear. "Five minutes," he says.

The woman stands up and walks toward the bathroom. John gets up and follows her. She shuts the bathroom door in his face. A minute later, when the water starts running, he steps inside and leans against the sink. From behind the drawn curtain, Florence lists what she hates most about the Northeast—the weather, people's lack of manners, too many cars and overweight men, a closed-in feeling she can't pinpoint, the price of marijuana, beer, and food. When the water stops running, John hands her in a towel and her blond wig. A few moments after, wearing the wig and with the towel snugly wrapped around her, she pulls back the curtain and steps out. Her legs and shoulders are pale white, smooth, and unblemished, as if they are fifteen years younger than her face.

In less than ten minutes, she's dressed, has put on fresh makeup and packed all her belongings. They walk down the back stairs to the rear parking lot and over to John's truck.

John opens the passenger door and waits for Florence to get in. He shows her his gun and tells her not to move, call out, or honk the horn. She says she wouldn't anyway. She wants to get back to Enid. John shuts her door, walks the fifty feet over to the lobby's rear entrance, opens it, sticks his head inside, and tells Skinny Leak, "Weren't nobody home."

Leak glances up from the set and shrugs. John pulls out his wallet, takes from it one of the hundred-dollar bills he had removed this morning from the sugar jar, and lays it on the counter where the old man can reach it. "If he asks—or anybody else—I weren't never here."

Leak sticks out a bony hand. He picks up the bill, pockets it, and hisses. "You's one the Fitch boys, ain't ya?"

John leaves without saying.

The bus station is on the south side of town in the first floor of a retired glue factory. Circled by a high metal fence, the terminal parking lot is potholed dirt. Two buses sit in it. Another, half full of passengers, idles in front of the depot. John parks the truck, then walks with Florence inside and asks the man selling tickets at the counter where the idling bus is headed to. The man says Buffalo.

"That west a' here?" John asks.

The man says it is.

Florence says, "I need to go to Enid, Oklahoma."

The man sneers like going to Enid, Oklahoma, is to him a personal insult. From a shelf below his waist, he picks up a little book, opens it, and starts tracing through the schedule with an index finger. After a few minutes, he says, "I can sell you a ticket there, but you'll have to get off in Buffalo, wait five hours, then change buses."

"What'm I gon' do for five hours in Buffalo, New York?" asks Florence.

"I don't know," the man tells her. "I've never been there."

"Give me the ticket," says John.

"This is a real hardship," Florence whispers to him.

Ignoring her, John pays for the ticket. Handing it to him, the man smiles sarcastically and informs them they've got fifteen minutes to say their goodbyes. Florence asks if there's smoking on the bus. The ticket seller says there isn't.

"Not even in the can?" asks Florence.

"Nowhere on the vehicle," the man tells her smugly.

Florence curses and says she needs a smoke now. She and John walk over to the benches against the far wall and sit down across from a large bulletin board with posters of wanted and missing people on it. There's no windows in the station. The stagnant air is hot and smells like body odor and the bad stink floating out one of the open john doors next to them. Florence lights up one of her little cigars. When she exhales, the smoke unwaveringly floats up to the ceiling, where it merges with an already thick, hovering cloud of it. She tells John again that taking such a roundabout route on a bus that doesn't allow smoking is a real hardship for her. Then she says she'll need more than three hundred dollars to make sure she gets to Enid all right. John asks her how much more.

"Two more ought to do it," she says. "Five, altogether."

"You mean, five hundred?" asks John, who has left in his

wallet, from what he took from the sugar jar, slightly over eight hundred dollars.

"No, dummy. Five million!" She chuckles derisively. "Hand it over."

"I ain't got that much," says John.

She gives him a weird look. "You're a strange one," she tells him. Then she says, "I don't believe you killed no one."

"I didn't on purpose," says John. "Was an accident."

"And you say someone's snatched your wife and kid?"

John stares blankly at the bulletin board, not answering. It hurts too much to think about it. Florence lightly places a hand on his wrist. "I get vibes sometimes—and I'm not just talking bullshit now—like life forces—positive or negative—and in your case I'm definitely sensing positive." She takes her hand from his arm and smokes more of her cigar. "Really. Don't ask me how I do it, though."

John doesn't. Every time Florence inhales, her lips make a wet, snappy sound. Two black men come out of the john, strut through the glass doors and onto the bus. The man at the desk says into a microphone that the bus to Buffalo is leaving in ten minutes. He frowns at John and Florence. John takes from his wallet five hundred dollars. It doesn't feel like money to him. When he hands it to Florence he feels like he's giving her scrap paper with scribbles on it. She rolls the money up, shoves it down her shirt, between her breasts, and says, "You ought to go the cops 'bout your wife and kid."

"Cain't."

"If whatever you done was an accident..."

"There's more to it than that," says John. He looks back at the bulletin board. A face there gnaws at him, though he can't put his finger on why. Florence drops her cigar butt on the floor and steps on it. John stands up. Blowing out smoke, Florence does, too. "I got to go to the can," she says.

John nods. He picks up her bag, watches her walk into the ladies' room, then strides over to the bulletin board and peers at a photograph of a girl with dirty-blond hair combed neatly over her forehead and ears, making her look even younger than the sixteen he had guessed she was. Her name is Ingrid Banes. She's from Rock Gap, Pennsylvania. Any remaining thoughts that John has of his being on an uncharted course instantly vanish. He feels a distinct pressure from a hand that is leading him along some path whose markers are known only to Him.

He tears the poster from the board, carefully folds it, and slides it into his front pants pocket. Then he takes Florence's suitcase out to the bus and hands it to the driver, who tosses it in with the rest of the luggage. He asks John if that's all there is. John says that's it. He imagines something like an invisible hawk flying circles above him. The bus driver closes up the luggage compartment and climbs into the bus. Florence comes out through the glass doors. John hands her the ticket to Enid. "I sense it'll be all right for you," she says. "Really."

John says, "What happened the one hit you with a bottle?"

She shrugs.

"You ain't got no idea?"

She gives him the weird look again. "He weren't from Enid, so how would I?"

John watches her get on the bus, sit down in a window seat near the back, and, a few minutes later, the bus leave. He waves at her, but she's already talking to her seatmate, and doesn't notice.

Lugging the heavy sack over one shoulder, he takes the side entrance up to the second floor of the J. J. Newberry building, tries the door to the lawyer's office, and finds it locked. He drops the sack and sits down to wait in the rickety wooden corridor whose yellowing wallpaper portrays farm scenes and emanates a musty, aged smell. He pulls all the coins from his pocket and, one at a time, rolls them across the corridor, trying to stop them as close to the wall as he can. Afterwards, he doesn't bother to pick them up. Staring at his feet, he imagines a flat, soundless field of high grass concealing dead bodies and the secrets they died with.

Soon he hears a thump–slide–grunt from the stairs, and a minute later, tightly gripping the rail and breathing heavily, Daggard Pitt appears at their top. Spying John, he flashes a big, toothy smile and, rattling the cardboard box he carries in one hand, gaspingly calls out, "I wonder if John Moon's a doughnut eater?"

John doesn't say if he is.

Wearing a lime-green suit that bags on his crippled side and is coffee-stained, the lawyer hobbles through the fallen coins as if they aren't there. He doesn't act surprised to see John or the sack. He leads him into the office, saying something about his secretary getting a molar capped. "Have a seat, have a seat," he tells John, placing the box on the desk and grabbing some papers from its top.

John, glancing warily around, remains standing just inside the doorway. On the wall across from him, a Syracuse law degree hangs between a photograph of Pitt waving from the deck of a sailboat John would never have guessed he could afford and framed words in a foreign language. A small metal plaque on the desk says "Thank You For Not Smoking," and just above it sits an ashtray. John thinks about his father, hat in hand, coming here to beg, and of Daggard Pitt tugging at his misshapen leg and regretfully clawing at the air with his frozen hand. Pitt says, "Did you know I once had political ambitions, John?"

John doesn't say. He smells alcohol on the lawyer's breath.

"I ran for three different offices—eight times, all told— and never came close to winning anything." He waves dismissively. "If you can't find anybody else, run the crippled midget, was the town joke—only don't vote for him!" He shuffles over and tries to hand John what he's holding, but his crippled fingers won't let go and finally John has to yank the documents from the lawyer's grasp. Laughing breathily, Pitt tries to make a joke out of it. "I don't want her, you can have her..."

John doesn't even smile.

Pitt weakly clears his throat. "That'll put us on an even playing field with her anyway, John." He hobbles back over to the desk, situates himself behind it, and from the box near his elbow pulls a cruller. John follows him to the near side of the desk, but doesn't sit down. The lawyer dunks the cruller into a half-empty coffee cup that was there when they came into the room, fishes it out, peers at the drenched pastry like it's a bug he's found, then half eats it. "Just sign there on the back, John, above your name."

John tosses the unsigned papers on the desk.

Pitt lays down the other half of the cruller. "They're no good 'less you sign them, John."

"I ain't goin' to."

"Why not?"

John takes the sack off his shoulder and drops it on the desk, where, with a loud thump, it lands on Pitt's cruller. The lawyer jerks his head back. "That was my last cruller," he says peevishly.

Verbalizing his fractured thoughts becomes too much for John. He silently stands there, his legs trembling, waiting for the lawyer to open the sack and look inside, but instead Pitt reaches into the box near his right elbow, pulls out a dough-nut, and bites into it. Red jelly squirts out two sides of his mouth. He catches the jelly in his claw-hand, then lays down the doughnut, picks up a napkin with his good hand, and carefully wipes his frozen fingers. "What a mess," he says, then matter-of-factly frowns at the sack. "I'm awfully glad you decided to nip this thing in the bud, John."

"Huh?"

"This sack doesn't belong to you, does it?"

John doesn't answer. No clear thoughts occupy his mind, only muddled images. And dark colors.

"Your wife came to see me yesterday afternoon," says Pitt, wrinkling his brow at John as if he's a young child or a retarded adult. "I told her that as your attorney I was prohib-ited from talking privately with her, but she insisted, and you know, John, I question whether we in the profession always best serve our clients by paying strict attention to the rules — after all, a family breaking up is one of the worst things any-one could go through, and the rights and wrongs of it are muddled and, it seems to me, different in every case." He nods at the desk drawer to his right. "A small one, John? I — perhaps both of us — could stand a small one?" Without waiting for an answer, he reaches into the drawer, pulls out a mug and a quart bottle of Jim Beam, uncaps the bottle, fills the coffee cup and the mug, then pushes the latter across the desk toward John. Afterwards, he seems to lose his train of thought.

"Your father wanted me to bend the rules, John — he wasn't in the hole so deep the bank couldn't have worked with him, but it was more profitable for them to sell the place — but I wouldn't do it, wouldn't go to bat for him because — in those days — I didn't want to make waves." He moves his crippled hand in a choppy line through the air to signify waves. "That was right before I ran for D.A. the first of three times." He picks up the coffee cup and holds it to his lips for several seconds. As he drinks, a thin line of whiskey dribbles from one corner of his mouth, and every swallow causes an exaggerated, painful-looking bob of his Adam's apple. John can see that he's bombed. "I hear tell the only candidate ever got less votes than me was Ralph Dolan running for sheriff that time."

John says, "This ain't about my father or your running for goddamned D.A."

Pitt tilts his head and purses his lips at John, and John, looking at him, suddenly thinks of Lois Copp, a three-hundred-pound girl he went to school with who would say or do anything just to get a boy to smile at her or talk to her for five seconds. "She was concerned, John, not just for you, but for her and the boy — all that money that you acted as if it had just dropped out of the sky into your lap made her think you'd maybe robbed a bank or even worse and what if you were to get arrested and her as an accomplice, what would happen to Nolan?" He jerkily wipes his mouth with the napkin.

"She asked me to talk to you. She said she'd tried and couldn't make sense of your answers and was so scared she didn't know what to do."

John's fear, confusion, and anger is such that it melds into a sort of clarity in which the only questions worth answering don't have to be asked.

"We're such a small town, aren't we, John?"

John doesn't say.

"An attorney with any sizable clientele at all often finds himself in these conflicting situations where one client's problems overlap with another's." More whiskey or maybe sweat slides down one side of Pitt's face. Several drops land on his desk. "Clients confide in me all sorts of things, John, some of them downright reprehensible, but as a lawyer I must look at the person behind the act, and do you know, in almost every case, I'm able to see the child behind the actor and to say to myself, 'There but for the grace of God, goes I'?" His hand shaking, he reaches for the bottle and refills the coffee cup, the glass and kiln-dried clay loudly clattering against each other. John again thinks of Lois Copp, how she'd once approached him and four or five other boys in the school corridor and in her sweet little girl's voice offered to blow anyone who would carry home her books and get introduced to her parents. John had felt as embarrassed for her as he does now for Pitt, and on the other hand, something in both of them made his flesh crawl. He nods at the sack.

"You represent the sons a' bitches wanting what's in that, Pitt?"

"In this business, John—particularly when you handle, as I do, mostly criminal and family-court work, seeing as how the upper crust prefers to take their civilized problems to life-sized, former football-playing lawyers—you engage all sorts of pitiable characters…."

"What's their interest?"

"I didn't ask."

"How come?"

"For the same reason I won't ask you exactly what it is, John, or how it came to be in your possession." The lawyer gravely purses his lips. "If, let's say, what you've brought me is ill-gotten gains of which I am made aware, I'd be legally obliged to turn it over to the law, and that, I think, is something all parties would like to avoid, yes?"

"I ain't smart 'nough to see your angle, Pitt, 'cept to figure you're gettin' a piece of it."

"I don't know what you mean, John." Pitt quickly picks up with one thumb and forefinger the other half of the jelly doughnut and dunks it into his coffee cup. "I'm a lawyer emboldened by whiskey, is all." He pops the doughnut into his mouth. "The image of your father, perhaps, has prompted me to take a more personal role than I ought to have…"

"You didn't give a shit for my father!"

"Not when it counted, I grant you, but I don't worry so much these days about strictly adhering to the rules, John. You see, I did some soul-searching after I went through my little political stage, and what I discovered is that I am an odd, ugly duck and that my gift is to represent other odd, ugly ducks—such as yourself, John—who don't comfortably fit into society's placid pond . . ."

Listening to Pitt, John is again reminded of his own cognitive shortcomings. Is Pitt a crippled devil or a deformed angel? Suddenly he feels as if all the world, outside of himself, is staring like a large audience at him—a deaf, dumb, and blind performer. Reaching down, he jerks the .45 from his belt and holds it loosely in one hand. Pitt, acting as if the gun isn't even there, mouths through his chewing lips, "You haven't discussed with anyone else the problems that have brought you here today, have you, John?"

John doesn't say.

"Talking in these situations is never good for anyone. Keep the body in the ground, so to speak, yes?"

John points the gun between Daggard Pitt's eyes.

Pitt exaggeratedly blinks as if struck by a sudden thought. "So, John, shall I turn the contents of this sack over to the other party entitled to my loyalty in this matter and instruct him, then, to consider it buried?"

"What about my wife and son?"

Pitt puts up his crippled hand as if to stop the anticipated shot from John's pistol. "That's the whole point of my involvement, John—to see that your impulsiveness in no way harms them."

"I want to know they're safe."

"Safe? Of course they're safe. Why wouldn't they be safe? Now, please, put the gun away."

"Where are they now?" asks John.

"I understand they're out of town through the weekend—she mentioned something about the Thousand Islands..."

John feels like he's floating, anchorless, in space. He reaches his free hand into the seat of the wooden chair behind him and picks up the cushion there.

"Call who's got them."

"Got them?"

"Do it now. Then I'll leave." John cocks the pistol. "On'y don't call Obadiah Cornish again."

"John?"

"He's had his throat sliced and things cut off'n him."

Daggard Pitt's face abruptly turns several shades paler than its normal blanched white. He picks up his coffee cup and jerkily gulps at the whiskey left inside, splashing most of it down his front.

"Call Waylon," says John. "Tell him you got the money."

Pitt pants breathily. John can see he's in shock and that's why he's not more frightened. "Not my client, John."

"How deep you in this, Pitt?"

"I, I... Obadiah, poor boy... odd, ugly duck... he..."

In front of John's eyes, the room starts to tilt again, like it did at the Oaks. An anticipatory feeling of awe comes over him, as when he was a kid and standing with his father at the Syracuse Airport, waiting to see, for the first time, an airplane take off. And he's scared too, as he was then, that his self might jump out of his body and take off with it. "You better call somebody, lawyer."

"...the only one I represent, John."

"What?"

"...there's nobody else..."

John shakes his head, but can't rid himself of the feeling, now almost a certainty, that he's standing next to his father again and that John's words and actions are no longer his own, but Robert Moon's. He places the pillow firmly over the lawyer's face. He imagines a switch blinking off, leaving an entire chamber dark and stone-still and its contents irretrievable. "You should've helped us, Pitt," he says, pushing the barrel of the .45 into the pillow.

"...ohhhn?"

John places his finger on the trigger.

"...ohnnn!"

The voice trying to transcend the pillow is muffled and strained, like an underwater shout. From its weightless haven, John's mind recognizes his own name, one syllable giving birth to a world of subconscious connotations. You are John Moon, whispers a voice. Farmer without a farm in a world that is as it was and always will be. The year is 199–. Two futures pulse in the muscles of your finger. Aloud, it says, "You ever see him cry?"

"Uhhh?" says the muffled voice.

"Robert Moon?"

There is no sound from the other side of the pillow, only the ripe pungent smell of the lawyer's feces. "Not me," says John. "Nor beg neither. I wished I had."

The weight behind the pillow goes limp.

Suddenly John realizes he is shaking. He looks at his hand and arm holding the pillow and sees they are tense with exertion. He pulls his finger from the gun's trigger, then jerks back the pillow. The face behind it is tinged blue. The head drops to one side of its neck. John's not sure how much time has elapsed. "Pitt?"

The lawyer doesn't answer.

"Who with, Pitt?"

The head lolls.

John slaps it.

The lawyer groans. His eyes flutter open. He takes several shallow breaths. Then deeper ones. Spittle rolls from the corner of his disfigured lips. His face looks like it's been pulled from a vise. "Who with in the Thousand Islands, Pitt? Who took them!"

"She...they...he—boyfriend..."

"Whose boyfriend?"

"I'm awfully sorry, John..."

"Huh?"

"Love's unraveling—so painful..."

John slaps him again.

"...they know nothing about"—Pitt's crippled hand flutters in front of his face like a defective parachute—"this..."

"They ain't kidnapped?"

"Kidnapped? No...ah, the note...Obadiah—bad child..."

"What?"

"...she ought to have told you, John." He starts panting faster again, as if suddenly remembering the nearness of his own death.

"...he, uh—boyfriend—apparently...on the water—a small camp?—you know, uh—for vacation?"

His small, simple world has turned ambiguously sinister. Heads have two faces, one visible, one not. Words, though spoken in proper linguistic form, don't mean what they ought to. From one moment to the next, nothing in this upside-down world is static. Even voices dichotomize, their bifurcating sounds clouding his thoughts, sending his mind reeling first down one path, then down another. Who can be trusted in this world? Humanity itself—the whole great mass—is mutable. John feels ill equipped to deal with it.

Avoiding eye contact with everyone he passes, he walks the three blocks back to the municipal parking lot, dangling the heavy money sack over one shoulder. The smell of hot tar fills the air. At the east end of the lot, his old crew works. As Cole Howard drives his roller over the freshly laid, steam-breathing tar, Levi Dean, his fat, sun-pink torso supported by a shovel, talks to a bald string bean who John guesses might be Gumby Talon. They strike John as three creatures out of a past life from which he has been catapulted like a small stone. He tosses the sack into the passenger seat, then, after ducking into the pickup, quickly pulls out of the west end of the lot.

He takes the less-traveled back river road out of town, passing by the old feed mill, closed nearly a decade now, where once a week he used to come with his father in their old flatbed truck. John remembers Robert Moon always opening each sack of grain, sniffing and running his fingers through the cool, sweet-smelling oat and barley mix to make sure he was getting what he paid for, and the prideful feeling when one day that task was turned over to John. He thinks of the dozens of farmers they used to meet and converse with at the mill, most of whom, like him and his father, now aren't, and suddenly John understands that whoever is to be blamed for his pitiful state, it is not his father.

Staring to his left at the serpentine course of the river wandering through mostly abandoned pastureland and virgin forest, he thinks of his wife and son, as far away from him as the rest of the life he lived before the dead girl, though he is thankful they are safe. He is not surprised—nor even really angry—that Moira has a boyfriend, though his heart aches with his own failure to be what she had wanted him to be and with the knowledge that she believes his very presence would be poisonous to their son. An odd, ugly duck Daggard Pitt had called him, as if John were the same as Obadiah Cornish or the rest of his down-and-out clients. He shivers at the memory of how he had nearly killed the lawyer—who maybe deserved it. He hadn't, though, and that's a thought worth holding on to.

But who had killed Obadiah Cornish? Waylon, maybe, after having discovered that Cornish—with his kidnapping bluff—was trying to recover the money without him? Or was it Simon Breedlove? But why? What was his connection with the other two? And where had the money come from? John remembers how Ira and Molly Hollenbach had been cut up and their throats slit, just as the Hen had been. Too many bad people in the world. Too many unanswerable questions.

He takes out the dead girl's picture and, driving with one hand, unfolds it on the steering wheel. She is five feet six inches tall, weighs one hundred eighteen pounds, likes motorcycle riding, outdoor sports, and is daughter to Bob and Melanie Banes, whose address and phone number appear beneath the words "Please help us find our daughter." The picture, he thinks, doesn't do her justice. She looks better with her hair behind her ears and wearing a little makeup, as in the Polaroids he took. He folds the poster and puts it in his pocket again, then abruptly pulls the truck off the road. He drives several hundred yards into an overgrown pasture of goldenrod and hawkweed and parks behind an abandoned bridge stanchion fifty feet above the river.

When he gets out, his limbs are rubbery and soft. To keep from falling over, he leans back against the crumbling concrete stanchion, then slowly sits down. The rest of the bridge, except for a similarly decrepit abutment on the far side of the water, is missing. The field before him is hip-high. Past it, the water is low and barely moving. A blue heron stands statuesquely at its edge. Where it still peeks above the horizon, the sun is blood red. Two hawks circle beneath it. John closes his eyes. His brain feels like mush sprinkled with raisins, in an indiscernible mass his few discernible thoughts.

His half-conscious imaginings become increasingly bizarre, though he doesn't recognize them as such. It strikes him that Waylon is not flesh and blood, but a devilish specter, always hauntingly present, but seldom seen. Ingrid Banes, from Rock Gap, Pennsylvania, appears before him as a winged messenger carrying God's personal agenda for John, but His handwriting's illegible. John falls asleep.

He wakes beneath a cloudless sky breached by stars. The windless air is pleasantly warm. A symphony of frogs and peepers plays. The field's flowered scent is like that from a greenhouse. A coyote bays somewhere on the mountain on the other side of the road, and in a tree by the river an owl hoots. John stretches his limbs, perfectly at ease in this world.

He's forgotten exactly where he is or how he got here or what he'd dreamed about. Until he remembers, he is just happy to be alive.

A thin mist covers the narrow road that curls like a looped rope along the east side of the river before crossing over a metal bridge five miles below the hollow where John lives. The truck's headlights pierce the mist-layered darkness for a hundred feet, giving objects a haloed appearance. He drives slowly, his arm out the window, smelling the night and half wishing he could vanish into it.

The few houses he passes are not lit. This late, even dogs are asleep. Inarticulable thoughts like voiceless music touch and rouse him in mysterious ways. The dead girl, in her deep sleep, her placid beauty frozen in time, is forever intricately intertwined with him, John Moon—alive or dead—a disturbing thought he finds oddly comforting. In this dynamic, ever-changing world, he suddenly can't wait to see her static face again. Did he think that, really? He's not sure. Images in the next moment are forgotten or change into something else. One thing is certain: she is the core around which his random thoughts now spin. The money doesn't matter anymore. It could blow out the windows and he wouldn't care.

A car passes him going the other way, causing him to snap straight up behind the wheel. The memory of zigzagging headlights are spots in his eyes. A drunk, he thinks, heading home after last call. Then he realizes he is traveling less than twenty miles per hour and is afraid to go home, afraid of what might be waiting for him. So why is he? Where else is there for him to go? he asks himself, only subconsciously aware—or able to admit—that the real reason is her, Ingrid Banes.

He is nearly in front of the dark one-story cabin that is Simon Breedlove's home, before he remembers it is on this road and understands his actual motive for coming this way. Now his mind's not laboring at all. Just acting or reacting. Striding moment to moment, a hiker on fate's predestined course. Two hundred yards past the cabin, he switches off the headlights and ignition and rolls the pickup down a dirt incline into a cornfield of knee-high plants where invisible cicadas make a cumulative buzz.

The smell is of fertilizer, damp soil, and adolescent growth. The sporadic spark of fireflies intrudes on the darkness. A night, in his past life, for hand-holding, duet whistling, blanket love. John pulls the .45 from the glove box, checks to see that it's loaded, shoves it down the front of his pants, and steps from the truck. Beneath his feet the dirt is powdery and soft. From his left comes a rustling sound. He wheels that way and sees four sets of glistening eyes that, in less than a second, are gone. Raccoons. He hears them scurrying through the field.

Standing fifty yards to the right of the cabin, concealed beneath a willow tree, he watches the dark house inhale the night air through its wide-open, sash-covered windows, and thinks how he doesn't really know Simon, and never did. A hard worker, hunter, drinker, with streaks affable, morose, and mean, he has, like John, few close friends. When was it that John had watched Simon, the two of them whiskey-shitfaced, hand-walk across the five-hundred-yard guide wire atop the Coxsackie Gap Bridge, screaming at John and the cars and river below that he had fucked, fought, drunk, and killed enough for one life and that John ought to shake the wire and knock him off? John can't remember whether it was before or after the Hollenbach murders, but it was right around then, and he remembers too, before the police had shown up to take Simon to detox, him standing on the far side, telling John, "After the first time, Johnno, even the worst things get like riding a bike…" which John had figured was a reference to Simon's war experiences, though now he wonders if it hadn't been meant to encompass more recent events.

Around back, on the dampened grass lawn, catercorner to the house, sits the Cadillac, its driver-side door open and its dome light dully flickering. Leaf-heavy branches, swaying from an adjacent ash tree, lightly caress the car's roof, creating a high-pitched mewl. Beneath the tree, amid scattered engine parts, lies a gutted motorcycle, and farther back, parked in front of the small, unpainted barn Simon uses for storage and to house two beef cows and a handful of pigs, goats, and chickens, is his dual-wheel pickup truck. From the barn come clucks, tired groans, and unshod hooves lazily shifting on the cement floor.

Tiptoeing toward the Cadillac, John is hit with an eerie sensation that this little one-acre patch with its unkempt cabin and barn, like the secrets in its inhabitant's mind, exists solely in a zone beyond the expected and civilized. The image of Simon, his childhood mentor and hunting buddy, becomes the mysterious man who, with no regular income, vanishes for weeks at a time and, upon his return, only gets together with John on his own terms, suddenly showing up at the trailer or by phone arranging to meet him in a bar or the woods somewhere. In the twelve years since Simon built his cabin, John can count on one hand the occasions he has been in it and then only to wait while Simon showered, changed clothes, or retrieved something he had forgotten. The last time, several years before, that he stopped by the cabin uninvited, Simon had snarled through a crack in the front door that he was busy and would call John when he wasn't, which turned out to be weeks later.

John steps on a slick spot in the lawn and his feet go out from under him. Exhaling a muffled grunt, he lands with a dull thump in the half-foot-high grass, then lies ten feet from the Cadillac, holding his breath, waiting to see if the noise has roused anyone in the house. Visible in the flickering shaft of light half-illuminating the interior of the car is the silvery reflection of keys dangling in the ignition and a white, shearling-covered seat. To his left, the back door to the cabin is ajar. Suddenly something bursts through the opening into the moonlit semiblackness between John and the building, charges noisily across it, and slams, snorting, into John's chest.

John punches the thing. Emitting a manic squeal, it backs off, then charges again; short-legged and bristly, its muscular body rams like a torpedo into John's ribs.

"Git!" hisses John, hammering the hard torso with his fists.

The beast runs off a few feet. John sees framed in a patch of moonlight, its blush-colored hide spotted on its head and neck by dark, moist blotches as if it's had a pail of paint thrown at it, a boxer-sized pig. He looks down at his hands. They are smeared with the same wet, sticky substance as that marring the pig. He smells his fingers, then touches them to his tongue. They taste sweet. Like molasses. He jumps to his feet. Throatily grunting, the pig scampers off toward the barn, its front door, John now sees, standing wide open.

He leans down and wipes his hands on the lawn. He looks at the house again. The dark shape of another pig darts out through the door. Releasing chortled grunts, the night-shrouded swine beats a grass-shivering path through the unmowed lawn toward the barn. His pulse hammering a staccato in his ears, John quickly strides over to the front seat of the Cadillac, in which an Albany banker and his teenage girlfriend had died before Simon salvaged it from a junk-yard, restored its body, and gave it a V-8 engine from a rusted-out Ford Bronco. Could he have imagined seeing it parked that afternoon at the Oaks? wonders John.

The car is in drive, as if someone had simply pulled it up as close to the cabin as he could, turned it off, pushed open the driver-side door, and, drunk, injured, or in a hurry, entered through the back of the house. The floor on the pas-senger side is dotted with empty beer cans, cardboard fast-food containers, a coiled rope, several hand tools. An unwound cassette dangles from a corner of the open glove box. The shearling smells like beer. On it lies a woman's sweater, san-dals, and a half-zipped gym bag, in which John finds one of Simon's hand-carved flutes, capable, in Simon's hands, of playing notes dreamy, sad, or that can transport your mind to a place a thousand miles away.

Now come to John more images of Simon, at about John's age, showing John how to whistle dozens of birdcalls, how to reassemble a rod-shot tractor engine, cut out a breeched calf without killing its mother, get downwind from a deer when trailing it, how to carve just about anything from a stick of dead wood. Rifling through the gym bag of clothes and toiletries, John remembers his father once saying of Simon—after he'd punched out that bull, maybe, or during one of his vanishing acts—"If that one were an ocean I'd take a boat clear crosst it but bet your ass I'd never swim in it."

He finds beneath the clothes more plastic-wrapped tools—various-sized picks, screwdrivers, wrenches, a hand drill. John wonders if they are burglar's tools. Then he remembers Simon's penchant for carrying tools, large and small, in his vehicles. Tools are an obsession with him. For lack of the proper tool, he once told John, a man might be stranded in a snowstorm, bleed to death, suffocate in an airless, locked room. John finds wrapped in a T-shirt and cushioned by a leather sheath a large hunting knife. He removes the sheath. The knife's blade is shiny and sharp. John remembers when Simon purchased the knife at a sporting-goods store in Ralston and how, after using it for anything—even to open an envelope—he meticulously cleans and polishes its blade and handle with a damp rag. Even if the knife had slashed Obadiah Cornish's throat, thinks John, the Hen's blood would not be on it.

He slides the knife back into the sheath, drops it in the gym bag, then pushes the bag toward the passenger door. On the vacated patch of seat lies a torn scrap of brown-and-blue computer paper that John recognizes as part of a monthly telephone bill, marred by someone's ink-scribbled words. He picks the paper up and studies it in the faltering dome light.

Halfway down the page, beneath Simon's typed name, address, and phone number, is written: "Oaks—room 229." John exhales a deep breath he isn't aware he'd been holding. He tries to fit this piece of Simon as torturer and murderer into the whole puzzle of the man. The piece fits only in a hollow, coreless world. A world lacking substance or a center. A world where images adhere more solidly than words to the mind. John drops the paper and backs out of the car.

Treading the grass-flattened path toward the back door of the cabin, he can taste the mist, a pollen-sweetened dew like the aftermath of a syrupy drink. He is fleshless in this soup, like the two shadowed animals—taller than the pigs and rangier—that, in the midst of John's approach, float like bearded specters through the half-open doorway before vanishing to his left into the darkened, fog-cloaked grass. John reaches down to his belt, yanks out the .45, and thinks, "Goddamn goats now. Sam Hell's left in the barn?"

Past the two-foot space between the edge of the screen door and the outer wall, he tentatively places a foot into the darkened house, which smells like the molasses earlier flavoring his fingers, varied manures, and gunpowder's pungent smoke. Though he can't see much of it, the room has the eerie sense of being alive. John can actually hear it breathing, or imagines he can, and feels its pulse steadily beating in the far corner to his left. His hunter's sixth sense tells him to back out of the house, as he didn't in the quarry, but a feeling even stronger assures him he is on fate's course.

He puts his other foot in front of the first one, and, holding the pistol out in front of him, starts to walk slowly. Suddenly he feels himself sliding, then, as if his feet have been grabbed by invisible hands, he's skating unrestrainedly across the floor toward a large, ominously rocking shadow fronting an even bigger one. Halfway there, he goes down and slides the rest of the way on his backside. He hears what he thinks is a moo. A half second later, he collides with the source of the sound.

For a moment he lies, panting, entangled in four muscular legs. He is close enough to see that he is beneath an emasculated bull. It swishes its tail, then restlessly shifts its stance. John carefully rolls out from under it. He's covered with molasses, manure, and whatever else is on the floor. He grabs onto the steer's tail for support and pulls himself to his feet. The animal lows and shakes its head, the motion creating a clanking sound in the small room. "Shhhh!" whispers John, reaching for its neck to cease the sway and finding the neck encircled by a chain. The chain is looped around and padlocked to the refrigerator before which the animal stands. In the center of the refrigerator, which is leaking water, are two circular, rough-edged holes that John guesses were made by shotgun blasts.

Leaning against the steer, John gazes in wonderment around the kitchen, his eyes now enough adjusted to the dark to see that the stove next to the refrigerator is also shot and that, above it, the food cabinets have been blasted or their doors torn open and the food that was inside thrown onto the floor for the pigs, goats, and whatever else to pick at. The oddity of this scene has an almost calming effect on John, as if he is in a dream in which the worst possible thing that could result is for him to wake up screaming. On the left flank of the cow is what looks to be a glistening wound or a large, glossy strip of paper. John looks closer and sees that a color photograph has been taped to the steer's hide. He pulls off the picture and holds it inches from his eyes, but can make out only the dark outlines of two people side by side and a smaller person or an animal crouched or lying between them.

He shoves his pistol into his belt, then reaches into his pocket, withdraws a packet of restaurant matches, and, holding the photograph between his teeth, lights a match. In the flame's dancing cone of light, he again looks at the picture. This time he sees a man and a woman sitting on a couch with their arms around each other and jointly holding a small child. The man is small and wiry, has a jack-o'-lantern's smile and something a little off with the left side of his head, as if maybe it's been stove in or he's missing something there. The woman is big-boned, pretty, taller than the man, and, like him, vaguely familiar to John, but more so. He can't fathom their pictures — or anyone's — being taped to a cow's ass in Simon Breedlove's kitchen.

John thinks the steer might be asleep. Its head rests almost on the floor and its only movement is a slow, steady, side-to-side list like that of an anchored ship. He tapes the picture back where he found it, then tiptoes past the refrigerator, careful not to slip again, and enters a wood-floored hallway where the molasses stops, but the boards creak beneath his feet. He remembers the hallway leads to a big catch-all room where, John had the impression, Simon does about everything but cook and sleep. He walks around a rounded corner and sees at the corridor's end a dull, steady light. He pulls out the .45 and tries to make less noise as he walks, though he's sure anyone in the house can hear his rapid breathing. He's a step from the doorway when through it rushes, in a mishmash of clucks and feathers, a large chicken.

"Jesus!" hisses John, flattening himself against the wall as the red-and-white pullet sissy steps its way down the hallway toward the kitchen. In the unblinking light falling from the room, the bird's flaming tuft reminds John, pressed against the oak-log partition abutting the doorway, of the crested hairdo on the woman he's just seen. As the fowl prissily trots around the corner and disappears, he suddenly remembers who she is. He wonders how Colette Gans's picture ended up taped to a beef cow's flank. Or why. Sweat oozes from every pore on his body. More clucking sounds come from the room.

He pokes his head around the corner of the doorway and sees, ten feet in front of a recliner facing it, a television noiselessly playing an off-air signal and illuminating two more pullets absently picking at what look to be kernels of hard corn scattered on the floor. Several open beer cans and an empty gin bottle lie on a throw rug near the chair. Resting atop the recliner's back, slightly tilted to one side, is the back of a human head.

Purged now of all conscious thought, John's mind fills with a single image of fate's darkened corridor whose light-flickering end might be a candle or a muzzle flash; in this narrow, one-way tunnel the sum of his earthly knowledge becomes the floating, transparent cells marring his vision. He slips into the room and, holding the pistol out in front of him in one hand, silently stalks the chair. He is less than five feet from it when a torturous moan sounds from the recliner and the head slowly lolls. John rushes forward and places the gun's barrel against the base of the head. It moans again, loosely bobs, then rolls back to where it had originally been resting.

"Who's it?" whispers John.

The chair's occupant groans. John pushes against the recliner's back so that it springs forward, then snaps to a stop, throwing its contents onto the floor. Loudly clucking, the chickens dance away from the body. It scrambles to get to its feet. "Don't try nothin'," says John.

A man laboriously gets to his knees, then slowly turns around. "Jesus, Johnno."

John points the gun at him.

"What the hell? Where—you? Son of a bitch, John."

"What?"

"Put the goddamn gun away. The bad guy's gone."

"Huh?"

"Bastard moved 'bout my whole stock in here." Simon lashes out at one of the chickens, which rises up, squawking. "You seen what he done my kitchen?"

John doesn't say.

"Plugged it eight times I counted. Mighta been more on'y drunk as I was, I c'udn't hardly see straight." He pushes himself with his hands into a semistanding position. John backs off half a step, aiming the gun at him. "What the hell, Johnno? I ought to kick your ass. Why you here?"

John waves the .45 at the couch. "Sit down yonder there," he says.

"What?"

"Got some questions for ya."

"You're holdin' a gun on me, John. And that's after you broke in my house. I think I'll jis' go back to sleep. Try wakin' up a whole 'nother way."

"I seen what you done the Hen," says John.

Simon straightens up the rest of the way. He runs a hand over his mouth. "Seen what?"

"Over to the Oaks."

"You seen a piece a' shit with his throat cut and figured I did it, that what you mean?"

"I seen what I seen. It looked a lot like what the cops said somebody done to Ira and Molly Hollenbach."

Simon shrugs. "Go 'head shoot me, Johnno. Been workin' up to doin' it myself here last couple a' days."

Suddenly John's hand holding the gun is shaking. He can feel his legs begin to quiver like fish flopping on a bank. He's afraid he's going to fall down. To prevent it, he puts his free hand on the back of the chair. "Why?" he asks.

"That ain't never as complicated as people like to make it out, Johnno. Years 'fore I ever heard a' Vietnam my daddy said I had the same wild hair's got him dead younger than I am now, o'ny I got far 'nough in school to know wild hairs is called genes and get a damn sight wilder a man's been drinkin'." He backs up to the television set. "And like everybody's mother always warns, I got in with some bad elements, baddest of which is that piece shit you found bleeding all over the Oaks' rugs."

"You worked for Ira. He treated you decent."

"Most times."

"Decent as my own daddy."

"Gon' turn off the set, Johnno."

"Don't!"

Simon abruptly reaches down and switches off the television. The room goes black. John hears a rapid movement. He tries to follow the sound with his gun. Simon chuckles. John says, "I know where you are!"

A dull light comes on behind him. "Boo!" says Simon.

John wheels around. Simon's standing before the couch, aiming a shotgun at him. "Shit, Johnno, din' you learn nothin' 'bout what I taught you?"

John lowers the .45. He feels physically and cognitively depleted. "Ain't like you," he says.

"Huh?"

"Don't shoot folks been good to me. Nor slit their throats neither."

"Ira was s'posed to be to a fireman's dance that night, 'cordin' the Hen." Simon points the shotgun at his own toes. He sits down on the couch. John's not sure if he's through covering him with the shotgun or is just taking a rest. "Him and Molly both. I run into Obadiah all growed-up over the Pink Lily in Raburn, this was maybe three, four years after Ira'd shit-canned 'im for skewerin' that cow and a coupla weeks after he'd done the same to me for not showin' up two mornings in a row, then wouldn't pay me no back wages. Hen says he'd been holdin' Ira's safe combination all these years—all we'd have to do is walk in and open it."

At a level deeper than conscious comprehension, John is thinking that the apparent palpability of words, acts, the whole process of human interchange, is a sham. He is mindful, though, only of his physical distress. His trembling extremities. His palpitating heart. "What I notice 'bout myself,

Johnno, is the drunker I get, the more reasonable the most un-fucking-reasonable things seem."

"Guess I'll sit down," John tells him, " 'less'n you'll shoot me for it."

"Christ, John."

"All right?"

Simon scowls.

John shoves the .45 into his belt. He takes a seat on the edge of the recliner, facing Simon. Simon sighs and says, "Them first coupla years after I got back I weren't hardly never sober 'cept when I worked for your daddy, who wouldn't tolerate it, but seems like the longer I'd go 'long his way, worse it'd be when I did let loose, and pretty soon a lost weekend 'id turn into a lost week or two or a whole damn month." He flicks the barrel of the shotgun at one of the chickens that's strayed too close to his foot. The chicken squawks and runs off. "Some mess, ain't it, John?"

John's not sure if he means his own or the cabin's. Anyway, he doesn't answer. It seems to him that Simon's voice has lost its uniqueness. It sounds like a million other voices.

"Hen drives out Route 9," it says, "and parks in the Conservancy so nobody'd see us comin' up the hollow, then we hike the woods trail over to Ira's, getting drunker as we go—I mean, I'm not even carryin' a gun, Johnno, because to me it's a sumbitchin' lark. I figure there's a safe at all, most'll be in it is the couple weeks' wages Ira owes me. We walk up the house whistling, through the front door, turn on a light, and go through the living room to Ira's office, where the Hen gets to his knees and yanks up a piece a' rug above where the safe is. He tries openin' it with some goddamn numbers he's got writ down but nothin' happens so he curses and tries 'em a few more times with no more luck and me giving 'im the raspberry 'cause I don't really give a shit and the Hen finally says fuck it he'll go upstairs and take some a' Molly's jewels and then we'll leave and though I'm not happy 'bout him ransackin' the place I go in the kitchen and drink a beer while I wait and maybe he's up there fifteen, twenty minutes tops and all I e'er heard, Johnno, was a little bangin' round and once or twice the Hen curse."

Simon stops talking and runs a hand back through his hair. He's wearing the same clothes he was two days ago. John wonders if he's slept in a bed or been less than half-drunk since then. "Look at this shit, Johnno." He waves the shotgun around the room. "Here's love makin' a damn monster out a' man. You think my homeowner's 'll cover what he done?"

John doesn't say. He's wondering who the monster is and how far wrong John had read Simon, what exactly his friend is capable of. Could it have been he who had shot Mutt and left the dead girl's body in the trailer? Was it possible that he had been involved with the Hen in threatening John's family? The belief that he might have been has on John's already tortured mind the excruciating pain-followed-by-numbness effect of frigid water.

Balancing the shotgun on his thighs, Simon reaches down with one hand and snatches an open beer can from the floor. "Hair a' the dog, Johnno," he says before raising the can to his lips and draining it. Afterwards, he scowls, fixates on a spot on the ceiling above John's head, and in a flat monotone says, "I hear Hen come back downstairs and I walk out and see 'im covered in blood with a look on his face like the devil's rooted up and found a home there and in one hand he's totin' Ira's bloody World War II bayonet and in the other his thirty-aught and when I ask 'im what the hell he's gone and done he walks by me toward the study and says, 'Ol' Ira was up there straightenin' me out on them numbers.' I run upstairs, Johnno, and find a mess worse than most of what I seen in 'Nam, and Ira, half butchered like he is, moanin' from Molly's lap and oglin' me out the one eye he's got left and the look he give me, Johnno, 'll follow me into the ground and a damn sight deeper, and I mumbled to him somethin' like I was sorry for it, then I took out my huntin' knife and done for 'im like I would for a wounded deer."

Simon tosses the shotgun onto the cushion next to him. Particles of dust rise up and, in the dim light around and above his head, spin in a circular pattern monotonous as his words. "Was Hen carrying the aught-six," he says, rubbing his temples, "so I din' argue much when he turns it on me and says we ought to split up, with him headin' with the money back over the Conservancy and me winding my way down the west fork the hollow where my pickup was stashed."

John reaches down and squeezes his left calf where it's cramped up. He wonders how long it would take Simon to grab the shotgun and aim it.

"We was gon' get together in coupla days to see 'bout divvyin' things up, but I figured from the start I'd seen the last of him and it ain't but a week later I hear he's pled to and been sentenced to a six-pack for a string a' burglaries up in Raburn he was out on bail for at the time the Hollenbach thing and I guessed he musta planned all along to stash whatever we took somewhere till he got out."

In the dark corners of the room, pieces of furniture silently sit like intrigued jurors. Sporadic clucks sound like the derisive barks of naysayers. "Coulda let the law in on it," mumbles John.

"In their eyes I'm guilty as him."

"You din' have to take the money."

Simon laughs contemptuously. "You know what a big pile cash does a poor man, don't ya, John."

John straightens up. He looks at Simon, trying to figure out if he's making generalizations or knows that John, in many ways, had come to the same crossroads as Simon and, as John now guiltily realizes, taken the same wrong turn. "Makes 'im greedy," says John.

"Like a rich man."

"More you talk, dumber I feel."

"Dead's dead, Johnno. On'y sense I e'er made a' life."

In John's mind, beyond fear and disillusionment, lurks his own culpability. Was his hiding the dead girl and taking the money as bad as what Simon had done? He's not sure. Nor of what Simon knows about John's own involvement. "Day 'fore yest'day I'm up to the Oaks where Big Colette Gans's hidin' from her old man and son of a bitch, Johnno, if I don't run smack-dab into Hen-shit-for-brains, still with his convict's tan and hellish s'prised to see me. Probably planned slippin' in and out town like a ghost with what he come for, though he gives me the song-'n'-dance 'bout lookin' me up soon's he had his hands on the cash on'y he swears after it got dug up from where he buried it somebody 'sides him snatched it."

John flicks his eyes at Simon. "Said it was him dug it up?"

"Din' say one way the other."

John glances nervously at the shotgun. "You shoot Mutt?"

"Wouldn't shoot no dog, John. Not your'n nohow."

"He say it was me took it?"

"Said he had a hunch. Then I drive up there and find you loaded for bear."

"Figured I'd be too busy studyin' on tattooed mountain lions see you'd searched the place?"

"Shit, John. Thought a' that money got like a cancer in my gut. I couldn't cut it out and couldn't live with it. Next morning I drove to town got even drunker. Figured you had it, after a while you'd get to feelin' scared or upright and give it the law. I weren't gon' shoot ya for it. And couldn't talk to ya 'bout it." Simon slowly picks up the gun. "'Cept I kep' goin' over what the Hen might do to you or your'n for it and finally I made up my mind go over there put a sick chicken out its misery."

"Done more'n that, what I seen."

"I wouldn't wasted so much effort killin' that sumbitch. How I left 'im's how I found 'im." He tosses the shotgun at John. John puts out both hands and catches it. "There's one in the chamber, Johnno. Be 'bliged you'd put it in me." He reaches down and starts untying his boots. Holding the shotgun, John watches him, acutely aware again of the living sounds and smells in the house, of animals, under darkness's blanket, eating, scratching, defecating, performing instinctual tasks as boundless as John's befuddlement. Simon kicks off his boots, then, sighing, reclines on the couch. "Headache weren't so bad, Johnno," he says, "till I passed out and was woke up half-sober in the same mess I passed out in."

"Was it Waylon killed 'im?"

Simon scowls confusedly at him. "Don't know no Waylon."

"Stocky guy with a beard? Got somethin' do with the money?"

"Not Ira's money."

"Was boyfriend to the girl."

"What girl?"

"Cornish din' mention her? Or 'bout havin' a partner?"

Cocking his head at John, Simon reaches down and picks up another half-dead beer. "Want to tell me what you been up to last couple a' days, Johnno?"

John shrugs. "Found some money, that's all."

Simon puts the can to his lips, drinks from it, then drops it on the floor. He scowls. "Why you here?"

"Was ridin' round confused."

"Guess Moira ain't come back."

"Got herself a boyfriend. My lawyer told me."

"'Member what I said 'bout the end of the world, John?"

"Yeah."

"That ain't it."

"Okay."

Simon turns sideways and puts his feet up on the couch. "Keep in touch with your son, though. My daddy never did with me like your'n did with you."

"Yeah."

"Mean somethin' to him later."

"Okay."

Simon sighs. "What you gon' do with the money."

"Ain't figured it out."

"I'd burn it's what." He puts his hands behind his head. "Less'n you want to end up that fiery place Old Ira already sentenced me to, I'd stick a match to her, John."

"Maybe I'll give it the cops."

"They can spend it good's anybody else."

"I'll keep your name out a' it."

"Don't matter either way, Johnno. Like I told you, I grew too old for this shit." He nods at the room. "Got to admire the man who can still feel the monster a' love this bad, though, don't ya?"

"You gon' tell me who or ain't ya?"

"Left his calling card on my steer's ass. Din' ya see it?"

"Gans?"

"Had that half ear, Johnno, 'member?"

John three-quarter smiles.

"Tell me ya do."

"I think maybe I do. Got a junkyard 'hind his house?"

"Filled with nothin' but American-made wrecks."

"Weren't barely full-grown?"

"Widdled-down son of a bitch din' know how bad the monster had him till Big Colette walked out." Simon reaches into his shirt pocket and pulls out one of his hand-carved harmonicas. "Guess he'da shot me too, if I'da been here."

"Prob'ly too drunk to aim straight."

"I feel kind bad 'bout it, Johnno. Man that afflicted."

John stands up from the recliner.

"Guess you ain't gon' do me no favor either, huh, Johnno?"

"Not tonight," said John. "Not never."

"Bring that 12-gauge over here then and put it down next the couch 'fore ya leave. And there ought be a pint a' Beefeater's lying there somewhere."

John finds the half-drunk Beefeater's. He carries the bottle and shotgun over to the couch and places them on the floor next to Simon's head. "You're a good boy, Johnno. Just like your old daddy taught ya. He don't call ya first, couple days you ring up Daggard Pitt."

John stares wordlessly down at Simon. "He ain't a bad little fella, John, for a lawyer. Just too easily took in, is all. Thinks all his clients—like you, me, and the Hen—is troublesome kids, gon' one day grow up." Simon rests his head against the arm of the couch, then reaches up and shuts off the light. "Good night, Johnno."

Feeling for objects with his hands, John starts blindly making his way out of the darkened house. Behind him the harmonica softly plays the sad but spirited tune that Simon often plays as the two of them, after a long hunt, exhaustedly tread their way back through the woods toward home. As John steps out of the cabin, the music, rather than abruptly ending, gradually fades out. Shivers of first light, like parasitic worms, riddle the night's dying body. The dispersing fog exhales a slumbering, organic smell. John crosses the road, then starts walking parallel to the cornfield toward his truck. From the cabin comes a single shotgun blast.

FRIDAY

ORGETTING HE had slept, he wakes with his hands gripping the wheel. In his head the memory of a gunshot echoes the last remnant of his fitful dreams. The unimpeded sun is straight up in a harsh blue sky. The truck is locked, its windows sealed. In a glade of red oak, it sits behind a large boulder draped in fox scat. The unregenerated air is stodgy and moist, hard to breathe.

John reaches down and jerks open the driver-side door. Fresh air enters like a shout. He stumbles into it, voraciously hungry all of a sudden. He walks over to the boulder, around the base of which grow Saint-John's-wort and raspberry bushes, and starts foraging for berries. A cottontail darts out of the thicket and the ground there is rife with deer and bear droppings.

John strips off his sweat-drenched shirt, twists it into a two-cornered sack, and tosses the picked berries into it. When it's full, he sits down with his back to the truck and eats what he's picked, once snarling at a chipmunk that wanders too close to his cache. Nothing in his recent memory has tasted better. When the shirt is empty, he fills and empties it again, remembering that he has not eaten in nearly twenty-four hours. Afterwards, partially sated, he climbs to the top of the boulder and gazes several hundred yards down through the trees to where his half-obscured trailer sits. His hunter's eye spots nothing amiss, but his brain is no more convinced now than it was hours before when he drove up the road in the fading dark.

Standing again on the floor of dogbane and clover, he is overcome by the enormity of his life's upheaval. He longs to be an anonymous part of the mountain's wildlife. Another nonhumanoid who at the merest whiff of man's odious stink retreats deep into the woods. He falls, trembling, to his knees. Inspiring his own foul-smelling exhalations, he sees his father, even while breathing death's rattle, mumbling, "Weren't no damn dog, tell ya. Was a wolf. A goddamn wolf!" What had he meant? No one in the family knew or had ever hazarded a guess. And Simon? While pulling the trigger on his life of excess, what enduring image had he tried to carry into the next world?

He lies flat on his back and stares up at a hole in the canopy of trees through which the sun peers, and imagines his former self sucked up into the cosmos through that corridor of light, leaving behind a flesh-and-bone shell free to be about anything.

He snarls, then reaches out with one hand and swats at the air. He unties his boots, kicks them off, stands up, and peels off his jeans and underpants. Naked, he feels freer than he had. Less encumbered by human plights. And stronger. He rakes his clawed hands through a patch of jewelweed. He bares his teeth and growls. He starts running a circle around the glade. In less than ten feet he trips on a root and pitches sideways into a briar thicket. He loudly curses. His stubbed toe hurts. So does his flesh where it is pierced by the needle-sharp balls. He feels foolish. And embarrassed. Two chattering squirrels seem to be laughing at him. He glances shiftily around to make sure no one else is. It takes him close to ten minutes painfully to extricate himself.

He quickly dresses, grabs the .45 out of the truck, and bushwhacks down through the woods to the edge of the mown field in which his trailer sits. He starts running in a semicrouch toward it. He is halfway there when, down the road, several blue jays start squawking. Then comes the sound of rapidly clopping hooves. John freezes. He is still searching for a place to hide when into the yard gallops a lathered-up Diablo, carrying Abbie Nobie.

"John Moon," she calls out, reining the horse in. "Brought you a home-baked apple pie and three loaves of Momma's oatmeal bread."

John shoves the .45 into his belt and waves.

"Got something to put on it?"

"Peanut butter maybe."

The horse shakes its head, spraying phlegm. "That all?"

"Ain't shopped in a while."

"Lucky for you I brought some sauerkraut and fresh-ground sausage." She swings down from the horse. John nervously glances at the trailer. "Make ya a hoagie."

"What?"

"For lunch." She's wearing blue jeans, riding boots, and a sleeveless black jersey that shows off her tanned, muscular arms. She's too pretty for John to even think about. She unfastens a saddlebag from the girth. "Momma's starting to worry you're up here fading away to nothing."

"I'm all right," says John. He starts walking toward her, keeping one eye on the house.

"Never said you weren't." She tosses the saddlebag over her shoulder. "Like to have lunch with ya, is all."

She drops the reins. Diablo puts its head down and starts to graze. John stops between Abbie and the trailer. He thinks maybe he sees something move behind the kitchen window. Then he's not sure. Abbie looks at him and wrinkles her nose. "You need a bath, John Moon."

John nods up the hill. "Was choppin' wood yonder."

"Where's your truck?"

"Up there with it."

"Whyn't ya jump in the shower."

"Huh?"

"While I make the hoagies." She smiles and walks by him toward the trailer.

Showered and in clean clothes, he feels more grounded to the world. Combing his hair in the bathroom, he hears Abbie whistling "Where have you been, Billy Boy." The events from the past five days give him a temporary reprieve. His recent behavior in the woods now strikes him as someone else's. He allows himself to pretend he is a man waking from a nightmare. The dead bodies dissolve in the morning light. Ghosts wing away like butterflies. He imagines it to be Moira fixing him lunch in the kitchen while the boy quietly sleeps in his crib.

The whistling stops. A few seconds later, it begins again, though lower-pitched than before. Or in a different key. Maybe the melody isn't the same. The sound gets weaker and weaker. The thought strikes John that it's a different whistler altogether. Not Abbie, but a third person. He runs out to the kitchen. No one is there. The basement door is open and the stair light on.

"Abbie?" he calls down.

The whistling stops.

"That you, Abbie?"

"Who else. A ghost, John Moon?" She laughs. John hears her pulling at the stand-up freezer door. His heart suddenly feels like a large bird caught in a tar bog, desperately flapping its wings to escape. He charges downstairs. "What you doing?"

She wheels away from the freezer. She's holding in her hand a plastic bag of sausage. "This ought to be froze," she says, looking at him oddly. "What we don't eat."

His reprieve abruptly come to an end, John snatches the bag from her. "I'll do it," he says.

She flicks at her hair peevishly.

"You don't open it right," says John, "everythin' 'll fall out."

"All the bodies, ya mean?"

John drops the sausage. They both squat down to pick it up at the same time. The fleshly, live smell of her makes him shudder, fills him with a combination of forbidden desire for her and remorse for the dead girl's contrary state. Abbie giggles as her hair brushes against John's cheek. John picks up the bag. "Your hands are shaking, John Moon."

"Ain't been myself."

"Sorry about Moira taking up with that professor."

John snaps his head back and cocks it at her.

"I've seen them together on campus." She reaches out and lightly touches John's shoulder. "He teaches in the same building where I take my empowerment course."

John abruptly stands up.

"He's not near as good-looking as you, John. Nor as nice, neither. He's got a haughty attitude. Like teaching freshman English makes him special or something."

John thinks he hears a noise upstairs. A door being quietly opened and shut maybe. He looks at the stairs, then back at Abbie, who looks like she's heard it, too. "What was that?" he asks.

"The wind knocking the shutters round, probably." She reaches her hand out for John to take. He does and pulls her to her feet. She holds on for a second longer, then walks by him and over to the stairs. Before starting up them, she smiles and says, "I bet a dollar she don't love him, John."

"Don't know," says John.

"I bet if you took that job with Daddy she'd see you've got a regular income and a future and she'd come back."

John shrugs. Suddenly it occurs to him for the first time that maybe she oughtn't to come back. Not that he doesn't love and miss her, and Nolan too, but he's not who he was a week ago and is not sure he trusts his present self to live with anyone. The thought makes him shiver. He watches Abbie walk up the stairs, then turns to the freezer and tugs it open less than an inch. He can feel what's in there pushing against the door. Without peering inside, he slides the sausage through the crack and quickly slams the door shut.

★   ★   ★

In adjacent lawn chairs facing the valley, they watch the slow sweep of a solitary white cloud across the horizon. John imagines the invisible wind pushing the cloud as the same relentless force propelling his fated course. What is soon will become what was, then will disappear. He thinks of life's short flush. Of Simon Breedlove's decomposing body lying atop his own chicken feed. Of his father dying angry. His mother dying sad. And the dead girl dying for a deer.

He looks at Abbie eating a hoagie, and fixates on her chewing. On the rhythmic pulse of the muscles in her cheeks, like the steady throb beneath her breast. He sees her emerging beauty evolving, imagines her blooming into a full-blown woman who will never again eat hoagies on John Moon's deck. This is not a guess, he tells himself, but a fact, like the sun coming up in the east and setting in the west. In his suddenly vibrant mind, more insights go off like sky-rockets. Moira will learn from her professor perfect grammar and compassion. One day she will come to pity John. And Nolan will come to view him as a dinosaur, a compelling character from backwoods lore. In their world, John will be more akin to the dead than to the living. "Been a murder in town," says Abbie.

To combat a sudden vertiginous feeling, John takes his feet from the railing and places them flat on the deck.

"Was on the a.m. news. Some fella up to the Oaks. Police aren't saying who, only that he's got a long record and roots in the area."

Past her head, a hummingbird, emitting a relentless buzz,

stabs at the honeysuckle. John pictures its needle-shaped beak slowly entering and narcotizing his brain. "They're searching for a woman was staying two rooms down from him who's disappeared without checking out." Abbie opens her eyes wide at him like she's staring into that dying place and marveling at its vacuousness. "They think maybe she's in the victim's truck. 'Cause it's missing, too."

Her studied gaze intimidates John. He thinks of Florence staring out her good eye at the endless flat terrain he imagines Oklahoma to be. And addlebrained Skinny Leak peering out from the depths of his slime-green, ravaged recliner, saying, "You's one the Fitch boys, ain't ya?" From around front comes a loud chortled neigh, then heavy foot-stomping. "Easy, boy!" Abbie calls out.

The horse sounds off again, then suddenly trots around the corner of the building, tossing its head. "What's the matter with you?" says Abbie, waving at him. "Wait for me out front. There's plenty of grass there!" She smiles at John. "Jealous, must be."

"Maybe somethin' spooked 'im."

"Could be turkeys. Been a bunch of 'em around."

Diablo turns and walks back around to the front of the trailer. John thinks he hears again the gentle banging he heard earlier, while in the cellar. He looks at Abbie, who apparently hasn't heard it. She breaks into a timorous laugh. "On the subject of trucks," she says, "that black Chevy Blazer went up toward Hollenbachs' again last night."

John subconsciously touches the empty place in his belt where, before he placed it on the bedroom bureau, his .45 had been. "When did it?"

"Late. Real late." Nervously, John glances into the woods behind her, then up the hill. In his mind, a fuse burns smaller and smaller. He hears Abbie take a swig of root beer, then loudly smack her lips. " 'Bout an hour 'fore you got home."

John looks at her again and this time sees one more of the human race better equipped and more informed than he. "I sleep light's a deer, John Moon." She smiles coyly. Behind her, the hummingbird is chased off by two sparrows, fighting. "A twig don't crack out my window I don't hear."

"Fell asleep at a friend's house," says John.

"Hope you were protected."

"Huh?"

She laughs uninhibitedly. "You know, John Moon. A rubber."

Her straight talk embarrasses John. He turns red.

"Having sex with one person's like having it with twenty-four. I learned that in health class."

"I didn't have it with nobody."

"Doesn't matter to me if you did." She shrugs. "Only you ought to be smart, is all. What's one second of pleasure worth?"

John scowls. He hears or imagines soft music playing somewhere.

"I could lend you one."

"What?"

"A rubber. I stole some from Eban's bureau drawer." She flicks playfully at her hair. "If Moira doesn't want to come back, John, you'll find somebody as nice if you're patient."

"What?"

"A good-looking guy like you, gentle and with a good

sense of humor?" She nods matter-of-factly. "Uh-huh. I think so."

"Go home," says John.

She laughs again. "When I decide to give up my virginity, John Moon, it's going to be to a guy as sweet as you."

John waves derisively at her. He's not sure if she's seducing him or making fun of him. Once he would have thought her incapable of either. Now no one's motives are clear to him. "You're almost the perfect catch, John Moon." She punches him firmly in the arm. Now John guesses she's only trying to be a good friend. "All's you need's a job."

"Maybe I'll take it."

"You ought to, 'fore Daddy offers it to somebody else."

The music, no longer imagined, gets louder. John abruptly stands up.

"Am I making you nervous, John?"

"I heard somethin' in the trailer."

"What?"

"Music, whatever."

She cocks an ear toward the kitchen, but the sounds John heard he can't hear now and neither can Abbie. "When'd he come back down?" John asks her.

"Who?"

"One in the black Chevy Blazer."

"He didn't. Unless it was while I was in the barn doing chores this morning." She gets a more serious look on her face. "Kind of a strange time to be searchin' for someone's missing, don't you think, John?"

"Yeah."

"What do you s'pose he's up to?"

John shrugs.

"Maybe somebody ought to call the sheriff."

"I don't think so," says John. Suddenly he wishes he hadn't left his pistol in the bedroom. He decides to go in and get it, just as the music starts in again. This time they both hear it. Somewhere past the kitchen, barely audible, a steel guitar, accompanied by a piano and a mewling, lovesick voice. Abbie looks uncomprehendingly at John. Behind her soft smile, maybe she's even a little scared. "You leave a radio on inside, John Moon?"

John wheels jerkily toward the door without answering.

"Sounds like it's moving from one place to another."

"You ought to get home," snaps John, turning back around.

"What?"

"Your folks'll be wonderin'."

She laughs shrilly, the sound seeming to inject life into a gnarled oak tree, down in the meadow, halfway to her house. As if limbering up for a race, the tree's foliated branches begin jauntily to bounce, then from them rises up, squawking, a grackle plague, its black smudge scarring the sky's perfect blue. Abbie, breathing heavily, jumps up from her chair. "Trash birds," she says.

"Go out this way," says John, gently shoving her toward the deck steps.

"Do what?" Enhanced by adrenaline, her vital smell provides an antithesis to the death's scent recently filling John's nostrils. His vertigo is enhanced. Vague disorientation becomes dissolution of rational thought. There's a ghost in the trailer, playing Willie Nelson tunes.

"No sense going out through the trailer."

"I'm not going out any way at all, John Moon," she says. Backing haughtily away from him, she puts her hands on her hips. Inside, the music is now a low, steady drone, sounding somewhere in the south end of the structure, where John's bedroom is. "Not till I know if you got a bogeyman."

John glances toward the room, forty feet to his left. A corner of its single window facing the valley is visible as a patch of mauve curtain, slightly pulled back from the open glass that last John remembers was covered by a screen but now is not. Into his chest enters a searing pain, like a ghost's bullet fired from that ajar place. He looks at Abbie and she is Ingrid Banes behind a briar thicket in the final moment preceding her death, and a tiny voice in his head says, "Don't shoot!"

"Got to be the transistor," he says. "Had it on changin' my clothes."

"Weak batteries," says Abbie with false bravado, "'ll make the sound fade in and out like that."

"I'll go turn it off." John steps toward the deck door.

"I'll come with you."

"You stay here."

"Give a holler if you got a band playing in there, John Moon." She laughs too loudly.

John opens the door.

Like a straining maestro's voice, his agitation rises as he steps into that airless, dark place he has inhabited these many years, though, once inside, he feels less as if he has entered his home than as if he's exited the world of light. Here, where the soul and body of Ingrid Banes rests, more dangerous than what eyes can see, is what the sun can't touch. Still, he wishes he had a gun. Halfway down the semidark corridor where

the kitchen smells loiter, and ten feet from the closed bedroom door beyond which Willie Nelson sings, he remembers the .22 automatic he had hidden behind the toilet. He
veers left into the bathroom, reaches down behind the toilet's back, and finds the pistol. He checks to see that it's
loaded, then, holding it out in one hand, reenters the hallway.

In front of the bedroom door he stops, inclining an ear
inward. The music abruptly ends. An ad for Agway fertilizer
comes on. "The transistor," thinks John. "I did leave it on."
He turns the knob and gently pushes the door open.

The radio sits on the bureau to his right. Everything else
in the room looks as it had, except the screen that had been
covering the window now stands at its base. A light breeze
ruffles the curtain and John imagines the softly probing fla-
tus to be a ghost's inaudible whisper. A foreign scent taints
the room, an organic stink concomitant to exorcised life.
Now he's not sure if the bed has been lain in or if the fault
marring its center was created in its making. In this spiritu-
ally vibrant place, he suddenly feels like an inorganic lump.
Like a stone marker in a cemetery. Even the tumultuous beat
of his own heart seems like a sound disconnected from his
static flesh. A frantic banging maybe, coming from the
closet. He takes a deep breath and walks over to it. Brandish-
ing the gun in one hand, he reaches down with the other
and yanks open the mirrored door.

A whoosh of dust-filled air exits.

John reaches in and runs a hand through the closet's sparse,
dangling contents—two pairs of dress slacks, his one suit
coat, half a dozen skirts or dresses left behind by Moira. He
exhales pantingly, then shuts the door. He turns back to the

bed. He thinks about looking under it but even in his reve-nant state thinks he won't find anything significant in the couple of inches between the floor and two-by-four-raised spring. On the radio, a promo for the upcoming County Fair ends. A loud whinny sounds from the front of the trailer. Diablo's uncharacteristic skittishness reregisters itself with John. He walks over to the radio, on which a Garth Brooks song now plays. He switches it off. Through the window, from the deck, he hears a sharp, dual-toned whistle like somebody calling a dog or remarking on a pretty girl. The sound repeats itself. John moves over to the curtain, pulls it back, and sticks his head out.

Standing on the deck behind a limp-looking Abbie, one of his hands holding a clump of her hair and the other a long knife against her throat, is Waylon. "I give you three seconds 'fore I make her look like the Hen, John," he calls out. "Have you seen the Hen lately?"

John doesn't say. His gaze is intent on Abbie's languid face with its closed eyes and slack mouth.

"Offers me buried treasure for drugs! I go along as a favor to him—even dig the shit up for him 'cause he's afraid a' snakes or some damn thing, then I give 'im his merchandise and when I come back for my money, not only is it gone, but my girl, too, and when I see the Hen about it, he can't under-stand how it's his problem and I tell him he'll understand if I don't get back the cash or the drugs in seventy-two hours— I even offered to let him keep Ingrid, who anyway was getting to be a pain in my ass." His speech is high-pitched and staccato, the clipped words running wild and tripping over each other in their hurry to get out, and listening to it,

John is furious at the dead girl for being infatuated with insanity.

"Three days later he tells me the drugs are sold, he hasn't got the money, my girl's been shot by a haybale, and basically, 'Fuck you, Waylon,' and that's what I get for trusting a guy I met in prison!"

"Why ain't her eyes open?" hollers John.

"What?"

"Abbie's eyes ain't open!"

"Choker hold'll do that, John."

"She ain't dead, is she?"

"She'll wake up when I start carving on her."

"I'll give you the money," says John.

"Of course you'll give me the money, you stupid cow-donged son of a bitch. Now drop the pistol and get your woodchuck ass out here!"

Waylon's handling of Abbie has a ritualistic quality. He lowers her to the chaise longue, then gently rolls her on her back. Watching from the kitchen doorway, John thinks of the dispassionate way his father's home health aides, their eyes slyly diverted, would hoist and turn his cancer-ridden body that to them might have been a side of pork or a car lodged in a ditch. "Gotta hand it to ya," says Waylon, straightening up and pulling from his belt a 9-millimeter pistol. "Not every half-assed dirt farmer seen a chance like what you did would take it."

He waves John out onto the deck. John steps outside. His hunter's eye automatically probes the muscular torso in front of him for its weakest link. He thinks it might be the knees.

Waylon signals him to a stop ten feet from where he leans against the rail, facing the valley. "Tell you the truth, at first I didn't believe Obadiah when he swore a woodchuck had stole my money and murdered my Ingrid—figured he had or they were in on it together." He's wearing dress chinos, a jersey marred by briars, and what look like brand-new L. L. Bean hiking boots. White froth stains his beard and armpits. He smells lathered up, like an exercised horse. John guesses he's bushwhacked through the woods from where he's dumped Obadiah Cornish's pickup. "Time I'd sliced off his nose, though, he'd convinced me."

"Was an accident."

Waylon smiles. "Which? Stealing my money or shooting her?"

"I took her for a deer."

"A deer? She didn't look anything like a deer."

"Was a mistake."

Waylon slides the knife into a sheath on the other side of his belt. "That crazy son of a bitch really dump her in your bed?"

John nods.

"Where is she now?"

"I buried her," says John, suddenly not wanting Waylon ever again to cast his eyes on her. "I dug a hole up in the woods and put her in it. I can take you there."

Waylon waves at him. "I don't like corpses. They give me the creeps." He frowns. "I'm just wondering, though, John, did you fuck her?"

"Did I what?"

"If you didn't, you really missed out on something. That

girl was three rolled into one." He shakes his head. "Was 'bout all I could do to hold on her once she took to bucking."

"Wrote in a letter how she loved you," John angrily says.

"What?"

"Said you was going take her to Hawaii."

Waylon glances curiously at him. His black, dilated pupils suggest oil splats in saucers of thick, heavy cream. "You read my Ingrid's mail, John?"

"Was tryin' to put a name to her. Was you gonna?"

"What?"

"Take her Hawaii?"

"Oh well, you know how women like to hear about sand and water, John. Now let me ask you—did you fuck her before or after you shot her?" He rolls his head exaggeratedly. "Or d'ya try her both ways?"

John rushes angrily forward. Waylon thrusts his pistol straight out. John comes to an abrupt halt three feet from the end of its barrel. "Come over here, John," says Waylon. Moving a few feet sideways along the rail, he points at the spot he's just vacated. John walks over to the spot and stops. Down on the pond, half a dozen ducks float motionless as decoys. Two oaks on the water's far side cast dark shadows on half its surface. The air smells like tansy and wild violets. "Put your hand there on the rail, fingers spread."

"What for?"

"If you don't, I'm going to shoot the girl in both knees."

"Ain't we gon' go get the money?"

"No. You're going to go get the money. I'm going to stay here with the girl—what's her name?"

"Abbie."

"She and I are going to stay here for the two minutes you're gone."

"It'll take more than that."

"More than what?"

"Two minutes."

"I'll give you ten, then I'll cut off one of her kneecaps." He nods down at Abbie's placid-looking face, which suggests she might be dreaming pleasantly. "Another five, another kneecap. A joint-to-joint thing, get it?"

John says, "I'll go as fast as I can."

"I know you will, John. Now, where exactly is it?"

"On the mountain side the trailer. Up in the woods."

"You'll point me there so that I can sit here with Abbie and watch you go up and come back."

"You'll have to move the far end the deck, past the trailer's edge."

"That's not a problem. Now, John, where's your truck? I'm told you have a truck."

"Up there with it."

"You'll bring it down for me, won't you? So that I can borrow it?"

"Yes."

He reaches into the sheath with his free hand and pulls out the knife again. "I'm not like the Hen, John, who gets off on cutting people up, okay? I admit, I'm not at all pleased that you killed Ingrid—she was a sweet kid and a tremendous fuck—and because of it I don't think you and I could ever be good friends, but you say it was an accident and that you gave her a proper burial and I accept that. So, about Ingrid, bygones are bygones." He nods at the rail. "Fingers splayed, John, like I asked. Unless you'd prefer I take an eye. Would you rather I take an eye?"

John doesn't say. Adrenaline and bile race into his stomach, so that for a few seconds he's afraid he's going to be sick. He glances at Abbie and wonders how long someone who's had done to them whatever Waylon did to her stays unconscious. "How do I know you won't hurt her once you got the money?"

"I've just explained to you, John, that was the Hen's trip. Not mine. I'm a businessman. That's all. Like every other employed slob in the world, I got people I got to answer to. I need my money back, John, or I'm the next one gets put in the ground. That's how life works. Get paid, so you can pay. You think what I sold to the Hen was a gift to me? No. Life is a big wheel—somebody fucks with a cog like you did, John, and the whole wheel is shot. So, I've got to fix the wheel, okay? How am I going to do that? First you need to know that the girl will look like a totem pole if you're not back with the money in ten minutes. Second, I need to know that while you're up there in the outback that should you get to feeling like Davy Crockett and scrounge yourself up a musket and a lead ball, I can feel secure that the ball won't end up in my brainpan. So what's it to be, John? I take one of ten fingers, leaving you nine? Or one of two eyes, leaving you a cyclops? I know what I'd do."

The focus of John's thoughts is like a kitten curled up in the only sun-warmed corner of a dank, dark house: he won't be responsible for another girl's death. He stares into Waylon's anvil–hard face, crisscrossed by pockmarks and tiny rivulets of sweat. "Did you think this son of a bitch was handsome?" his silent voice angrily asks Ingrid Banes. "Din' ya see them eyes, colder than anything wild I ever hunted? Or was you just drunk with all his danger?" He lays an unwavering hand palm-down on the rail, then slowly spreads his fingers. Against searing pain, guilt will be his amulet.

"Nice try, John."

"What?"

"I watched you open the door earlier, remember?"

John gazes blankly at him.

"You're right-handed, are you not?"

John nods grudgingly.

"That's the one needs altering, then." Waylon smiles knowledgeably. His teeth appear well cared for and straight. His slicked-back hair is black as a beaver's pelt. Momentarily sliding the knife beneath his gun arm, he reaches his free hand into his back pocket and pulls out a linen handkerchief. "You know, John, trigger finger."

John takes his left hand from the rail and replaces it with his right. He spreads his fingers so that, of the five, his index finger is the closest to Waylon. He remembers his father once telling him about an old Iroquois trick whereby a captured brave, to divert pain inflicted by his torturers, would will the pain into the empty shell of a turtle. Waylon flaps the handkerchief in the air, then carefully lays it over the rail next to John's hand. Still covering John with the pistol, he takes up the knife again. John empties his mind of everything but an orange-and-black box-turtle shell. Waylon quickly leans forward and, just above the lowest joint, deftly slices off John's index finger.

John reaches out, grabs the handkerchief, and wraps it

around the bleeding stub of his finger. He's completely for-gotten about the box-turtle shell. He pulls the mutilated limb into his chest and bends his knees with the pain, which is throbbing and deep. The white handkerchief is stained red. His breathing is shallow and fast. He hears his severed finger bounce off the deck floor and looks up in time to see it tumble into the grass below. "It'll be there when you get back," says Waylon. He wipes the knife blade on a napkin he's picked up from the table, drops the napkin, and returns the knife to its sheath.

Doing semi-deep-knee bends, John applies pressure to the hand. Sweat pours from his brow. He swallows what tastes like the crest of vomit. He remembers, during his only attempt at factory work, seeing Burton Doomas lose two fingers in a machine that made bowling pins. One of the fin-gers had squirted blood like a bottle of hot Coke. The other had barely bled.

"Ten minutes," says Waylon.

"Less'n I wrap somethin' round this," pants John, holding out his injured hand, "I won't be able to lug the money."

"Go in get a Band-Aid, whatever," says Waylon. Aiming the pistol at John, he walks over to Abbie. "But if she wakes up and sees me, all bets are off." He leans down next to Abbie and, with his non-gun hand, picks her up beneath the armpits and starts dragging her to the road side of the deck.

John turns and walks rapidly through the trailer to the bathroom. Feeling woozy, he removes the handkerchief. Blood oozes rather than spurts from the stump. John is briefly saddened by the look of his four-digit hand, which reminds him of a lizard's webbed foot. He stanches the wound with hydrogen-peroxide-soaked cotton, wraps it with gauze, and tapes it. From a jar in the cabinet, he pours into his mouth half a dozen aspirins, chews and swallows them. He looks at himself in the mirror, slaps his cheek with his good hand, and quietly tells himself, "Think, son of a bitch!"

On the deck, he finds Waylon sitting on the chaise longue, facing the mountain, the unconscious Abbie, gagged and blindfolded with two handkerchiefs, reclining between his legs. Waylon's got his knife pressed to her throat. "How far up's my money, John?"

"Five hundred yards give-take."

"Is it with the truck?"

"Near 'bouts. Gon' have to dig it out from 'neath a rock."

"Drop your pants."

"What?"

"Get 'em down."

John unbuckles his jeans and yanks them down to his knees.

"Turn around."

John twirls a slow circle on the deck.

"Okay, get 'em up."

With his uninjured hand, John pulls up his pants and buckles them.

Waylon puts the knife blade next to Abbie's left kneecap and makes a sawing motion. "Stay in sight long's ya can, John. Right?"

John nods.

Waylon glances down at his watch, then scowls up at him. "Nine minutes fifty seconds, woodchuck."

* * *

He finds it least painful to run with his bandaged hand tucked like a football against his stomach. Even so, with each jarring step he takes, the missing finger throbs as if being severed anew. Seeing his full-throttled approach, Diablo rears up, then gallops across the road, into the woods there.

At the meadow's north edge, John plunges into the bushes and scrub pine, where, for another hundred yards or so, until the trees get thicker, he is still visible from the deck. As the forest gets denser, the grade steepens and he is forced to walk, but at least now he is hidden from Waylon. He follows a deer path several hundred feet east through a stand of sugar maple, then again veers north, scrabbling up a leaf-slick berm underlaid with patches of granite and bluestone, where, for purchase, he grabs with his good hand at saplings and grapevines. Seventy-five yards from the giant boulder behind which the pickup is concealed, he stumbles on a root and catches himself with his injured limb. The pain is so severe he howls. A moment later, he hears echoing up through the woods Waylon's emotionless shout, "Seven minutes, John, 'fore I start playing mumblety-peg!"

Heavily panting, his body drenched in sweat, John starts toward the truck again. He tries emptying his mind of all thoughts except getting there, but he keeps envisioning a glistening knife blade against Abbie's throat, and eyes as black as the interior of the quarry cave where the dead girl once rested and he knows that, in those eyes, Abbie is already dead and, if he returns with the money, so is he. As he scrambles around the west base of the boulder, where the bushes that had earlier fed him dig at his face and arms, and into the oak glade, he fights a strong desire to keep on running. Suddenly he views his inability to be as conscienceless as Obadiah Cornish or Waylon as an exploitable weakness, for had Waylon not surmised that John possessed what Waylon did not, he would not have sent John alone into the woods. He understands that John will return with the money, even realizing it will cost him his life, and for that, Waylon surely considers him a weakling.

After scrabbling to the top of the boulder, John peers through the trees to the trailer deck. From this distance, the two intertwined figures in the lounge chair are indistinguishable. They might not be alive except that John can see one of them—probably Waylon—waving something over his head. Even with the use of his normal shooting hand, John, sighting through the high-powered scope of his .308, would have to fire a near-perfect shot to hit either of them. Below the boulder, though, his view to the deck would be blocked by the trees, and past the trees, in the rock- and bush-laden field, Waylon would see him. "I'm gettin' nervous not knowin' where you're at, John!" Waylon yells. "Give me a holler, something!"

John leans forward on his knees and puts his hands to his mouth. He knows he's not visible from the deck because he'd looked for the boulder from that same spot earlier. "Yo!" he calls out. "I'm at the truck!"

"Ya got the money?"

"Gotta dig it out first! Take me a few minutes!"

John sees the two figures stand up, but can't tell if Abbie is doing so of her own volition or is being assisted by Waylon;

then he sees the larger figure kneeling next to the smaller one, doing something with its legs. "I'm pulling the girl's— I'm pulling Abbie's—pants down, John!" John sees the glint of something from the deck that might be Waylon's knife blade reflecting the sun. "If you make like a hero—try circling back on me, whatever—I'm gon' fillet her like a brook trout!" Congruent with the hammering in his mutilated hand, anger pulses in John's temples. He finds himself involuntarily hissing.

"I'm comin' 's fast I can!" he screams.

"You got five minutes get my goddamn money and drive it down here!"

John turns from the valley, drops onto his butt, and, faster than he had anticipated, plummets down the slick, moss-encrusted side of the boulder; three-quarters down, to avoid crashing headlong into the raspberry bushes, he springs upward and out. He lands on his feet in the glade, then pitches sideways into a witch-hazel shrub, its woody fruit, like a gauntlet of blackjacks, painfully pummeling his mutilated stub. His consequent thrashing upsets a possum family, who, screeching in protest, scurry out from beneath him.

John exits the shrub and, still moaning, stumbles the fifteen feet across the glade to where the truck sits. He unconsciously reaches to open the driver-side door with his bandaged hand, sending additional pain waves through the stump and reinforcing in his mind the many tasks made easier with an index finger. The word "cripple" flashes through his mind. He thinks of Burton Doomas gripping cigarettes between his pinky and his fourth finger and the odd, rubbery feel of his three-digit handshakes. John's internal organs tense at the thought of the human monstrosity who blithesomely commits such mutilations. Fiends are found only among men. Never in the wild has he encountered a creature as evil. If John fails in his one slim chance to rescue Abbie, Waylon, for all his jesting tone, John knows, will inflict on her body every act he has enumerated, and several more.

Pushing horrific images from his mind, he opens with his left hand the pickup door, reaches above the cab's rear window, and takes down his .308. He leans the rifle against the truck, then, absently shoving the money sack to one side, crawls across the seat, yanks open the glove box, and takes out a carton of shells. He opens the carton, removes four bullets, then crawls out of the truck and, with his one good hand, spends more seconds than he can afford getting the shells into the clip and the clip into the gun. Afterwards, he hastily slings the rifle by its strap over one shoulder and again runs through the glade, reaching the base of the boulder just as he hears shouted up through the dense foliage, "Three minutes, John, till I have a slice!"

Several times while clambering up the boulder, he bangs his wound and curses. He's halfway to the top when the rifle falls from his shoulder. Suddenly remembering he has forgotten to check the gun's safety mechanism, John, as the weapon slams into the rock, braces himself for its discharge. The gun doesn't fire, but he loses thirty seconds retrieving it. From the bottom of the boulder, he restarts his assault. Pain throbs from his stub to his right ear. John envisions the absent finger, inverted in his flesh, cannibalistically headed toward his brain. All traces of white have vanished from the gauze covering the stump. Out of the soaked dressing, sporadic drops of blood fall.

By the time he reaches the boulder's crest, he feels feverish. He's not sure if the flush he is experiencing is from infection or the afternoon heat. His head spins. Maybe he is delirious. In his mind the bloated image of Ingrid Banes presents his severed digit to him like a conciliatory gift. It strikes John that she views his mutilation as partial recompense for her death. Then he thinks maybe he does, too. In a body-sized indenture in the rock, he lies flat on his stomach, giving himself, through the tops of two trees, a narrow view of the trailer deck. He pulls the rifle into his right shoulder, then quickly realizes that the pain and swelling in that hand, now half again the size of its mate, have rendered the four remaining digits useless as trigger fingers. He tries reaching back with his left hand to manipulate the trigger, while steadying the gun with his right, but it is too cumbersome and impedes his aim. "Talk to me, John!" yells Waylon.

The shout to John seems inflected this time with hysteria. He envisions a new paranoid monster, more dangerous even than the old cocksure one. He switches the rifle's stock to his opposite shoulder, so that now his left eye peers through the scope and his good hand falls naturally on the trigger. "I've got the money!" he hollers.

The view through his off eye is skewed. Or the world is. Objects look as if they have inclined slightly toward the valley. This affects his depth perception, negatively or positively. He's not sure which, only that his take on things is slightly altered.

"Don't fuck with me, woodchuck! Your voice ain't moved none!"

"I'm luggin' it back the truck!"

Through the magnified glass, it takes him several seconds to locate the deck and its occupants. He no sooner zeros in on them than they disappear again. Twice more, he finds, then loses, them as, beneath his mummified hand, the rifle's stock bounces precariously. Sweat drips into his eyes. He envisions pulling the trigger and seeing his awry shot slam into the skull of Abbie, who is being held like a shield in front of Waylon's body.

"I don't hear an engine start in sixty seconds, John, I'm cutting off everything sticks out from her knees up!"

John lays down the rifle. He hastily eyes the top of the boulder for a makeshift stand. To his right, he finds a fallen Y-shaped branch. He snaps off the stem of the branch, leaving about six inches, then quickly inserts the stem into a small crack at the front of the indenture. He picks up the rifle again, lies back down in the crevice, places the gun's butt against his left shoulder, its stock onto his injured hand and its barrel into the Y, then peers through the scope.

This time he quickly locates the deck. With an unwavering base supporting the gun, he is able to focus on the two figures. He is shocked at how close to him they seem, how physically intertwined they are, and how, in less than ten minutes, their appearances have so drastically altered. Waylon is visible behind Abbie only from the shoulders up and mid-calves down. His godless eyes dart left and right, as if expecting at any moment to see John come rushing out of the bushes. His tongue squirts repetitively back and forth like a small fish across his lips. His knife is pressed against Abbie's throat. A thin line of blood is visible there. John thinks he looks about ready to crack. Like he is on the verge of mania.

The white skin of Abbie's legs is made to seem even more so by her shockingly black tangle of pubic bush. Her jeans and underwear lie around her ankles. John's thoughts of the second are quadrangular—rage at him who has exposed her; guilt for John's own part in contributing to her predicament; fear that he will not be able to save her; and, like the abrupt onset of a scratchless itch, blood-quickening arousal that shames him. Even looking at her, he feels he is violating her. Suddenly one of her feet jerks backward, as if she is kicking at Waylon. Then the other. John sees Waylon's knife blade flick upward like a silver tongue and Abbie's shirt and bra fall away, exposing her taut belly and pink-tipped burgeoning breasts. The kicking stops. John instantly shifts his gaze back to Abbie's face. Now he sees that the blindfold dangles from her left ear, though her eyes are shut tight, and the mouth gag pulsates as she breathes. He moves the crosshairs slightly above the top of her head, locking them in on the furrowed brow of Waylon.

The rifle is John's sole inheritance from his father, who used it to hunt deer. Though he keeps the gun in his truck as a constant reminder—good or bad—of Robert Moon, John has only occasionally shot it at paper targets. For hunting he prefers his 12-gauge, finding the shorter, more wieldy weapon handier in this thick mountain foliage, where normally one must get close to his prey before shooting it. Until now, he has never had need of the rifle's magnified scope. When last he used it, it sighted slightly north or south of the crosshairs, making the gun fire high or low. Now John can't remember which. If he guesses wrong either way, Abbie is dead. From John's bullet or Waylon's knife.

"I've stripped her naked, you goddamn raccoon-balled son of a bitch!" Waylon's strident shout cracks the thin air like a hawk's shriek. "You're two minutes past the deadline! Where hell you at?"

John thinks the gun shoots high, but is not sure. He lowers his aim to the point of Waylon's chin, thinking—or hoping—if the bullet rises, it will enter his forehead, and if it sinks, the top of his sternum, inches above the crest of Abbie's skull. He places his finger on the trigger. Now his hands begin to shake like two days ago when he was aiming at the wild turkeys in his yard. John closes his eyes and silently prays that, at this juncture in his fated journey, he be allowed a steady grip. He takes a deep breath, then gradually blows it out, trying not to think what Waylon might be doing during those few seconds.

He opens his eyes again. Through the scope he sees side by side on a single neck, like the faces of victory and defeat, the heads of Ingrid Banes and the wounded buck. In less than a second, he is made to understand that triumph and tragedy always travel coterminously like this. He sees the dead girl bleed. Imagines her pain. Watches it ooze from her chest and, in a thin stream, trickle down her pale front. She opens her eyes, which, through a moist fog of hurt, beg to be saved. They look straight at John. John raises the rifle's scope above their gaze. He squeezes the trigger. He watches, almost congruently with the rifle's report, Abbie and Waylon tumble backward onto the deck.

*   *   *

His eyes won't open. He cannot say for how long. From that internal dark place, he screams—silently or aloud—at the plague of injustice fated to him; at the curse of history repeating itself. Wordless ruminations, like large, swooping shadows of predatory birds, are reminders of invisible forces more powerful than he. In muted words, he begs, pleads, beseeches, one of these to alter its course. But they are heartless. Pain lopes as athletically as the unwounded buck through their umbrageous world. Fear is the rustling of branches. Death is what lies on their far side.

An external shriek returns him to sound and light. At first he thinks the noise is self-induced. Then, with his eyes open, he hears it again from a far-off place. A nightmarish screech that in its escalating tone incarnates terror. With his good hand still cradling the rifle, he falteringly lifts the scope to his left eye and peers toward the source of the sound.

His blood-soaked redeemer cowers on the deck; on her haunches against the trailer wall, she stares outward in paralytic horror at a half-headless creature staggering toward her on its knees. But for its exposed teeth, frozen in a garish clench, the right side of Waylon's face below the nose is gone. He still grips his knife. He externalizes his internal monster. John can't believe he isn't dead and thanks the invisible forces Abbie isn't.

He grips the rifle's stock between his chin and right shoulder, then with his left hand pulls back the bolt and shucks out the empty shell. He levers in another bullet, fits the barrel back into the twig's crotch, tucks the gun into his shoulder, and puts the crosshairs just beneath Waylon's right eye. With as little effort as breathing, he pulls the trigger.

*   *   *

Abbie attempts to push John away as he tries to calm her. She looks at him as if he is the monster who has inflicted her pain. That look strikes him as the stare of all humanity and it suddenly frightens him to have this small, naked child in his arms. Finally, she collapses like a felled tree on the deck. In a cataleptic trance, she trembles and begs for Mommy.

John hastily examines her and determines that the blood on her body is mostly Waylon's, and her cuts, though several, are not severe. He cleans and dresses the wounds as best he can with only one functional hand. Then he wraps her up in one of Moira's old bathrobes.

She can't—or won't—even talk. He worries what her parents will surmise of her condition, let alone the law, which he doesn't even consider calling. She is his only witness to what has occurred and she looks at him with the same blank stare as she does the half-headless cadaver on John's deck. He puts her in the front seat of the pickup and drives to her house, to find no one home. He continues directly to the hospital in town, stopping the truck in front of the locked red emergency-room door. He jumps out, hurries round to the passenger side, and helps Abbie down. After walking her over to the door, he pushes the call button and, before running back to his truck, says, "Just say to 'em you need tendin', Abbie. You'll be all right!"

The few people he sees on his way back out of town look like rail-thin coyotes circling a kill. He drives the back way up Hollenbachs' mountain. Halfway to the top, he turns left onto Carter Sey's old rock-infested lumber road. After a while the terrain flattens out into a field of saw grass and white birch widely spaced enough to drive the pickup between. The earth gets gradually softer and damper beneath the truck's wheels. A pair of ducks fly overhead. He can smell water. Now he can hear it. Finally he can see it, a small stream trickling off to his right. He fears the pickup will mire down. He parks it on a dry plateau behind a high field of weeds, gets out, and follows the cascading water upward to its source.

He sits on the shore, where as a boy he had sat with his father and watched a loon swim underwater the length of the pond. On its sky-blue surface, lily pads are pandemic. Frogs here are huge and have baritone croaks. His father said this is because they are old, retired frogs. Fish sporadically jump. John gives them scores, one to ten, for height and splash. Hours pass. His right arm so pains him he threatens several times to kill it. He condemns to hell his missing finger. He blocks from his mind all thoughts but those relating to his corporeal self. His hurt. His mutilation. The odd way that his four remaining fingers will suddenly jump of their own accord. Other thoughts hurt too much to think about.

Darkness falls. He listens to a hoot owl and watches a fox and two deer come to the pond and drink. The new moon is a wisp of itself. He grows light-headed and tired. He fears his hand is infected and will become gangrenous. He tries and fails to recall for pain an old Indian recipe—something made of mud and a certain kind of crushed leaf. Like a wounded animal, he retreats several feet into the woods, crawls beneath an upturned stump, and sleeps.

He dreams of fire, acres of orange flames high as the trees they devour. A conflagration, pushed by a strong wind. An entire mountainside going up like a Roman candle. A burning that wipes out plants, animals, people; fouls the air with its breath; raises the earth; turns flesh to smoke and bones to ash; that spares no life, large or small. In the blaze's aftermath, on God's charred field, lies only dead silence. A dog doesn't bay. A bird doesn't chirp. A breath isn't breathed. On this hardpan, a piss stream would emanate like rifle shots, but there is nothing. Only mute souls in this graveyard, until from the black skeletal remains of a pine break comes a barely audible rustling. Then footsteps, like the harsh popping of virgin snow. Now a buck's snort, loud as a trumpet blast, and life's horror begins anew....

SATURDAY

H<small>E WAKES</small> feverish in the deep woods, half buried beneath the roots of a giant upturned oak. Did he hear voices talking? He's not sure. He quietly lies there, inhaling the smell of rich humus and rot that makes him think of an exhumed grave. Only a narrow shaft of sunlight penetrates this cool, dark cocoon in which tortured horseflies twist in a brown spider's web and where slugs and beetles are riveted to the decaying walls. The throb in his hand is a reminder of pain's continuum.

He slowly rolls toward the entrance, unintentionally applying pressure to his injury. The pain is searing. He envisions a pair of tongs gripping his skin below the stub and tearing upward to his shoulder. He bites his lip so as not to scream. Now, beyond the enclosure, sounds splashing water.

John tentatively pokes his head through the opening. Several wood ticks and a mole scurry away. He blinks in the sudden midday glare that reflects harshest off the pond fifty feet to his left. A woman's head floats atop the water. Then John understands her body is swimming beneath it. Her hair is wavy and long and trails her skull like a tangle of black snakes. A pair of wood ducks float a few feet behind her as if she is one of them.

Suddenly a loud whistle comes from the shore closest to John. The swimmer glances that way. She exhales a sharp bark that sounds like cold ice breaking. From a high stand of pussy willows wades a naked man. He is muscular and tall, with hair the same color as the woman's, in a ponytail at the nape of his neck. He walks toward her until he is in up to his knees, then stops. Treading water twenty feet away, the woman warily watches him. The man reaches down with both hands and splashes water at her. The woman takes in a mouthful of the pond and spits it his way. The ducks nervously flap their wings and back up several feet.

John is immediately transfixed by the couple. He wonders who they are, how they got here, and in what manner they are intertwined with his fate. He thinks maybe they are predisposed to interact in a way that will determine the course of his own life.

The man splashes more vigorously at the woman, almost as if he is angry. Now John sees that the man's penis is erect; long and thick, it curls steeply upward and back, touching his stomach above the belly button. The woman rasps stridently. She paddles several feet closer to the man, rising up out of the water enough so that her unclothed breasts float atop it like two more heads. Like the rest of her, except for her blood-red areolae and nipples, they are the color of fresh cream. They strike John as being filled with that substance. She hisses at the man.

John thinks maybe they aren't acquainted. But how could that be? Out here, in the middle of nowhere, strangers colliding? Still, their manner of circling one another suggests two wandering curs sniffing each other. They are to John beautiful and ugly at the same time, like the corpse of Ingrid Banes.

With her chin the woman beckons at the man, challenging him to come farther into the pond. The man slaps more water at her, but doesn't move. The woman swims to within five feet of him, then stands up and darts her tongue at him. The pond is halfway up her thighs. Drops of it trickle from her pubic bush, which is dense as briars and comes to a sharp point an inch below her navel. She reaches down and runs several fingers through it. As if in response, the man wraps a hand around his penis.

The woman haughtily tosses her head. Then she pointedly slips a finger into her vagina and begins steadily thrusting it in and out. Her hips increasingly pulsate. The man snorts. He starts yanking at his erection. The water's surface gently ripples from their movements, which are like an intensifying dance. Neither has uttered a word since John has been watching them. Their openmouthed, wide-eyed glaring at one another suggests two cats vying for the same spot on a couch.

Precipitately they rush toward each other. Releasing himself, the man grasps at the woman, who throws her arms out to the sides like someone doing a swan dive. The man loudly slaps his hands on her buttocks. The woman lets out a loud yelp. The man jerks her out of the water, his prominent deltoids rippling, and hoists her breasts up to his face. He starts biting and suckling at her nipples. The woman gyrates side to side so that he can't keep one in his mouth for more than a second. She wraps her legs around his waist and starts baying like a hyena. He sounds as if he's growling.

John tells himself that these are Conservancy hikers fucking, but in his feverish state he doesn't believe it. He feels as if he's being made to watch two devils mating or murdering each other. Or both. Now they are turned sideways to him and the woman is gripping the man's penis, which looks big as a bludgeon. She points it straight up toward her crotch and the man, in a way that makes John wince, pushes her down onto it. The woman yelps again. Then she's throwing her whole body at him as if she's trying to knock him into the lake. Their splashing heightens. In a rush of wings, the ducks take flight and John, witnessing this hell's dance, suddenly wants to do the same.

With his good hand he hefts himself up out of his dark den just as the couple spin another half circle. Suddenly the woman faces directly toward the shore. At first John's not sure that she sees him, standing fifty feet back from the water, then, skewered on that great hook, she thrusts her head straight at him and John imagines her piercing, devilish eyes purloining his worst thoughts. Then she throws back her head and, not altering in the least the harsh pumping of her hips, bays twice as loud as she had before.

John starts to run. Behind him he hears, echoing off the water, that awful hyena's bark. Once he looks back and sees her, still astride the man, intently eyeing John as he crashes through the trees and bushes on his way downstream toward the truck.

As he drives back down the lumber road to where it intersects with the cleared swath leading over the mountain to the Nobie side of the preserve, his behavior is no longer determined, if ever it was, by deliberate thought. He is the artist striving to complete a mosaic for which no blueprint exists. Not that he is acting aimlessly. On the contrary. Each of his actions, like a domino, follows by rote the act preceding it.

Barely wider than the pickup, the steep path through a stand of white pine said to be among the oldest in the state is not intended for vehicles. Several times he has to stop and get out to drag fallen trees from the road. Even with four-wheel drive and all-terrain tires, the truck gets hung up in a creek bed. Next to the water lies a mound of bear scat so fresh it steams. John listens for the bear, but can't hear it. With his one good arm, it takes him half an hour to wedge enough flat rocks under the pickup's tires to free it.

Beneath the weald's dense canopy, headed for the mountaintop, he is like an exhausted homeward-bound horse spurred on by a single thought—the piercing eye of the mounted woman in Hidden Pond: in his mind it becomes the omniscient stare of Ingrid Bancs, to whom he has given his solemn oath not to abandon her. Though his mind is not altruistically pure. What if the law discovers her in his freezer? Far better for him that they find her someplace else or not at all. And if she is found already? He tries not to think about it. Either way, they will be out combing the woods for him. Possibly they are waiting for him even now at the trailer.

At the top of the mountain, the forest tunnel empties into a rolling plain where, before the Conservancy requisitioned it, John's father and grandfather grazed the few sheep they owned. The brown blanket of knee-high grass is stained purple and yellow by Indian paintbrush, goldenrod, and tre-foil. Up here, Simon Breedlove and John once saw a mountain lion, though they're supposedly extinct this far east. They were sitting in a deer stand in the pines when it loped through the snow—a huge cat—twenty feet from them. It was like seeing God's light. For the rest of the day, they didn't want to shoot anything. They kept looking at each other and shaking their heads. Then Simon told John about the only girl he ever loved, Ling something or other, a Vietnamese girl whom, Simon said, if she hadn't stepped on a land mine and been killed, he would have married and had about a dozen babies with. The memory causes in John a sharp pang of grief for his friend. No one, he thinks, ever knows anyone else's real story.

He drives across the field to the east edge of the pines, where, six days before, with the sound of trodden branches, his nightmare began. Turning right and skirting the woods for another mile or so would bring him to the dirt road heading down the west side of the mountain to the hollow. Instead, he veers left several hundred yards before easing the truck through a narrow opening in the trees that leads to a half acre of void forest razed by a lightning fire. Blurred by a thin layer of clouds, the sun's light casts a greasy veneer on this dead hole striving to be reborn. The few sounds are magnified—a hollow wind whistling through the charred remains, small animals rifling the new growth, the chirps of passing birds finding few trees to land in. John pulls the pickup into an abrupt swale concealed on either side by yarrow and briars, turns off the engine, grabs the .308 and the money sack, gets out, and scrambles up the steep embankment to the forest floor.

He carries the rifle over his right shoulder, the money sack over his left. His footsteps make a crunching sound on the charred earth. As he exits the fire zone, his pain mysteriously subsides. Suddenly he is aware only of an erratic, surgy pulse at the end of his right arm and, emanating from his torso, a moist heat like the internal steam from a heap of corn silage. He looks down at the blood-soaked bandage, beneath which his injured hand, hanging like a butchered loin by his side, is purply and fat. For maybe five minutes, his mental state is close to euphoric. Then the pain comes back. And he begins to sweat. By the time he steps from the far side of the forest into the scrub pasture a half mile above the trailer, his whole body is drenched.

He drops the money sack and sits down on a rock. Through the scope of the .308 he eyes the trailer below. Everything looks the same as it did, except from this high up he can't tell if Waylon's body is still on the deck. There are no vehicles in the drive and no signs of life but for two hawks circling above the structure. It strikes him that he has spent most of the last six days sneaking into or out of places. He thinks of his father, who always walked upright, chin jutted out, into a room. "Must be the world one day just twisted under him," thinks John, "like it can to anybody. Weren't nothing he could do, probably."

He stands up, grabs the money, and looks around for a place to hide it. Beneath the rock, he finds a crawl space big enough to put his head and shoulders into. After making sure there are no animal footprints or droppings near the opening, he lies down on his stomach, holds the money sack out in front of him, and pushes it as deep into the hole as he can. Then he gets to his feet, slings the .308 over his shoulder, and starts for home.

In the woods south of the trailer, he passes a hundred yards by it, then cuts north and crawls on his belly up to the west shore of the pond. From behind a cluster of hop hornbeams, he surveys through the rifle's scope the front of the structure until he is as certain as he can be that no one is there. Warily, he stands up and moves closer. In the meadow, only a dove's coo interrupts the shrill buzz of cicadas. He quickly walks to the back of the trailer and onto the deck.

Where Waylon's body had lain is a circle of half-dried blood and a chalk outline of it. John's feverous brain abstractively paints a picture of his demise—a glowering troll guards a bridge; a white goat tries to cross it; a lead mallet wavers over the heads of both. Gore tones, harsh yellows, pinks the color of flesh predominate. The cumulative effect is blur; life, suffering, death swirl in a tripartite dance. Two cigarette stubs have been stamped out near the chalk.

John hurriedly enters the kitchen, which smells like exhaled smoke. Now his heart begins to pound. The police have been in the trailer and probably searched it. Have they looked in the freezer?

He lays the rifle on the table and hurries down the cellar stairs. The basement light is on. John stops in front of the freezer, his body suddenly racked by chills. In minute detail, the dead girl's face comes back to him. He pictures her ceaseless, open-eyed stare, reflecting to the whole world the horror of her death and the identity of her killer. "No matter where I'm at," he imagines her whispering in his ear, "my soul will always torment you." He grabs the door and yanks it open.

Abbie's pound of sausage and half a dozen venison steaks tumble out. John pushes away several more packages to reveal a human hand, an arm, then, where it's wedged against the roof of the freezer, the dead girl's skull. John loudly gasps at the sight of her. "Wouldn't b'lieve what's happened since I put you in here!" he says. In five minutes he has her sitting on the basement floor, her upper body, with its fractured spine, inclined at a nearly 180-degree angle to her feet. She's froze solid. "Gotta get you outta here," he says. "Put an end to this."

John leaves her there, walks to the rear of the cellar, and takes down from the wall a coil of rope and the toboggan he and Moira bought each other for Christmas one year. He slides the wooden sled across the floor and places it parallel to the cadaver. "Wouldn't be able to lug ya wit' on'y my one arm," he says.

He wrestles her onto the sled so that she's facing forward, with her head steeply inclined and her feet under the bow, as if she's plummeting downhill through a snowdrift. He turns away to pick up the rope and hears a loud bang. He wheels back around and sees the dead girl lying sideways on the cement floor next to the sled. John winces as if she's still alive. He thinks there'll be no end to her, or his, pain until she's properly buried. He gets her sitting upright on the toboggan again, then loops the rope several times around her body and the sled's front, before securing it.

He pulls the toboggan over to the stairs and, with his left hand gripping the circular twine around its bow, climbs laboriously to the top. To maneuver the corner into the kitchen, he has to coincidentally hoist and push the bow, causing the cadaver's skull to collide loudly with the banister. He tugs the sled into the center of the floor and, panting heavily, sits down at the table next to it. "Sumbitch weren't even gon' take you Hawaii," he says, exhaling derisively. "That's who you died for. Now I'm in it up my neck!"

He goes into the bathroom and takes the dressing from his wound. It oozes blood still, along with a white pussy substance. The flesh surrounding it is the color of a purple tulip. John's not sure if the cut's gangrenous. He pours peroxide on it, rebandages it, and eats another half a dozen aspirins. In the cabinet mirror, his face seems paler than the dead girl's. Rivulets of sweat pour down his cheeks. His eyes look like they're drowning in the depths of kettle ponds. He's about used up, thinks John, unless he sees a doctor pretty quick.

He walks back into the kitchen, picks up the phone, and dials the number of the only person left alive he thinks might still be able to help him. Suddenly remembering it's Saturday, he is about to hang up when the call is answered. "It's John Moon," says John.

A long silence follows.

"You mad at me, Pitt?"

"Lots of folks are wondering where you are, John." The lawyer's voice sounds hollow and faraway—almost sad—though partly that could be John's perception and that Pitt is on a speaker phone. "Sounds as if your world's turned into an awful mess."

"It's why I'm callin'."

"The police found one of your fingers."

"Ain't doin' so good without it."

"I'm afraid it's too late to sew it back on, John. I'm awfully sorry."

"You still my lawyer, lawyer?"

"I wasn't clear that you hadn't fired me, John."

"Was confused 'bout things—my family, the Hen. I weren't gon' shoot ya."

"I hoped not, John. Still, it shakes a man up." Pitt delicately clears his throat. John imagines the lawyer's tiny Adam's apple bobbing as his apparently constant pain exits through his eyes. "Did you know, John, that poor little Obadiah was raised by about eight different people because his parents didn't want a thing to do with him, and one of them—an aunt, I believe—used an electric cattle prod on him and, when she caught him eating in bed, made him sleep in a cage with live rats?"

"I know he sliced up Molly and Ira Hollenbach."

"...He was ten—cutest little fella you ever saw—when the court first assigned me to represent him."

"You drunk again, Pitt?"

"Just tired, John." The lawyer sounds like he's about to cry. John thinks he's made a mistake calling him. "I'm not a very good lawyer, John. All my clients lie to me. I allow them to play on my good graces."

"How's Abbie?"

"Recovering well, I'm told. And wondering about you."

"I made a mistake 'bout a week ago, Pitt. Don't seem to be any end to it."

"... And did you know our good friend Simon Breedlove is also gone?"

"Was how he wanted it," says John.

"A few years ago—five, to be precise, right after... well, you know—he had me draw up a will. He's left everything he owned to some Vietnamese immigrant family in San Francisco."

"I din' know him so good," says John.

Pitt clears his throat again. "There's lots of dead bodies, John, and you're still alive. My guess is, the police aren't sure what to think."

"How many, 'xactly?"

"How many what?"

"Bodies."

"Well, John—they count three. If you include Simon and Obadiah."

"They ain't lookin' for no others?"

"Bodies?"

"Whatevers."

John hears a slurping sound on the other end of the line and guesses Pitt's emboldening himself. He glances over at the dead girl, touching her toes, and thinks if lives could back up, the world would soon be out of room. "Maybe you ought to call a real lawyer, John. One of those ex-football types. I know you've got the money to pay for it."

"That's good as buried."

"Are you sure you want to do that, John? Even gullible old Daggard Pitt requires a substantial retainer for a mess like yours."

"How much?"

"Ten to start, I'd think."

"Thousand?"

"I'd guess, yes."

"Would it keep me out a' jail?"

"Well, John, I'd feel more comfortable about that if the arithmetic didn't keep changing."

"Whadda ya mean?"

"I'm afraid one more body would push credulity beyond its limits."

John thanks him for the advice, then hangs up the phone.

He walks down the hallway into his bedroom, yanks open the top drawer of his bureau, and reaches beneath his underwear. He pulls out the envelope there, then goes back to the kitchen and from cold tap water makes a thick cup of instant coffee. He sits down with it at the table and pictures a southward winding road that never ends, just gets narrower and narrower. Outside the window, darting swallows filch flies from the air. Perspiration drops from John's brow onto the tabletop. His scent is gamy. As they thaw, the dead girl's bones creak and groan. "Must be you figured Waylon as your best chance for somethin'," he tells her, "even if he weren't much a' one. That it?"

She doesn't answer.

From the envelope John takes the Polaroids he snapped of her and aimlessly shuffles through them. He envisions the world as a populous plain interwoven by a network of tiny creases in which man's evil little secrets hide. He imagines the worst retribution as a self-inflicted paralysis. He thinks of the physical aspects of being incarcerated—prodding hands and clubs, restraining iron bars, the close smell of so many people, even sunlight rationed like a scarce commodity. He finds himself shivering. Tears mix with the sweat exiting his body.

Falteringly he stands up, walks over to the dead girl, and runs a hand through her hair, which is cold, with an oily texture. He bends forward and hugs her frozen, soulful torso. His field of vision starts to blur. He feels like he's looking down through a haze of smoke at the imagined life of Ingrid Banes. What if it were possible to alter history—even emotions—with only words? To manipulate talk into facts and verbalize facts into dreams? Even for those—like John and the dead girl—born on the wrong end of it, this would be a world worth living in. "You're gon' make it Hawaii, Ingrid," he says, kissing her on the cheek. "Ya lucky girl, ya."

Fearing someone might drive up the road and spot him, he takes the same route back up the mountain as he did coming down. Fueled by adrenaline and a belief that from fate his own feebleness cannot swerve him, he pulls the heavy toboggan with his good hand, allowing the other to swing loosely by his side. Over the grassy field leading to the woods, the sled's slick bottom passes unrestrainedly. The pollen is thick in the air. Several times, John stops to catch his breath or sneeze.

Entering the forest, he is struck by the unusually large number of crows and grackles perched or circling above him. Or else he is suddenly more attuned to their presence. There are seemingly hundreds of the birds, all of them black as night. Their cacophony grates on his ears. Though the toboggan still slides with relative ease over the needle-and-leaf floor, the going is slower. In the eighty-plus-degree heat, the cadaver, beneath its tarpaulin, melts more rapidly. Soon the increasingly flaccid flesh begins shifting side to side, making the job of tugging it harder. Thawed some, the half-rotten corpse again exhales its gone smell. John temporarily engages himself in searching for a nonblack bird.

At the start of the steep grade leading to the pines, the number and size of rocks multiply. John's upward course becomes more serpentine, and the work intensely taxing. He has trouble keeping his feet beneath him. Every five yards or so, he falls to his knees. Finally, instead of standing up again, he loops the lead rope around his shoulders and, with his three functional limbs, scratches and crawls his way toward the top.

His hand lands on a nest of fire ants. Abruptly rearing back from their bites, he hears behind him a distinct crack. He turns around and the cadaver, now half unveiled beneath the tarpaulin, is sitting upright. John watches its upper torso, the spine completely severed, creakily ease backward until the dead girl is supine on the sled, staring straight up at the sky. A crow drops down and hovers above the body. John shoos it away. He thinks what awful things happen to flesh once it's dead. More awful even than when it's alive.

It takes him another half an hour to reach the scrub pasture where the money is stashed. Gasping for air, the rope still circling him like a cinch, he sits down on the rock concealing the sack. Hanging half off the sled, the cadaver, where it has banged against impediments on its upward journey, is scuffed and bruised. One of its eyes, half-dislodged, peers at an impossible angle behind it where two of its teeth must lie. In a way that he can't describe, John, while eyeing the body, is struck by the irony in mankind's vainglorious-ness, that day-to-day conceit which, like air from a puffball, is instantly expunged by death.

After retrieving the sack, he tucks it, alongside the shovel, between the dead girl's legs, then once more pulls her upper torso forward, folding her like a wallet over the money. He loops the rope twice around the corpse so it won't flop back-ward again, re-covers it with the tarpaulin, and heads into the pines. On the flat terrain, he doesn't have to work so hard. He has more time to think and feel his pain, now more like a general sickness infecting his body. One minute he is hot. The next, cold. In between, he has surges of energy.

He begins to suspect that he is being followed by the birds. Perched high in the canopy, they chatter among themselves as if making plans. One will occasionally swoop a few feet above his head, stridently squawking. To avoid thinking about them, John converses with the dead girl. He tells her in these woods is where their paths began to coincide. He points to the thistle patch behind which he first saw the dead buck's antlers as the spot where her death was first assigned to him. He explains to her how he chased the deer for miles before it limped, as if preordained, into the quarry. Beneath these pines, he tells her, is a nice place to be buried. There's plenty of shade, a gentle stream nearby, and it's not far from a good view of the valley. Here is where he would be buried, he says, if the state would allow it.

Her response is to plant a snapshot of her parents in his head, as if she is demanding to know why he is hiding her from them. John refuses to answer. Instead, he tells her of his belief, recently arrived at, that souls are liberated by the earth. That once she is in the ground, she will be free to move easier than the wind. She can visit her parents or, if she hasn't already, go to Hawaii. He realizes that he is talking quite loud, that maybe the fever is causing him to rave. The crows and grackles are yelling back at him. Suddenly he is angry at the dead girl for making him see that he is as much a coward as most of mankind. He stops walking and puts the back of his hand to his forehead. It feels like room-temperature beef. "You're dead and I ain't," he tells her, "and I don't want to go to jail, all right?"

She doesn't answer.

John starts lugging her toward the truck again. He's on the edge of the fire zone. Although it's been razed nearly two years, the area still breathes a faint odor of smoke. A hundred feet ahead, he can just see, nearly parallel to the ground in the brush-tufted swale, the pickup's roof, dully reflecting the sun. Now he starts to consider the difficulties of performing his task. Though the fire-dead earth should be softer to dig, in John's weakened state, and with only one functional hand, doing so will be torturous at best. That his pain should be commensurate with his deviousness seems to him exactly right.

At the swale's edge, he drops the lead rope, climbs down the indention into the pickup, starts the engine, pulls the truck up onto the flat terrain, then shuts it off.

For several seconds he can hear his raggedy breathing and rivulets of sweat splashing onto the seat. Then the birds start in again. Out the windshield, John sees more crows and grackles than he can count perched in the live trees encircling the dead zone. He jumps from the truck and nearly lands on a porcupine. He leaps back. The porcupine doesn't move. John prods it with his toe. The varmint just lies there. John rolls it over and sees that only the animal's head and quills haven't been eaten. He kicks the carcass into some bushes, then hurries over to the toboggan, draws back the tarp, unties the dead girl, and grabs the shovel from between her legs. "In a coupla years," he tells her, reentering the swale, "this spot'll grow up to be beautiful again. And you'll be a part of it."

The digging is even slower and more painful than he had imagined it would be. After each one-handed shovel thrust into the dark loam at the swale's bottom, he places a foot atop the metal blade and pushes until it sinks to the hilt; then, simultaneously yanking back and lifting the handle, he extracts the blade and, using for ballast the forearm of his injured limb, shakily dumps to the left of the hole what soil he manages not to drop, usually less than he doesn't. From start to finish, performing the procedure initially takes him close to half a minute, and, as the grave gets deeper, necessitating even higher hoisting of the shovel, successively longer, while each time he removes less dirt. So that he can easily stand while working, he makes the hole about four feet wide. Having started close to five feet below ground level, he soon can't see beyond the swale's borders.

Whenever he stops to rest, he hears the ceaseless yakking of the birds; intermittently one or more of them will dive down out of the trees to peer curiously into the depression. Once, a noise resembling asthmatic wheezing begins above him. John abruptly drops the shovel and scrabbles from the grave to find a pair of red foxes sniffing at the dead girl. He chases them off with a volley of rocks, then ascends to the forest floor, grabs the lead rope of the toboggan, and yanks it to the swale's edge. He climbs into the grave again and recommences digging. After a while his left arm hurts as much as his right. He suffers periodic dizzy spells; his eyes blur; in his gaze, objects vacillate; rocks become people drowning in the knee-deep pool of blood that he bales. He begins ascribing to the birds' toneless squawking a blend of poetic insight and cold intelligence. He imagines their varied flights composing silent funeral marches. From the shovel's blade, his father's face screams at him, "Was a wolf, I tell ya. A goddamn wolf!"

The birds abruptly turn mute. A moment later, they start in again, even louder. In that brief interlude of silence, John is certain he heard voices—real ones—from somewhere above him. Once more he exits the grave, this time with more difficulty. With his eyes, he circles the woods and brush above him. To the west, a patch of yarrow sways harder than he thinks this gentle wind could cause it to. Or is it his imagination? He's not sure. It surprises him to see that the sun is three-quarters of the way toward the horizon. How many hours has he been digging? Three? Four? Reaching up to the toboggan, he whisks several horseflies from the dead girl's face. "Gotta put ya in deep 'nough," he tells her, "where somethin' don't dig ya up."

Again he descends into the grave. He has no idea for how long. Time is like recycled water rising and falling, and John dead wood on its surface. Even his physical distress isn't reliable; like all human conditions, it can't maintain its intensity. His pain loses its sharp edge and becomes merely monotonous. Periodic pangs, twinges, and abnormalities remind him he is unhealthily alive. When he spits or swallows, his swollen tongue feels like a live fish wriggling in his mouth. A loud throbbing sound fills his ears. His sweat tastes like bitter almonds. He urinates a burning, dark yellow froth into the bottom of the grave. Twice more he thinks he hears voices and maybe branches cracking at ground level, but, after crawling out to see, spots nothing amiss. The third time, he doesn't even bother to look; recalling his dying father's hallucinatory wolf, he dismisses the sounds as audible phantasy.

Beyond a certain depth, his one hand can barely heft to the lip of the hole an empty shovel, let alone a dirt-loaded one. His efforts prove fruitless. Abruptly dropping the tool, he gets down on his knees and begins scooping up single handfuls of soil, then tossing them out of the grave. At some point during these labors, he becomes convinced that a carnivorous animal is trying to exit through his throat. Gagging, he tries to heave the beast, but having eaten nothing but berries for forty-eight hours, can't. His skin temperature drops from hot to clammy. An almost peaceful mood attends him. He believes he is dying and is not overly troubled by it. After several seconds he is able to breathe again; then the experience upsets him terribly. "This is gon' have to do!" he yells up at the dead girl. The floor of the swale is maybe six inches below his shoulders. Shadows half-fill the indenture. John tries to exit the grave, and finds he is unable to.

Worn out from shoveling, his uninjured limb trembles

like jelly while failing to pull him up. His right arm is even more useless; monstrous-looking in its tumescence, it radiates enough pain from even the slightest pressure to present John with a phantasmagorical longing for death as life's first prize for suffering. He nearly faints. Then, emitting a whimpering sound, he exhaustedly sits down in the grave. Though he's not seriously concerned with being infinitely trapped there—he can, after all, always refill a portion of the hole with dirt and walk out—the idea of being imprisoned in a pit not even up to his chin infuriates him. He thinks of the hours of labor he spent to confine himself and wonders if burying Ingrid Banes will result only in more suffering for him, rather than less. Then he recalls his father saying that "life is for the living" and John's own determination at least to try, as had Robert Moon, to be a presence in his son's life. And how can he do that from a jail cell?

Rejecting the disheartening and painful prospect of refilling what he has dug in order to escape, he stands up, grabs the shovel, and lays it on the swale's floor near the edge of the hole. With his good arm, he pulls himself as far as he can up the wall, then grips it with his knees, the swale's floor with his elbow, and the shovel's handle with his left hand. Slowly he inches the blade toward the toboggan's lead rope where, six feet from him, it dangles from the forest floor into the swale. Several times he falls back into the grave. Each failed effort brings the blade closer to the looped rope. Finally, he manages to work the blade into the loop and, pulling the rope gradually toward him, removes most of its slack. Hoping to stop the sled next to the grave, he begins easing it gingerly down the steep bank of the swale. Suddenly he again loses his balance and, still holding the shovel, tumbles backward into the hole. In the split second that the toboggan and its contents career down the abrupt embankment toward where he lies face-up in the grave, John is aware of the birds' heightened screeching and, once more, voices, real or imagined.

Either he has been unconscious for a day or only for a few seconds, because the hole is still half filled with dying light and overhead the crows and grackles swoop and cry. There are other noises, too. Snapping brush. Frantic whispering. Wedged by the sled's bow against the grave's floor, John stares into the nondislodged eye of the dead girl, catapulted by the collision onto him. She reeks a stench that begs for the warm blanket of mother earth. Spoken words float like pollen in the air above them.

"He dead?"

"Looks to be."

I'm not! says John, only he can't hear his own voice or feel his mouth speaking it.

"Couple peas in a pod, their eyes open that way."

"Think he killed her?"

On'y killed one person in my life purposeful, John inwardly yells, and that one needed it!

"Blew a hole in her chest, I'd say."

"Was a while ago, by the smell of her."

"Wonder where he's been keeping her at."

"Someplace wet by the look of her."

"Jesus, baby, you don't suppose he had her in tha...?"

"Nah! She's been froze, then thawed, looks like."

John is no longer aware of the pain in his hand. In fact, none of him hurts at all. He envisions his body as a car wreck, being appraised for junk.

"Where you guess all that money came from?"

"Someplace it oughtn't to have, for sure."

He's not quite certain where all his parts are or which of them he can move. Then, horrified, he suddenly realizes he is—and has been for several seconds—trying and failing to make all or any of them move. He screams a cry as muted as a shout from the center of the earth.

"Jump down there, baby, and gather up the cash. Put it back in the sack."

"Not me, brave boy. Something spooky 'bout that hole."

"It's just a hole with a sled, a mountain of dough, and two dead people in it."

"Like you see corpses every day, right?"

"It's not doing them any good."

His eyes won't move left or right, forward or back. He can see only straight up, which is why he can't see who's talking. Beyond the dead girl's face, past the tops of the trees, the sun-setting sky resembles in his slightly fractured vision a gently blowing field of goldenrod.

"Promise you'll fuck me on the plane to Paris, lover?"

"Once in the can, then in the cockpit. Now get your cute ass down there and help me."

A thud vibrates in his ears. Then another. A moment later, he is aware of the dead girl being rolled from his chest onto the ground next to him or maybe onto his legs, he can't tell for sure. Then the toboggan is lifted from him and two pairs of arms thrust it over his head toward the swale's floor, where it lands with a wooden slap. For a few minutes he hears the two people picking up the bills and stuffing them back into the sack from which they must have spilled.

"Jesus, let's get out of here. The stench is killing me!"

"We haven't got all the cash."

"We've got most of it. You believe this amount of cabbage?"

"Like manna from heaven!"

"Hey, look at this. Snapshots." John hears someone pull the Polaroids out of the waterproof envelope he'd placed them in. "Of the girl, I guess."

"Christ, she looks half dead in 'em."

"Why would he bury them with her?"

"Who cares? Let's get out of here. This whole scene gives me the creeps!"

"There's some kind of note stuck in with 'em."

"Do me a favor, will ya? Don't read it."

"Whadda ya mean, don't read it?"

"It's bad luck."

"Bad luck?"

"Stick it back in the envelope with the pictures and leave 'em, lover, or count me out of the whole thing!"

"All right, all right!" John hears the envelope fall next to him, then the labored breathing of one or both people rearranging the cadaver in the hole. Seconds later, female legs straddle his head; above them are a body and a face out of which poignantly stare the black she-devil's eyes that followed John's frantic flight from Hidden Pond. "Jesus," she says, "you sure he isn't alive?"

"He's dead as this one," says the man. Another dull thump

sounds in the ground, followed by one of the dead girl's slightly swollen hands flopping across John's face and staying there. He hears the man and the woman exit the grave and, after a slight pause, the shovel being picked up.

"Earth to earth," intones the man.

"Dust to dust," adds the woman.

A scoop of falling dirt lands on John's face. Then a second. And third. Mother earth numbly slaps his cheeks. Blackens his vision. Fouls his throat and nostrils. His mind is as disconnected from his body as a circling hawk from the world. He understands he is out of time. His panic becomes a panacea. He gives thanks for being granted on this journey the touch and scent of another human being. He fears not what comes next, but only that the dead girl might. John mutely assures her that her soul is headed to Hawaii and that only her spirit-abandoned flesh will rest here with his own, the Polaroids he took of her, and a handwritten note, telling the world:

A terble thing happned here. Weren't nobody's fault, but a bad turn of events. This was a pretty girl, as anyone can see from her pictures. Her name was Ingrid Banes. She died on 6/18/95. She knows the truth of things and so do I. I didn't tell nobody bout what happned—even her parents who maybe are better off thinkin she's still alive and happy—cause I was fraid I'd not be blieved and would spend my life in jail for it. I din keep none the money cept twenty thousand dollers for my lawyer, round four thousand I tried to giv my wife, and five hunred to a one eyed lady from Oklahoma. It was stoled in the year 1990 from Ira and Molly Hollenbach by one bad man and another not so bad, who was my best friend. How it ended up with me's a long story.

John Moon
6/24/95

About the Author

Matthew F. Jones's 1999 novel *Deepwater* was adapted for a 2006 film of the same title. He lives in Charlottesville, Virginia.

BACK BAY · READERS' PICK

Reading Group Guide

A SINGLE SHOT

A novel by

Matthew F. Jones

An conversation with
Matthew F. Jones

A Single Shot is in many ways a different breed of noir than other, less daring works of crime fiction—particularly in regard to the way the novel ends. Was choosing a fate for Moon difficult for you? Or did it simply seem like the natural conclusion all the way through your writing process? (Did you have this beginning in mind right from the start?)

I had no idea how the novel would end when I began it or, in fact, until the moment it unfolded while I was writing it. Once I have the characters I'm writing about in mind—i.e., once I feel that I know them—I try to think as little as possible while writing. And I never outline or plan out in advance what will happen in a novel or to the people in it. Once I've created the characters, the story as I see it comes more from them than from me. I do my best to follow wherever they lead me and, through my own filter, accurately record their accounts. I've never had much luck in trying to manipulate anything to come out a certain way in my own life, and doubt I'd be any better at it in the lives of fictional characters. Plus I can't imagine the monotony of writing from an outline. I sit down to write each day with only a vague idea of where I'm headed—and never knowing where I might end up—which for me makes writing more of an adventure than a task.

What are some of your personal favorite novels, and do you see any of their influence in A Single Shot, *looking back on it now?*

I'm an eclectic reader and a lover of many novels, though two unifying elements are found in the ones I admire most: indelible characters whose stories are compelling because of who they are; and a rich evocation of the particular world they live in. In that vein, some that, in no particular order, come readily to mind are *Of Mice and Men, The Grapes of Wrath,* Flannery O'Connor's short stories, *The Postman Always Rings Twice, The Collector, To Kill a Mockingbird, The Spy Who Came in from the Cold, The Sheltering Sky, Augie Marsh, A Flag for Sunrise, The Quiet American, The Stars at Noon, Suttree, The Killer Inside Me, The Risk Pool, The Cement Garden, Paris Trout, The Professional, Mystic River, Affliction, Fat City,* etc.

I don't in truth see the influence of anyone else's work in *A Single Shot* (or, for that matter, in any of my work except possibly in my novel *Deepwater,* the opening scene of which, in retrospect, may have its inspiration in a favorite novel of mine) any more than I think the way in which I speak is influenced by the voices of other people I admire or care about.

More objective readers of the work might see something I don't, I'm not sure. It would be interesting for me to know.

Were you struck at any point by parallels in your writing to your own experiences, or was A Single Shot *created, out of necessity, from deep research?*

A Single Shot came directly out of my own experiences and/or knowledge, though obviously the actual events (anyway, most of them) are fictional. I grew up in that world and with the people who inhabit it. The mountain, the quarry, the farm were all based on the actual mountainside I grew up on. Daggard Pitt's law office above Newberry's was modeled on the office I practiced law out of for three years. The only research I ever do in my writing is for technical purposes (the caliber of a particular gun, the model of a car or tractor, for example).

Have you known anyone like Moon in the course of your life? How did you go about creating the character—and the situation in which he finds himself?

John was formed partially out of a composite of a few people I knew growing up. I knew, for example, several people who hunted deer all year long. They did it to feed their families and to live on. Jobs were—and are—scarce in that part of the country and deer nearly as plentiful as squirrels.

I went about creating John the same way I do every character I write about. Before starting the book I put him in a number of imagined situations and wrote pages of him conversing with various people in those situations. When I felt I knew him well enough to have an idea, without having to think about it, of how he would react in any type of circumstance, I wrote the opening scene to the book and, from there — from John walking up the mountainside with his twelve gauge at the crack of dawn — I trusted my knowledge of him enough to follow him into whatever he led me to.

Daniel Woodrell, author of Winter's Bone, *was kind enough to contribute a foreword for* A Single Shot. *What are your thoughts on how he's prefaced the new edition? Would you say you're as much a fan of Woodrell's work as he is of yours?*

Well, I'm not sure what to make of him calling me "a twisted motherfucker," though in context of the rest of what he wrote I'm pretty sure he meant it as a compliment! In all honesty, when I heard Daniel had offered to write a foreword to *A Single Shot* I was thrilled, largely because — as I told him when I thanked him after I'd read it — I didn't have to pretend I was a huge fan of his work, I actually am one and have been for a good long time. A review he wrote in the *Washington Post* of *A Single Shot* when it came out in 1996 first alerted me to his work. Not long after that I purchased a copy of *The Ones You Do,* and from there I was hooked and have gone on to read all of his novels. He is one of a very few authors whose release of a new book is an event I eagerly anticipate. In my mind he is "the voice" for that part of the world he writes about. If I hadn't been such a recluse I would have contacted him to thank him after he wrote that first review of *A Single Shot* — I'm glad he didn't hold it against me! And I'm honored that he feels about my work the way I do about his.

Your novel Deepwater *was made into the 2006 film of the same name, and* A Single Shot *is currently in development as well. Were you consulted as part of the filmmaking process for these two projects? Did you adapt them for the screen yourself? What are your thoughts on book-to-film adaptations—of your own work, and in general?*

I had nothing to do with the screenplay for *Deepwater,* which had a lot to do with why I accepted an offer to write the screenplay for *A Single Shot* when it came along and, after that, the screenplay for my novel *Boot Tracks,* which is also in production. Not that I believe *Deepwater* is a terrible film (for what it is, it's fine); it just isn't close to an accurate representation of the novel or, in truth—and, more important—anywhere near as good a film as it could have been. In fact, the main producer of that film, after reading the screenplay I'd written for *A Single Shot,* told me he wished he'd hired me to write the script for *Deepwater.* I told him I wished he had too! So when the *A Single Shot* job was offered to me I felt I had to accept despite a few novelist friends warning me off of it based on their unpleasant experiences in trying to cross over into the film world. The truth is, though, I love movies nearly as much as I love books and, as a novelist, have always considered writing dialogue one of my strengths, which is a lot of what a good script is. The two forms, though, are very different. Novel writing in my view is an art in which the writer touches every one of a reader's five (or, I guess, six) senses, whereas script writing is more of a craft in which my self-imposed rule is "if you can't see it or hear it, don't write it." One quickly learns too that movie making, in direct contrast to novel writing, is very much a collaborative endeavor. Everyone—from the director, to the producers, to the actors, even sometimes the DP—gives their input on a script. Then there's the money people who worry, is it too dark? Is it too graphic? Is it too anything that might negatively affect their investment? So, the writer, while making compromises, has to work hard to keep in the script the true core and essence of his story. The only way I believe that a novelist can do a good adaptation of his own novel is to always bear in mind that the movie will not be the novel. And it shouldn't be. It should be the novel seen through a different prism and experienced in a different medium.

You've written six novels to date—1992's The Cooter Farm, *1994's* The Elements of Hitting, *1997's* Blind Pursuit, *1999's* Deepwater, *2006's* Boot Tracks, *and, of course,* A Single Shot. *Is there a particular novel of the bunch of which you have the fondest memories—either of the writing process; how it was received by friends, family, or more generally; or because of its association with a particular period in your life?*

Each one is special to me for a different reason. I'm sure this sounds strange to people, but I feel in many ways as if a different person wrote each novel. I suppose that's because I was at a different point in my life during the time I was intimate with each one. By that I mean while working on a novel I'm fully consumed with the particular world and people I'm writing about. It's as if you're spending a very intense period of time with a group of people you've been marooned on an island with and then they're all rescued and go their separate ways into new lives. So each book, you're with a new group of people, and even if you're on the same island (i.e., writing about the same locale, which I often do), it's through these new people's eyes and perspectives. Or, looked at in a different way, each book is an exploration of the same world through a different writer's viewpoint. *The Cooter Farm* had a unique impact on me not only because it was my first published book (after a long struggle) but because in the weeks leading up to its publication my wife gave birth to our first and only child and shortly after that my father died after a long, excruciating illness. So, I was dealing with all these conflicting emotions. And when it came out it seemed like half the people in the town I grew up in saw themselves (in a good or bad light) in it. In retrospect, I could see why some of them thought so, though no character in it (or in any of my novels) is based on any one particular person.

Have any of your working experiences had an influence in the events depicted in A Single Shot?

Well, I grew up working on dairy and horse farms and did so for many years, so I have a very close understanding of that way of life. And for a few years I practiced law in the rural upstate New York town I grew up in, which is very much the town I modeled the town in a *A Single Shot* after. A small-town lawyer specializing in criminal and family law can't but help, to a certain extent, to have their finger on the pulse of the community or be attuned to the intimate details of his or her clients' lives. And being a criminal defense lawyer—there, and in a larger city for a time—I learned a lot about criminals. And I learned the difference between people who choose, as a way of life, to be criminals (and how they think or look at the world) and people (such as, in my view, John Moon) who are basically good people who for a myriad of reasons end up committing criminal acts.

In giving interviews or answering questions in front of readers, are you surprised by the frequency of any of the topics that come up—both about your work in general and A Single Shot *in particular?*

Oftentimes a reader will wonder if I intended a specific passage or event in one of my novels to have a particular symbolic meaning they've attributed to it. Usually, once it's pointed out to me, I see exactly why they would think so. But those sorts of thoughts never cross my mind when I'm writing; all I'm thinking about is creating the best story I can. In relation to *A Single Shot*, I'm probably asked most often about the ending, and why I chose the one I did. And my answer always is, I didn't choose it, the writing of it did—and sometimes I wish it had come out a different way for John.

What would you have done in Moon's shoes? Would you have followed the same path as Moon throughout the course of A Single Shot's *events?*

That's the question hopefully every reader of the book asks—or will ask—of him- or herself. What would he or she have done had it been them? And I don't think that any of us can do more than speculate on the answer. Based on what I know about myself and how I think I view the world, I can guess — or hope — I would have reacted one way or another. But without being in that actual moment — in the immediate wake of having fired that single shot (and in John's particular circumstances) — I can't know for sure what I would have done. I've long suspected — and maybe it comes across in *A Single Shot* — that only in the most dire circumstances — when one's back is to the wall, so to speak — does one truly get to know oneself.

What books, music, and art inspire you? What are you reading and listening to right now?

Art that inspires me most — through whatever medium — creates for me characters or scenes so indelible that I'm drawn to know more about them the way I'm drawn to know more about a new person — or stranger — I meet who in some way (often indefinable to me) sparks my interest. In the visual arts I find this most in certain photographs (often black and white) of people in their everyday surroundings or in the best Impressionist paintings that magically ignite my imagination to see a world and story well beyond what is on the canvas. Great blues music (from the pioneers of it up through today's masters) inspires me in the same way. I spend far more time and money than I care to admit searching for, collecting, and making blues playlists to exercise or mellow out to. The newest one combines cuts from, among others, R. L. Burnside, Odetta, James Blood Ulmer, Otis Taylor, John Lee Hooker, Son House, Big Mama Thornton. And on my nightstand right now are two books I'm a ways into: James M. Cain's *Mildred Pierce* (it doesn't, in my opinion, measure up to *Postman,* but few novels do) and *The Snow Leopard* (a great piece of nature writing by Peter Matthiessen about a trip he took into the Himalayas in the 1970s in search of the elusive snow leopard, but that is about so much more than that).

Questions and topics
for discussion

1. John Moon does much of what he does in *A Single Shot* because of a sense of obligation—either to the girl he has killed, or to his wife and young son. Do you find Moon to be a moral man? If so, why? If no, why not?
2. Is there anything about Moon's decisions or behavior that, if done differently, might change the way you feel about him?
3. Do you think it's okay for Moon to poach game when destitute and desperately in need of food to live on?
4. Moon is presented with a long series of difficult decisions throughout *A Single Shot*—whether to follow the deer he has been illegally hunting into the woods, whether to fire into the brush, what to do with the body of the girl he has killed, what to do with the money that could change his life, and how to make things right once they begin to go horribly wrong. Reading *A Single Shot,* were there any particular decisions that struck you as foolish or poorly thought out? If so, do you understand Moon's reasons for acting the way he did regardless?
5. If you were in Moon's shoes, do you think you would have acted differently? If so, where and when in the story? If not, how does this affect your reading of the novel?

6. Given the same skill set as Moon, would you have taken the shot against Waylon that saved Abbie from death, torture, or disfigurement? If so, why? If no, why not?

7. Is Moon a better man for having pulled the trigger and killed Waylon? Is this death more excusable than the one that opens the novel? Why or why not?

8. Does Moon's success at saving Abbie justify the risk he took in firing his weapon?

9. Did the ending of *A Single Shot* surprise you? If so, why? If not, why not?

10. Is Moon right to turn down Nobie's offer to work for him? Clearly the decision has to do with pride, as the land he would be working used to belong to the Moon household. Does this decision to turn away money honorably earned affect your opinion of how Moon handles the money he has unlawfully obtained? What would you do?

11. When *A Single Shot* begins, Moon and his wife, Moira, have already separated, though we experience snippets of their time together in Moon's many vivid flashbacks. It's clear that Moon cares deeply for Moira, even though she wishes to end their marriage. Do you accept Moon's reasoning for why she wants to leave him? Is she right to seek a divorce? Who do you sympathize with more, Moon or Moira?

12. When Moon holds his little boy seemingly for the first time after he has broken into Moira's apartment, he discovers he is less capable of comforting the child than the babysitter who has made a wreck of the place and invited a man over as Moon's child sleeps in the next room. Do you think this is evidence enough to show whether

Moon would have made a good father to his son? Do you think Moon, like his father before him, would have been viewed as a disappointment to the generation he raises?

13. Daggard Pitt, Moon's lawyer, appears at first to be on Moon's side. Later, Moon finds out he has been representing the interests of the thieves who have come after Moon at the same time. Do you find this to be moral behavior? How much does Pitt's job as defender of the accused affect how you view the nature of his decisions?

14. What do you make of the many hallucinations Moon experiences of the woman he has killed? Particularly, do you find the sexual nature of many of them to be expected? What reason, subconsciously or consciously, do you think Moon has for giving the dead girl a personality and thoughts of her own, despite having never met the girl before her death?

15. To what extent is Moon's assertion that the "bad thing" he refers to in his letters "was nobody's fault" accurate? Is Moon culpable? Who in the novel is most culpable? Who is least culpable?

16. *A Single Shot* has something in common with the plot of a Greek tragedy. Do you consider Moon to have a tragic flaw? If so, what is it?

Also available from Mulholland Books

The Bayou Trilogy

Under the Bright Lights • *Muscle for the Wing* •
The Ones You Do

By Daniel Woodrell

Collected for the first time in a single volume—three early works of crime fiction by a major American novelist.

"A backcountry Shakespeare.... The inhabitants of Daniel Woodrell's fiction often have a streak that's not just mean but savage; yet physical violence does not dominate his books. What does dominate is a seasoned fatalism.... Woodrell has tapped into a novelist's honesty, and lucky for us, he's remorseless that way." —*Los Angeles Times*

"Daniel Woodrell writes with an insistent rhythm and an evocative and poetic regional flavor." —*The New Yorker*

"Woodrell writes books so good they make me clench my fists in jealousy and wonder." —*Esquire*

"What people say about Cormac McCarthy goes double for Daniel Woodrell. Possibly more." —*New York*

Mulholland Books • Available wherever books are sold

Also available from Mulholland Books

A Drop of the Hard Stuff

A novel

By Lawrence Block

"Good to the last drop...a Great American Crime Novel.... The perfect introduction to Scudder's shadow-strewn world and the pleasures of Block's crisp yet brooding prose....*A Drop of the Hard Stuff* reads like it's been jolted by factory-fresh defibrillator pads, as Scudder recalls his first, nerve-rattling year of sobriety. Block makes the hard work of sobriety totally gripping....A bracing distillation of Block's powers." —Ed Park, *Time*

"Moving...Elegiac...Satisfying....Right up there with Mr. Block's best." —Tom Nolan, *Wall Street Journal*

"Block is a mesmerizing raconteur....[The book is] a lament for all the old familiar things that are now almost lost, almost forgotten."
—Marilyn Stasio, *New York Times Book Review*

Mulholland Books • Available wherever books are sold

Also available from Mulholland Books

Fun and Games

A novel

By Duane Swierczynski

"Insanely entertaining."   —Josh Bazell, author of the
New York Times bestseller *Beat the Reaper*

"More exciting than whatever you are reading right now."
—Ed Brubaker, author of *Criminal* and *Incognito*

"Cool, suspenseful, tragic, and funny as hell, *Fun and Games* is Duane Swierczynski's best yet. I haven't had this much fun reading in a long time."
—Sara Gran, author of *Dope* and *Come Closer*

"A white-hot nuclear explosion."
—Joe R. Lansdale, author of *The Bottoms*

Mulholland Books • Available wherever books are sold

MULHOLLAND BOOKS

You won't be able to put down these Mulholland books.

A SINGLE SHOT *by Matthew F. Jones*

THE REVISIONISTS *by Thomas Mullen*

BLACK LIGHT *by Patrick Melton, Marcus Dunstan, and Stephen Romano*

HELL AND GONE *by Duane Swierczynski*

THE HOUSE OF SILK *by Anthony Horowitz*

ASSASSIN OF SECRETS *by Q. R. Markham*

THE WHISPERER *by Donato Carrisi*

SHATTER *by Michael Robotham*

A DROP OF THE HARD STUFF *by Lawrence Block*

BLEED FOR ME *by Michael Robotham*

GUILT BY ASSOCIATION *by Marcia Clark*

POINT AND SHOOT *by Duane Swierczynski*

EDGE OF DARK WATER *by Joe R. Lansdale*

Visit www.mulhollandbooks.com for
your daily suspense fiction fix.

Download the FREE Mulholland app